CRIME CITY NIGHTS

CRIME CITY NIGHTS

J RAZOR – BACKSTROM

PALMETTO
P U B L I S H I N G
Charleston, SC
www.PalmettoPublishing.com

Paperback ISBN: 979-8-8229-4361-2

ONE

My mother Mia Laurent, worked for a local pub; it was there she claimed she met my biological father, Leo Dubois. She also claimed he was dashing; with a manly chin and a good physique. He found her attractive as well. Allegedly, the two instantly hit it off and began dating. Shortly after that, they began living together and nine months later, I was born. From an early age, I knew my mother had an important job, because she was always in a rush to get to work. Later, I found out it was because she worked at a bar and if she was late, she would have to contend with angry drunks, demanding more alcohol! I didn't know what my father did for a living. There were times he would argue with my mother, right after dinner. Sometimes, I would be told to leave the table and go to my room. Most of the time, I would leave the kitchen without hesitation, however, there were a few times that I just hid and listened to hear him tell her he needed to go to work, because his job was important. According to her, she knew what he did for a living, but married him anyway, because she was in love. At the time I had no idea what his career entailed; all I knew was he didn't want to talk about it. He would always leave, slamming the door as he went! I never got used to my father's temper; it only made me fear him. One day, before my mother left to go grocery shopping; she told me to be good and don't make any noise, because my dad was resting. It was the first time I remember her leaving me with such responsibility; and at the time it was a huge deal! I had the entire downstairs to myself, as long as I didn't wake my father. Curiosity, eventually led me to the kitchen, where I remember my mother cooking at the stove. I remember her telling me to never touch the burners; because they're extremely *hot* and could harm me! Well, my imagination got the best of me and I began to tinker with the oven's door handle, pulling it open and looking inside, before closing it and grabbing a nearby chair to stand on and reach the dials. For some reason, I wanted to see how far I could get my skin to the surface of one of the burners; before pulling my hand away. It was my first attempt at playing chicken. Without realizing, I made enough noise to wake my father when I dragged the chair across the floor. I managed to reach the closest dial and turned it too high. The burner visually heated up right in front of me. In fact, it glowed red hot! I then extended my hand, inching my way *closer* and *closer*. I already made up my mind that I would stop if it got too intense. I just wanted to test my resolve – I wanted to see if I could do it. Could I get close enough to feel the intensity of the heat – without cowering and pulling my hand away? My dad was always the one who claimed that the measure of a man is determined by his ability to overcome difficult times. Just as my hand got within maybe two inches of the burner, I felt someone grab my forearm! It startled me and when I looked at who it was, I saw my dad and he wasn't happy!

"*Que fais-tu*?!" my father demanded to know what I was doing? Due to fear – that I had woken him and of what he might do – my mind went completely blank! I tried to recoil from his grip; as I protested! "I'm not doing anything!" All I could do was hope my mother would be home soon, so she could put a stop to his abuse. Or at least hold him accountable, with a few choice words, which would ultimately redirect his anger away from me and he would be forced to leave – either to return to his bedroom upstairs, or go for a walk to cool off. "Why is the stove on?" He was determined to get an answer! I honestly didn't have a good reason, so I just lied, "I don't know! Maybe mom forgot to shut it off."

"Really? Then why did you have your hand near one of the burners?" he asked, expecting a viable answer. Not knowing what to expect, and realizing he was growing increasingly impatient with me. I did what any frightened young boy would do, I lied again, "I was reaching for the dial, to turn it off." For a moment, I actually believed I sounded authentic, enough to convince him that I was telling the truth. I didn't like lying to him, but I felt I had no choice. It was either tell a lie, or face the consequences of being scolded, for my curiosity.

"I don't believe you."

"But it's true, *honest*!" I could see the storm clouds growing in his eyes. His face was utterly expressionless, and it sent chills down my spine. "Sebastien, I watched you from the hall. You moved your hand slowly over the burner; you probably wanted to see how close you could get your hand to it, before pulling your hand away. Am I right?" It was obvious, he had played similar games as a child. "Listen to me carefully, if you tell me the truth and stay away from the stove until your mother gets home, it will be as if nothing happened. On the other hand, lie to me and there will be *severe consequences*." He purposely emphasized the words, "severe consequences," frightening me even more! I could feel my heartbeat faster, as my pulse rapidly increased. I knew from experience; he had a bad temper. I also knew he demanded honesty from those around him. I figured he was only trying to entrap me, so he could scold me for telling him a lie. Again, fear compelled me and I continued with the previous lie. "Honestly, I saw the stove was on and I was going to turn it off, when you grabbed my arm."

"Sebastien, I'm very disappointed in you! I'm disappointed that you felt the need to lie to me. I'm also disappointed, because I gave you an opportunity to redeem yourself and you chose to continue with a lie. You know how I hate to be lied to! Your mother and I have always tried our best to teach you never to lie, because a liar can never be trusted to tell the truth. And you never want to get the reputation of being a filthy rotten no-good liar!" I now know, this anger was coming from the roots of his childhood, when he was abused by his old man. His father didn't want him to turn out like him, unfortunately, his parenting skills were nothing more than *mental* and *physical* abuse, and that same abuse was passed down to the next generation. "But I didn't lie!" I proclaimed! It was no use; my father didn't want to hear another word. It appeared as if what I did, stirred something evil inside him, because his eyes grew moody and foreboding, as he took ahold of my wrist. Those same eyes peer down upon me, unconcerned how I was going to react to what he was going to do next. "Sebastien, let this be a lesson...one you will never forget," he vowed with a calm, yet unforgiving voice. It was at that moment, I felt him pull my hand toward the lit burner. I reacted instinctively, trying to pull my hand away! He over powered me and pulled me even closer. I struggled to free myself, with every ounce of my being, but he was simply too strong! Suddenly, I felt why I couldn't get close to the burner - the pain grew *exponentially*! I pleaded for him to stop! He ignored my cries, while pushing my hand closer and closer to the stove's glowing coil! Finally, I felt it's bite! It was a feeling I'll never forget – a searing feeling, with the unforgettable odor of burnt flesh. He released his grip, before any significant damage could occur. I recoiled my injured hand and he told me to go upstairs to the bathroom, and run cold water on the damaged skin. He claimed it was just a superficial injury. A little burn cream and bandage would suffice. From that day forward, I replaced the fear I had for that man, with shear hatred. Yet, for some reason

I respected his principals. I knew he was correct, when he told me no one trusts a liar, and that I should never allow myself to get comfortable being dishonest. At that time, I wasn't aware how ironic it was, because my dad was not a man to be trusted. It was just a façade he showed to the public. Later that summer, I finally got the opportunity to find out for myself, what he did for a living. My mother was busy in the kitchen preparing what would be dinner. She complained again that the kitchen sink was leaking, at the P-trap. She told me it was something my father could fix, if he were here. Since he wasn't, the task was passed down to me. She explained, I would need to go down to the basement and grab a plumber's wrench. The basement was where my father kept all his tools for fixing things around the house. He was quite handy with a wrench, and could have easily been mistaken for a plumber. There were two access doors to the basement. One, attached to the hallway going to the kitchen. The other door, resembled a root cellar, attached to the side of the house. My dad mainly used the root cellar, which was nothing more than a metal door with a padlock, that only he had the key for. While down in the basement, I struggled to find what I thought would be the right tool for fixing the kitchen sink. I recalled my mother saying, it was some kind of wrench. I had no idea what kind of wrench was needed to fix a leak, so I just perused the tools on the surface of his workbench. I moved from the bench, to the wall of hanging tools; then I searched a rather large tool chest. Each draw of the tool chest was labeled. The bottom draw had a label that read: plumbing tools. My father had every type of tool imaginable. He had hand tools and power tools, sockets and tools for measuring angles. I heard someone unlock the cellar doors; it had to be my father! I felt like I was doing something wrong by being down here, even though my mother had asked me to find a wrench. That familiar feeling of being afraid, overwhelmed me and I quickly reached up, pulled the chain cord to the overhead light and moved quietly into the shadows, where I believed I'd be safe. I witnessed the cellar doors open and the sudden sunlight temporarily strained my eyes, making it difficult to see the stairs. My eyes adjusted, to see my father coming down the stairs, carrying a rather large cloth sac. I watched as he pulled the cord to the overhead light and went directly over to his workbench. There he laid the cloth sac down and opened it. He poured the contents out onto the workbench. Immediately, I saw sparkling images of what could only be described as diamonds and fine jewelry – I even spotted a few gold watches! I was so nervous I consciously slowed my breath, believing if he knew I was down here, he would surely kill me! That's when I heard my heartbeat faster. Next, someone else came down the stairs, by way of the cellar doors. It was a thin man, with a deep voice. I knew this, because I witnessed him call out my father's name. He asked if my dad was down in the cellar? I watched as my father turned and hissed, "Yes. Come on down, but be quiet!" The stranger, who was apparently well-acquainted with my father, met him at the workbench and the two appraised the jewelry. I watched as the stranger picked up different items, and carefully looked at them more closely with what must have been a jeweler's magnifying glass. "Very nice, Leo! You have impeccable taste." The stranger smiled, pleased with my dad's efforts.

"Thank you. I told you they would be high end."

"What was the price you agreed on?" asked the stranger. I moved because I didn't want to be seen. Having moved, I couldn't see his face, due to where he was standing. However, I did get a good look at the back of his head and noticed he was rather mature – with a significant bald pattern.

"A million for everything," my father boasted rather confidently, "in U.S. dollars."

"That's far too much! Besides, these are hot items. You do realize it's going to take me a while to find a home for all these gems. I may have to hold on to them for a while too."

"That's not my problem. My source told me you were the one who wanted stuff like this and would be willing to pay top dollar."

"I pay within reason. I'll take everything off your hands for a hundred thousand dollars...that's American currency." The stranger spoke with a uniquely European accent – a mix of German, with a little evidence of the effort to speak clear and concise French. My father on the other hand, spoke clear and concise French and dabbled in German, for reasons concerning business. "A hundred thousand! That amount isn't even in the same neighborhood. I agreed to a million and was told you were on board with that figure!" I could see in my father's body language, that he was growing increasingly anxious, and I could tell by the tone of his voice he was beginning to build up pressure! The only relief valve for my dad's temper was to *lash out*! I became increasingly worried for the stranger's safety, hoping he would stop pushing my father closer and closer to the edge of no return.

"It's a hundred thousand dollars, take it or leave it!"

"I'll have to leave it then."

"You do know it's not wise to stash such stolen items? You never know if the authorities are looking for such missing merchandise," asserted the foolish stranger, obviously taunting my father.

"Are you threatening me?"

"Not exactly. I'm just explaining that one could inform the authorities about the whereabouts of such stolen merchandise, that's all. That is if we can't make a deal."

"That would make you an *accomplice*," grumbled my father, with that calm and unforgiving tone in his voice. The same tone I remember when he wanted to teach me a lesson.

"*No*. You must have heard about anonymously tipping off the authorities. I would actually get a reward for turning you in. Either way, I *win* and unfortunately, you *lose*."

"Is that so?! Is that what you plan to do?! You plan to *rat* me out?!" Shortly after I heard my father say the word rat, I noticed him reach for a nearby tool. The tool was a hammer, located near him on his workbench. He cleverly concealed it at his side.

"Honestly, I haven't yet decided."

"What possessed you to come to my home and appraise my goods, only to back out on the deal? Do you do this a lot? Do you enjoy ratting out others to the authorities?"

"I don't consider myself a rat. I'm a business man."

"Do you have any idea the amount of effort it took me to get these items?"

"I'm sure it wasn't easy."

"*No*, it wasn't! Have you thought about what it would do to my family and I, if you were to go tell the authorities about me and what I have here in my basement?" My father repositioned the hammer, making it possible for it to be seen.

"No, I haven't and to be totally honest, I don't care. What do you intend to do with that hammer?" The stranger noticed my father holding the tool at his side, like he was getting prepared to use it. "You do *realize*, now that you told me what your plan is, I can't allow you to leave?"

"Are you the one threatening *me*, now?" would be the last words coming from the stranger. I watched with sheer terror, as my father brutally beat the man next to him. Striking him repeatedly, over the head, with the hammer. I attempted to move quietly, only to bump into some carpentry stock. Mainly 2x4's stacked together. The stranger was left lying lifeless on the cellar floor, with my father standing over him. He heard the wood move and turned in my direction. "Who's there?!"

he shouted. I remained still, hoping he would think it was mice or something; but he didn't. Instead, he walked over to where I was standing. He found me near the wood pile, with my eyes closed. "What are you doing down here? Look at me when I'm talking to you!" I quickly opened my eyes, half-expecting to see the hammer directed at me! My father looked down at me; directly in my eyes and shrieked, "What did you see?" My legs went numb, and at that moment, I couldn't even utter a simple phrase – not even a word! I was completely *terrified*! Afraid of him lashing out at me; due to the stranger causing it to rain. Those storm clouds remained in his eyes, like a swirling cyclone, which could cause more damage, if I didn't try and appease the god of fury!

"Sebastien, tell me what you saw! Do you hear me?"

I finally overcame the fear that immobilized me, and I answered, "Nothing!"

"Sebastien, tell me the truth!" I could see in my father's eyes he was growing increasingly impatient with me. I decided lying wasn't an option. "Okay, I saw everything! I saw you put those jewels on the bench. I saw him come down stairs and you wanted a million for the stuff and he refused to pay that. Then I watched you hit him with your hammer."

"I did what I had to do. He was going to rat me out to the authorities, because he was a no-good bum. Why are you down here anyway?"

"Mom wanted me to get a wrench to fix the leak under the kitchen sink."

"Well, you gotta help me first," he groaned. It was then I noticed the storm clouds slowly dissipate in my father's eyes. The pressure in his blood, tapered off like a warm front gradually moving away, allowing the sun to return.

"With what?"

"*Him*." He pointed to the dead man, lying on the cellar floor. "We have to get rid of the body."

"How?" I asked.

"Don't you worry about that. I have just the stuff to eat away the flesh. It'll take a few days, but it will dissolve him, leaving just his bones. After that, we'll have to gather up his bones and I'll crush them with my hydraulic press. Then you can dispose of his ashes."

"Where?"

"The river," he explained. He then ordered me over to where the dead man was lying. He told me to take hold of the dead man's feet. I couldn't help but notice the man's expensive looking penny-loafers. Even his socks looked expensive. He told me to grab the dead man by the ankles and lift. I did what was expected of me. He directed me over to a rather large metal drum. He claimed it was triple sealed, for just this purpose. I helped him get the dead man's body inside, head first. Then I watched as my father went and retrieved large containers, containing high concentrations of different acids, including sulfuric. He then put on a pair of industrial gloves and goggles, before pouring the contents of each container into the metal drum. Immediately, I could smell the repulsive odor! The fumes even began to irritate my eyes. I watched, hoping he would hurry and put the lid on, sealing it and all the foulness inside. Within about twenty minutes, he seemed confident that there was sufficient acid solution inside the drum. He lifted the lid, putting it on the top of the drum and tapping it with the hammer, securing it in place. The following weekend, he reminded me about the dead man inside the drum, down in our basement. He wanted my help once again. This time, he was going to show me how to get rid of the bones – that afternoon, I lost my innocence. I no longer viewed life the way I had; even days before all this madness. While I pulled out both femurs at once, my dad queried, "Aren't you gonna ask me?"

"Ask you what?" I replied, handing him one femur at a time.

"Have I done this before? Have I murdered anyone before?"

"I wasn't going to ask you that. Since you mentioned it, have you?"

"I have! It's not something I'm proud of either. It comes with the job though." He continued to explain, whenever possible, he would ask his victims why they tried to do him harm? Whether it be like the stranger, wanting to go to the authorities, or others, who attempted to kill him first. For the life of me, I didn't understand what he meant? Or why he was telling me such details. Later, I realized he was trying to tell me, he wanted to know what made these men tick?

He wanted to know why they felt it necessary to go against him. Within a week, he was back trying to sell his stolen merchandise. From what I was told, he became desperate and tried to sell the jewels to an undercover policeman. That was the beginning of the end, because the authorities raided our home, found the drum and containers. They ran DNA tests and determined, the man whom I knew only as the stranger, was really a middle-aged man named, Hugo Schroeder. The authorities had reason to believe my father was responsible for two dozen other murders. He was sentenced to life in prison, and my mother divorced him. The scandal of being married to a convicted murderer was far too much for her to bear, so she decided to seek citizenship in the United States. We left France, with no intention of ever returning.

TWO

We could have moved anywhere in the United States, but my mother decided to bring me to Chicago, after hearing about all the opportunities, in the windy city. As the son of an immigrant, my mother and I had to overcome not just the language barrier, but also the cultural differences. It was difficult for her to enroll me in grade school, she wound up seeking assistance through child services, along with temporary financial support, through social services. We were fortunate, because we managed to get assistance for housing, food, clothing and I received the necessary help to get me enrolled in the proper classes, to help accelerate my learning. I had to take extra courses to help me learn and understand English. There's nothing worse, than feeling out of place; and that's how I felt attending grade school. I admired the students who were fortunate enough to accelerate in class. Later, I realized they did so well, because they had a strong family foundation, in which to work from. Some were more blessed than others, with parents who could afford nicer shoes, along with, shiny instruments for the after-school music program. I desperately wanted to measure up to that clique, but couldn't. I didn't have successful parents. In fact, I was embarrassed that my mother was still accepting welfare benefits, when she promised me, it would only be temporary. I knew I could never be accepted by the successful students, so I adjusted my aim and focused my attention on the athletic ones who could hit a fastball, or catch a football, like it was nothing. As much as I tried to fit in, by jogging and doing dozens of sit-ups and pushups, I was still at a disadvantage. I hadn't yet reached puberty, and my height and weight were anything but athletic. Finally, I found the group that accepted me for who I was, whether I was tall and lanky, like Todd Fritts, or unambitious, like Matt Fields, Pete Summers and Mike Grimes. Nothing was expected of me and surprisingly, I was ok with it. That was until that Friday afternoon, when a bunch of us decided to skip class and go steal. I was led to believe, it was okay to steal, because we were victims of the system. It was rather ironic, because even though my father was a thief and went to prison for it, he didn't want me to wind up in trouble with the authorities, and here I was about to commit a misdemeanor. I guess he knew the life he chose was wrong and he wanted a better life for me. Today was going to be a challenge, because it was my turn to steal and to show the other guys, I had what it takes to be brave and get what is mine – after all, I was told I deserved it. The target was the Derenis Convenient Store, located on the corner of 45th street. It was an old two-story brick building, with two apartments on the second-floor. One apartment was for the owners, the other apartment was for their grandson, by the name of Jimmie, he was one of Chicago's finest, or so I was told. I never actually seen him, but the word in the neighborhood was that he had been a patrolman for ten years. I was told it wouldn't be easy to steal anything from the Derenis Store, mainly because of the security cameras and the fact that everyone in the neighborhood was scared of being caught by Jimmie. I was told, I would need to steal as much candy as I could stuff into my pockets, without getting caught and that would prove my worth to the guys. They also mentioned, if I was really brave, try to steal some beer! Stealing beer was simply out of the question. I knew that was a fool's errand and would definitely get me into trouble. However, stealing dozens of candy bars wasn't out of the realm of possibility, and I was somewhat confident and ready to prove my worth! "You ready to do this?" howled Pete Summers. He was a seasoned thief, or so he liked everyone to think. He told us how he and his nephew stole electronics and sold them to a guy they knew, for good money. It seemed he already decided to make this a career. I on the other hand, was having second thoughts, because I didn't want to turn out like my old man, with a criminal record. I knew that would just devastate my mother – she had great hopes for me! She wanted to see me attend medical school and become some wealthy surgeon, so she would have someone to care for her when she got older – that's what she kept telling me. She's told me more than once, how she was saving her *nickels* and *dimes*, to help pay for my tuition. I knew if I backed out now, I would look like a coward in the eyes of my friends. There's nothing worse than being called a chicken! "I'm ready," I offered, looking right at Pete. He smiled and snapped, "Good! Now go get us some candy."

I walked off, even though my head was telling my legs to stop and think about what I'm about to do! I entered the convenient store for the first time. The security cameras were just where Todd said they'd be, one over by the front of the counter, where the cash register was located and two others positioned down both grocery aisles. Immediately, I thought it wasn't possible to steal anything without being seen. It didn't help that the owners, an elderly couple watched everyone that came in and they didn't take their eyes off you, until you paid for what you wanted and left the store. I went over to where the candy was located and began looking over what looked appealing to the eye. While doing that, I heard the little bell over the door; ring, signaling a customer had entered the store. Whoever it was? They knew the owners, because they were busy chatting, giving me ample time to decide what I wanted. I began stuffing my front and rear pockets, with as much candy that could possibly fit, without looking obvious. I was about to leave the store, when a clean-cut guy in his late twenties stopped me, by grabbing my arm and then standing directly in front of me, so I couldn't pass! "Hey, get your hands off me and get out of my way!" I snarled, putting my free hand up in front of me, just in case he planned on hitting me – my friend Matt Fields taught me that. He's into street fighting, and said if anyone gets directly in your way, preventing you from moving, or verbally threatens you, then put your hands up to protect your face and head. I noticed he saw the scar on the palm of my hand, where my dad placed my hand on the top of the stove when I was younger, to teach me a lesson.

"How did that happen?" asked the clean-cut guy, looking directly at the scar.

"None of your business! Now let me go!"

"Actually, it is my business, when you come into my grandparent's store and steal from them. You know who I am?" Right after he asked me that question, it dawned on me, this must be Jimmie, the grandson cop, everyone in the neighborhood talked about! He let go of my arm, but remained standing directly in front of me, preventing me from leaving.

"You're Jimmie the cop, aren't you?" I bleated, feeling nervous.

"Yes, I am. And who might you be?"

For a moment, I contemplated whether or not to lie to him about my name. It was then, I realized he could check and find out I lied. I decided to be honest, and tell him my real name. "My name is Sebastien." I didn't bother offering my last name, and it seemed he wasn't interested anyway.

"Where are you from, Sebastien?"

"I live here in Chicago."

"*No*, I mean where are you from? You have a noticeable accent?"

"Oh. I was born in France. My mother took me here, to start a better life."

"I wonder if she knows you're doing this? Stealing candy? You think she knows?"

"No, she doesn't. She would kill me if she found out!"

He reached out, took hold of my hand, turned it, so the palm was facing up. "Is she the one who did this to your hand?" he got a better look this time. I could tell by the expression on his face, he was genuinely concerned. "No, my dad did this to me, when I was younger. I was playing in the kitchen, with the stove and he caught me. He asked me what I was doing and I was so scared, that I lied. He told me if I lied, there would be severe consequences! Then he asked me again and I lied again, out of fear. I guess he knew I was lying to him, so he did this, to teach me a lesson, not to lie to him."

"That's awful! Does your dad abuse you a lot?"

"No, not anymore."

"Why is that?"

"He's in prison, back in France. He was arrested for murder."

"Oh, nice," Jimmie cackled, sounding a little sarcastic. "So, why are you doing this Sebastien? You following in your father's footsteps? You looking to be a career criminal?"

"No. My friends put me up to this."

"Are those the guys I saw outside? Are they waiting for you?"

"Yeah," I answered. I watched helplessly, wondering what he was going to do next? It took a moment for him to make a decision, and he uttered, "I'll tell you what I'm going to do."

"Please don't tell my mom!" I pleaded!

"I'm not going to tell your mom. I'm gonna pay for the candy you have in your pockets, but I want you to promise me, you'll never steal again."

"You're gonna do *what*?!" I gushed, finding it hard to believe he would be so kind, especially after all the rumors I've heard about how he treated criminals.

"I said, I'm gonna pay for the candy in your pockets and forget this ever happened, as long as you promise me, you'll never steal anything, ever again? okay?"

"Okay!"

"Promise me. Say, I promise I'll never steal again."

"I promise, I'll never steal again!" I repeated.

"You need to find new friends Sebastien. Friends who won't get you into trouble."

"I don't have any other friends."

"Well, I know I'm a lot older than you, but I could be a friend, if you want?" The moment he suggested he could be a friend to me, I immediately thought of him as a great big brother! An older sibling, that I never had. Someone with his background, who could teach me the difference between right and wrong. It was an offer I wasn't about to turn down. It was as if he was heaven sent, and this was an opportunity to change my life completely.

"Okay," I answered.

"You like baseball?" he asked. I didn't want to be rude, but I knew as much about baseball as I knew about aeronautics. I knew in baseball someone threw a ball at the one holding a bat. The one holding the bat was supposed to hit the ball into the air and run. That was my knowledge of baseball. I could tell he expected me to say, I loved baseball, every child my age should love baseball, but I didn't. I didn't even like it! Instead, I politely explained, "Sure, I like baseball!" After I told him that, I began to wonder if that could be construed as a lie? For the first time in my life, I was truly beginning to see what lying had done to me, because I was finding it difficult to be honest. Had I become the person my dad warned me about? The liar nobody trusted! If I had, I wasn't about to remain a liar, not now. With Jimmies help, I could redeem myself.

"Ever play baseball?"

"No, I've watched it though!"

"I coach a Little League on weekends. You should come and watch. Meet some of the kids, they're young like you."

"I don't know if they'd like me."

"Why do you say that?"

"Because, I'm not athletic."

"You don't have to be, just be yourself."

"Okay."

Jimmie walked me over to the counter, where his grandfather was and suggested, "I'm gonna pay for the candy, Sebastien has in his pockets." The old man looked confused; his eyebrows prove he was not at all pleased with what his grandson had just told him. "*You're* gonna pay for his candy? *Why?*"

"He has candy in his pockets?!" the old woman ranted.

"Why has he got candy in his pockets?" asked the old man.

"It's ok grandma and grandpa, I'm paying for the stuff."

"He tried to steal from us?" the old woman fumed. "That's a crummy thing to do to a couple of old folks." She looked directly at me, "we don't earn a lot of money. What we do earn; plenty of it goes to keep this store open. Do you realize when you steal from us, you effect our ability to pay to keep the store open. Where are you gonna shop if we have to close?"

Jimmie tried to defend me, "Grandma, it was only candy bars."

"Candy bars *today*, beer and cigarettes *tomorrow*! Eventually, he'll grow up to demand money out of the cash register! I tell ya', with kids like that, stealing all the time, your grandpa and I should just close the store and move to Florida."

"Grandma, he's promised me he'll never do it again."

"I don't want him back in this store," the old man blurted. Jimmie turned and urged his grandfather, "Grandpa, he's just a kid. We've all made stupid mistakes in life. He promised me he's never going to steal again and I'm willing to trust him.

Why don't you and grandma, give the boy a second chance?"
The old man wrinkled his lips, like he was struggling with the
thought of a child stealing from him and his wife, "Where
does this boy live anyway? I'd like to have a few words with
his parents!"

"Grandpa, calm down," Jimmie insisted.

"*Calm down*! This hoodlum thinks it's okay to steal. I'd
like to know who taught him it was okay to behave this way?
What's his name? I want to speak with his father in fact, I
want you to find his father and bring him here, so I can give
him a piece of my mind, before I file a complaint!"

"Grandpa, it's okay, it can all be resolved."

"Says who?"

Jimmie pointed at me and cautioned, "Grandpa look at
him...you really want to be the one to destroy his future?"

"Destroy his future! How would I be doing that?"

"You want to ensure he gets a juvey record?"

"No, but I don't want him stealing from us either."

"I agree. He's given me his word that he won't steal ever
again. Do you think you could find it in your heart to give
this child a second chance?" Jimmie asked, and his question
left me on the edge, because I wasn't sure what his grandfather
would say. I was somewhat relieved, when I heard the old
man say, "I suppose I could, if it's okay with Margret. Dear,"
he turned to his wife, "what do you think? Should we give
this young man another chance?"

"Jimmie, what's the boy's name?" asked the old woman.

"Sebastien."

"That's a nice name. Do you mind if I ask him a question?" she asked, looking over at Jimmie.

"I don't mind. What do you want to ask him?"

"Why did he steal?" she mumbled.

"Why don't you ask him yourself?" After Jimmie spoke, she turned to me and cawed, "Why did you steal from us?" I could see the years of arduous labor; embedded in the wrinkles of her forehead. Even her eyes showed decades of tenuous means, where she and her husband had to survive on a measly income – nothing short of austere.

"I didn't want to. My friends put me up to it."

"They don't sound like friends to me," she waffled.

"Well, I have a new friend," I replied.

"And who is your new friend?" asked the old man.

I pointed and offered confidently, "Jimmie."

"Yeah, we're friends now, I'm gonna walk him home, to show the guys waiting for him outside, that he's not going to be stealing anymore."

"You're not gonna tell my mom though, right?" I begged, feeling worried.

"No Sebastien, I gave you my word. That's something I guess I'm gonna have to teach you – the importance of giving someone your word. It's like an oath of honor. You know what an oath means?"

"No, not really."

"An oath is a promise, witnessed by someone else. When

I asked you never to steal again, and promise me...that was an oath. You gave me your word."

"Oh, okay."

"I have a lot to teach you, if you're willing?"

"Sure."

When we left the store, I saw all of my so-called friends, have run off. Jimmie turned to me and declared, "See, there's no honor among thieves. Those kids, your so-called friends, couldn't care less about you. They only care about themselves."

"I see that. I gotta question for you?"

"What's that?"

"What do I say to my mom? I mean, how do I explain, *you*?"

"Tell her the truth."

"You mean, *everything*?"

"That's up to you. I gave you my word that I wouldn't tell her you attempted to steal. You could just say, we met at the Derenis Convenient Store. You didn't have enough money for candy, so I paid for it and we got to talking. I told you I was the grandson cop of the owner of the Derenis Convenient Store, and I mentioned I coach kids' baseball on weekends. I offered to have you come and watch some weekend and you agreed. You're not lying if you tell her that."

"Your right, I'll tell her that. Thank you!"

"For what?"

"For buying me the candy, even though I was intending to steal it."

"Just remember, you gave me your word – no more stealing, ever again!"

"I know."

"You know, you're pretty lucky kid?"

"Why?"

"Because if I wasn't there, and my grandparents caught you, they'd clobber you! My grandpa has a bat behind the counter – he's not afraid to use it either."

"I'm sure!"

THREE

The day Jimmie Derenis and I became friends, was truly a turning point in my life – the event changed me forever. He truly became the older sibling, I never had. Every weekend, without fail, he showed up at my residence, knocked at the door and told my mother, he was there to take me to baseball practice. I enjoyed going to watch each game, and he taught me a lot about baseball, like the right way to throw one. The elements of a catcher's mitt, like the pocket and the bridge; where the baseball lands – if caught properly. He explained the importance of the outfielder and their job to catch pop-ups or fly balls, and to hold the runners at their bases and stop anything from getting past them. He also taught me the proper way to hit the ball, using my hips and turning with my ankle in the direction I want the ball to go. Finally, he coached me on running the bases and pitching the ball. His guidance didn't stop there. He even helped me with school work and when I became a freshman in high school, he helped me navigate my way. He got me interested in wrestling and music. He thought learning to play the piano would be a great way for me to express myself and teach me the importance of discipline. I had no problem tackling wrestling, because it allowed me to bring out the beast inside me – the beast I never knew existed. On the other hand, learning to play the piano, took me in a totally different direction. The first few months were difficult, because I had to learn to use not only all my fingers on one hand, but incorporate the other hand into practicing, along with my feet. Jimmie attended both my wrestling events, and the days I practiced piano. He noticed I wasn't putting in the same effort, in piano as I was with wrestling. One day while practicing piano, he mentioned it. "Excuse me," Jimmie uttered, to my piano teacher, "I've noticed Sebastien is having difficulty getting both hands to work in unison. Are there exercises he can do to help him overcome that?"

"There are, but I think what you're looking for is an instructor who is the master of improvisation. Someone who combines performance with communication of emotions and instrumental technique, as well as spontaneous response to other musicians. I really think that's what he needs and I believe that's what you're looking for," explained the piano teacher, "I could give you the number of a very talented and accomplished jazz pianist, if you want. I believe he's currently accepting new students. However, I should warn you, he's a little expensive."

"When you say a little, how much are we talking?" Jimmie asked.

"Two hundred dollars an hour."

"Wow! That much?"

"It's money well spent, if you want Sebastien to learn from an iconic professional. I mean, the difference between learning from me and learning from Neil, is like your child attending the university of Illinois, which is where I attended. Or Juilliard, in New York City, where Neil attended and graduated."

"What's Neil's last name?"

"Markowitz. Neil Markowitz. If you want Sebastien to learn from the best, he's the one to see."

"Really?" Jimmie hooted, before he turned to me, "What do you think of learning from Neil Markowitz?" It was if he was willing to overlook the fact that the guy charged two hundred dollars an hour, by the expression on his face. "He's *expensive* though," I replied.

"Not if I can get you a job, working for my grandfather, around twenty hours a week. I'm willing to pay half of whatever he'll charge for lessons for the week."

"I believe he offers up to three lessons a week. One hour each lesson," explained the piano teacher, "but most students only do one hour a week, because there is so much material to cover and you need to have time to practice."

"Does he have any students that do up to three hours?" asked Jimmie.

"He does, but their *exceptional.* I mean they *live, breathe* and *sleep* piano sheet music. They practice nearly all day long. They're the exception and not the rule, but the choice is up to you. I know he does offer from one to three hours a week. It really all depends on Sebastien. If he thinks he can do three hours a week, then by all means try it. However, if it were me, I would probably try just the one hour a week. It will take longer, but it might be worth it."

"What do you think about three hours a week? You wanna see how that goes?" asked Jimmie.

"That's six hundred bucks a week!" I was surprised!

"No, it's three hundred a week from you and three hundred from me. Like I said, I'm willing to pay half."

"You'd do that for me?" I was utterly at a loss for words, because he was willing to do so much for me.

"As long as you put in a hundred and ten percent."

"Sebastien will have to be able to practice a lot. So, I'd advise you to consider buying a used piano."

"What does a good used piano cost?"

"Depends on the condition. I have an old Baldwin, upright. I'd be willing to sell it for fifteen hundred," explained the teacher.

"I'm sorry, but I live on a cop's salary. Hoping to make detective soon. If I pass the exam that'll be a bump up in pay."

"I didn't know you were a Chicago cop."

"Yeah, it's not something I go around telling everyone," Jimmie said, politely with a smile.

"You being a cop, I'll let you have it for free. Consider it a thank you for your service to the city."

"Really?"

"Yes. However, you'll have to come and get it and transport it to wherever you plan to keep it."

Jimmie looked over, "Sebastien."

"Yeah," I turned to see him staring at me. I was about to apologize for being distracted, because I had allowed myself to be captivated by a very beautiful young girl; around my age. I didn't know her name, all I knew was that she practiced piano as well, with another female piano instructor.

"You think your mom has room for the piano at your place?" He then turned to the teacher and said, "How big of a piano are we talking?"

"An upright, doesn't require a lot of space. It can go in any room, or bed room."

"Sebastien, what do you think? You wanna make arrangements to pick it up and bring it home?" he asked, looking at me. It was almost as if he expected me to say *yes*, otherwise he was going to be disappointed. The last thing I wanted to do was disappoint him. On the other hand, I needed to be sure my mom would allow me to have a piano in our home. "I probably should ask my mother first."

"Okay. If she won't let you have it there, I can bring it to my apartment and you can practice before or after work, because I'm going to convince my grandparents, they could use the help and you need the work; especially *now*, seeing how you're going to have to pay half, for your more expensive jazz piano lessons."

FOUR

Jimmie managed to convince his grandparents to allow me to work five days a week in their convenience store, around my already busy schedule, which included: lessons with Neil Markowitz, after school wrestling, homework and practicing the piano until my fingers ached. The old man, Lloyd Derenis, warned me if I ever stole from his store again, he'd see to it that his grandson, would bring me out in handcuffs, so everyone in the neighborhood would know I was arrested for stealing. I gave him my word, I would never steal another item from his store, not even a piece of chewing gum. The old man was very generous, even though I had given him every reason not to be. My wages were just enough to cover the cost of my weekly obligation to pay for lessons with Neil Markowitz, along with the unfair and in my opinion, unnecessary taxes my employment would incur.

My job included helping unload freight, with a pallet-jack, stocking product on shelves and inside the two main refrigerated coolers. I was also responsible for rotating product, to prevent expired items from winding up on the back of the shelves. Deliveries arrived twice a week. Every Monday at 5 p.m., there was a scheduled delivery of soda and dairy products for the coolers. Every Thursday at 6 p.m., there was a huge delivery of product, from toiletries to bread and flour. First thing I had to do, when a delivery arrived, was look over the driver's inventory sheet and match it with Lloyd's list. If there were any discrepancies, the old man told me to tell the driver to take whatever wasn't ordered off the pallet, before I helped move it inside. Once inside, it was my job to help customers who might enter, while stocking product. Mondays and Thursdays were the worst – a real grind! I had to get up at 5:30 a.m., to do my school work, have breakfast and shower, before going off to school. Classes ended at 2 p.m. and I wrestled for a full-hour, before rushing off to work, at the convenience store. After work, I spent several hours practicing piano. I asked my mother if I could bring the Baldwin to our apartment and she wasn't thrilled by the idea, mainly because she wasn't sure how long we'd be living in the building. We lived under what was called, Section-8. It was very affordable housing for those with limited funds. My mother wanted us to live in a better neighborhood, one where she wouldn't have to worry about me. Her anxiety about my safety had convinced me to ask Jimmie if he'd show me some self-defense moves, he learned while attending the police academy. He offered to show me a few things over the weekend. (The Baldwin piano found its home in Jimmie's apartment.) He told me I could practice on it as much as I wanted; for as long as I wanted. However, I would have to be finished with homework, wrestling and work at the store. Jimmie worked nights, so practicing after work, wasn't an issue. Most weekends, he stayed over at his girlfriend's apartment. Her name was Vicky and she lived in Wicker Park, in a three-story brown stone. Most nights I didn't finish practicing piano until around 11 p.m. My mother claimed she spent most of the evening waiting for me to get home, worried I might become another neighborhood statistic. I had told her several times, not to worry, because I was a senior now. Besides, I wrestled and had filled out my T-shirt rather well. I tried to assuage her anxiety, by trying to reassure her that I could defend myself, but anything I said, wasn't effective. That evening, I managed to practice all the jazz compositions, Neil had asked me to work on. I had even managed to improvise some; adding a little spice of my own to the material. The piano was located in Jimmie's living room. It faced the outside wall, with an adjacent window to its right. I only had to lean over a foot or so, to look out the window. Normally, I kept the window closed, due to noise pollution, from passing vehicles, with their stereos blaring loudly, or kids out in the neighborhood, when they should be home. I covered the piano keys, with the keylid – it protected the piano keys, when I wasn't practicing. I was amazed at how large his apartment was – it had to be twice the size of the apartment my mother and I lived in. He had nice furniture for a cop; he even had a large screen TV. My curiosity got the best of me and I wound up turning on the

TV, just to see how many channels it had. I slowly scanned through each channel, until I came to a commercial for the military. It was an ad for the Marine Corp., looking for *a few good men*, who were brave enough to join! The ad showed what it took to become a marine – the training, the discipline and the result – a warrior! It mentioned a phone number and website, before the channel returned to the local news. I mentally recalled the phone number, and decided to write it down. First, I had to find a pen; than a piece of paper. I found a pen, but no paper so I decided to write the number above my wrist, where it wouldn't smudge.

FIVE

Usually, I used the weekend to catch up on some much-needed rest. However, I had promised Jimmie, I'd meet him in front of his grandfather's convenience store, around 10 a.m. The plan was to go to Fuller Park and practice some self-defense moves. He told me he knew the Fuller Park Supervisor very well – they both attended the Marshall Metro High School and played on the football team. At that time, Jimmie was a first-string quarterback and his friend Terry, was a defensive lineman. Apparently, Jimmie got permission from Terry, the Fuller Park Supervisor, to let us use the boxing gym exclusively for the entire afternoon. (The boxing gym was within the Fuller Melville Park.) The park itself was approximately 11.41 acres, with a fieldhouse, a fitness center, along with two gymnasiums. The park also featured a swimming pool, refurbished patio and fountain area. People like Jimmie, who enjoyed athletics, had their choice between: basketball, baseball, soccer or tennis. When I got to the convenience store, I saw Jimmie outside, waiting for me. "You beat me," I conceded, as I approached him. "Well, I do live here," he replied.

"Yeah, but I thought you spent your weekends with your girlfriend, Vicky?"

"I do. I mean, I will be spending the rest of the weekend, with her later. Today's the start of the weekend. So, you ready to learn some self-defense?"

"Yeah."

"I figure since we have the entire Fuller Boxing Gym to ourselves, I can also show you the elements of boxing."

"I've never been to the Fuller Park, what's it like?" I watched as he kneeled down, picked up a gray colored gym bag and added, "You've never been to Fuller Park?" He walked to his classic 1966 Chevy Impala. The car was in mint condition. Its exterior paint color was midnight black, with two red racing stripes running up the entire length of the engine's hood, and car's roof, ending at the end of the vehicle's trunk. I've asked on a few occasions, if he would ever keep this gorgeous car in a garage, or at least covered? His reply was always the same, 'If I treat it like a classic, I'll wind up never using it. What's the point of having a car, if you're not going to use it?' I followed after him, "No, I never had a reason to go to Fuller Park."

"Trust me, you're gonna love it," he insisted, stopping at the rear of his vehicle, opening the trunk and tossing the gym bag inside, before closing it.

"What's in the gym bag?" I went around to the passenger's

side. He looked over the roof at me and divulged, "I got you a pair of wrist wraps and weighted gloves, to help with your self-defense training."

"Cool!" The interior of Jimmie's car was absolutely spotless. There was no sign of wear or damage, from the seats to the vehicle's dashboard. In fact, it appeared as if it just rolled off the assembly line. I looked over as he got in, closed the door and put the key in the ignition. He was about to start the car, when I noted, "Graduation is coming up in three months, are you gonna be able to make it?"

"Your high school graduation?" he replied, looking over. "Yeah."

"I wouldn't miss it for all the gold in Fort Knox!" His reply, put a smile on my face – a smile the length of the car. He turned the ignition, starting the engine. The car's supercharged V8 was equipped with a chrome CAT-back exhaust system. The dual pipes were tucked nicely under the rear bumper. The engine fired up with a loud roar, before tapering off to the sound of a galloping horse. Inside the Fuller Boxing Gym. Jimmie showed me how to properly put on my wrist wraps, by having me watch him put his on first. I only watched him wrap one hand, before attempting to wrap my own. I followed exactly how I saw him wrap his wrist. He made a comment: "Wow! You got it, on your first try! You just might be a natural." He directed me away from the ropes into the center of the ring. "Let's start with you getting used to throwing one's and two's, okay?"

"Sure."

"Keep your hands up, to protect your head," he said, then showed me what he meant. He told me to jab. "Come on, throw a jab!"

"What's a jab?"

"It's just a punch. Throw a punch."

"Oh. Like this?" I clinched my fist, and struck the air in front of me.

"Exactly!"

I threw another punch, and he immediately commented: "Nice! *Powerful!* Keep going. After a few more, I'll show you some combinations."

"Jimmie." I clinched my fist again and punched forward.

"Yeah?" he replied.

"You mentioned to me before that you knew a lot of fighting styles. Did you learn all that at the police academy?"

"When I was your age, my dad got me involved in boxing. Then when I got really good, he felt I needed more of a challenge, so he got me to take Jiu-Jitsu and Krav-Maga. I excelled in all those fighting styles and found myself buying DVDs to learn more about things like wrist-locks and how to successfully take a gun or knife away from an attacker."

"Really?"

"Yeah. Then when I went to the police academy, I learned even more techniques."

"Can you teach me everything you know?" I asked, thrilled and excited to learn everything and anything about defending myself. "Yeah, kid. I'll give you a little advice one of my instructors said to me, while at the police academy. His name was Trent Rogers; a real nice guy – sharp as a tack. Book smart, from being a college grad and street smart, from being very aware of his surroundings. His advice to me was, be like a sponge and absorb everything that I hear, see or am exposed to, because it will ultimately be a tool for me when I'm out on the streets. He was right! Everything he taught me was absolutely vital and to this day, I can't thank him enough, because his training saved my butt many times."

"So be a sponge. I can do that," I replied.

"Today, we're going to go over a ton of material, so if you have any questions, don't be afraid to interrupt me and ask me whatever's on your mind; okay?"

"Okay."

After about thirty minutes of boxing, he decided to teach me about the elements of Krav-Maga. He explained, there may come a time, when I'll need to defend myself with my knees. He showed me how to properly use my knees in a fight. He also covered the importance of covering the face, eyes and ears when needed. He mentioned it didn't take much to permanently damage the eardrum by cupping your hands and striking the ears of your opponent. After about two hours of going over techniques in Krav-Maga, which included successfully taking away a gun and knife, he then showed me the importance of understanding Jiu-Jitsu.

"You never want a fight to end up on the ground. However, you may wind up there, so you have to know how to defend yourself. I'm just going to go over some key points today. Everything I've shown you; we'll go over every weekend if you want; for as long as you want."

"Really! Thank you. That would be great."

He told me to lie down. Then he showed me a guarding position and told me to protect my face, while maneuvering my knee in front of his stomach, for a sweep. He showed me what he called an elevator sweep. He directed me to use my ankle and hips to push him off. I managed to get him off me, before he hollered, "Don't stop! Get up on my chest and pin my arms down, so I can't move."

"I don't want to hurt you though."

"You're not gonna hurt me. Just do it!" he cried out and I leaped up, straddled him and pinned him down so he couldn't move.

"Nice! A couple of more weeks and you'll be ready for the UFC."

"What's that?"

"You never heard of the *UFC*?"

"No, sorry."

"It's the Ultimate Fighting Champion. You ever see a cage match on television?"

"No."

"Wow, okay!"

"Jimmie," I sighed, letting his arms go and getting up off the ground.

"Yeah," he followed after me.

"What do you think of the Marine Corp? I'm thinking of joining recon right after graduation." He stopped dead in his tracks and looked at me. "What do I think of the marines?" he repeated. "They're an elite fighting group. Especially recon. Why recon?"

"I think it would be a challenge and a great experience for me to develop my fighting skills."

"You mean killing skills. The only thing recon will teach you is to be an efficient killing machine."

"So, you're saying you don't think I should join the marines?"

"No, I'm not saying that. You do what you think you need to do. What does your mom think about the idea of you joining the military?"

"I haven't mentioned it yet. She wants me to go off to college to study *medicine* or *law*."

"She just wants the best for you kid."

"I know. I don't know how to tell her."

"Just be honest. Tell her you want to get the experience that only the military can provide, then you'll go off to college. Tell her, the marines might even offer college classes. I know they offer the G.I. Bill, which helps veterans go to school afterwards."

"Yeah, I'll tell her that. I'll tell her it could help me with college expenses."

"Sounds like a plan. Now let's get back to training, leatherneck!"

"Leatherneck? What's that?" I asked. I was curious, because I had never heard the term before.

"That's a nickname for a marine, get used to it!"

We spent the rest of the day going over more fighting techniques. Jimmie not only managed to show me all the important elements of ground fighting, he also sparked an interest for wrist-locking techniques. He warned me only use wrist-locking in the event someone grabs me. He also mentioned I could use it too if someone threw a punch and I blocked it, tracked down my attacker's arm and then ended with a lock. I was equally impressed when he showed me some explosive training to help build endurance. It was literally running in place, with my arms out in front of me. I had to run for five minutes, with both arms out in front. After five minutes he told me to stop and do twenty-five jumping jacks. When I was finished, he ordered me to run in place again, with my arms over my head and my hands straight up in the air. After about ten minutes of doing this exercise, he gave me a ten-pound weight to carry. While we ran in place he reminisced, "I remember training at the Titan Gym, I was the youngest member at the time; a lot younger than you. It was there, that I excelled at Krav-Maga, boxing and martial arts." He stopped running in place, so he could take a moment to catch his breath. He noticed I was about to quit too, "Keep going…I didn't tell you to stop!"

"Yes sir! Jimmie what's Krav-Maga?" I was curious.

"It's a form of Israeli martial arts, for Israeli soldiers. As you now know, it involves using your knees a lot and striking fast. If you train to become a Marine Recon, you'll be exposed to it, along with plenty of other fighting skills."

"Really?"

"Yep. Sebastien, with that knowledge though – comes plenty of responsibility."

"I know, realize that...." I managed to get the words out, even though I was practically out of breath.

"Okay, you can stop running."

I was feeling exhausted; even more than when I wrestle. My legs were fatigued and I wasn't sure how much more of this grueling exercise I would be able to endure. That's when he said, "We're not finished yet. I just want to say something and make sure you understand what I'm about to say."

"Okay."

"I want you to promise me that what I teach you, you'll only use to help defend others and yourself against an attacker. You'll never use any of it, to bully others. Especially, someone weaker than you. Everything I'm teaching you; I want you to use to help defend those who may need your assistance. I want you to promise me you'll never use what I teach you for anything evil. Anything that would harm an innocent person."

"Yes sir, I promise!"

"There may come a time when you just need to walk away, never even using anything we've gone over. Promise me that too – promise me that you'll only use force, as a last resort. Ideally, you just want to get away from your attacker."

"Okay."

"So, say I promise I'll only use force as a last resort. I will never start a fight and I will live by a code."

"I promise I will only use force as a last resort. I will never start a fight and I will live by a code," I repeated. "What's a code…?"

"I'll tell you all about it on the way home," he said, before asking me if he taught me enough for one day? Honestly, I was a little confused, "You said we weren't finished yet."

"I was just testing you. I wanted to see your level of commitment. I know you're exhausted. You could have complained, but you didn't. You hung in there, like a marine would. Now, you ready to get outta here?"

"Is this another test?"

"No, I'm starved and I wanna put my feet up when I get home."

"In that case, yeah I'm ready…"

On the way home, Jimmie explained what a code was. He told me, if I say I'm going to do something, I do it, no matter what! *My word was my code. I need to learn to convince others that my word is as good as gold. Also, he made me promise never to strike a female, or a child and I must learn to listen to older people, because they're mature and wise, which in the long run benefits me and develops genuine character – something people notice immediately!*

SIX

I was the last Marist student to receive my high school diploma. It was handed over to me and I waved to my graduating class, before exiting the stage. I finally felt all the effort of studying and working hard to achieve good grades, had finally paid off! I knew both my mother and Jimmie were proud of me, and I was very happy about it. "You look so handsome in red!" my mother praised me, referring to my academic regalia; better known as cap and gown.

"You did it!" Jimmie extended his hand to shake mine. "You should be really proud of yourself son." It was at that moment – the moment he used the word *son*, that I felt an even stronger bond toward him; almost as if he was the father I should have had. Instead of shaking his hand, I gave him a hug and said, "I wouldn't be here if it weren't for you! Thank you." Just as I released my hug, I noticed out of the corner of my eye, one of my high school friends named, Rudy Brennan. He came over, with his year book in hand. "Hey Sebastien! You never signed my yearbook. You mind signing it?"

"Not at all," I replied. "What should I write?"

"Say something funny," he insisted, with a simple, yet priceless expression on his face. He reminded me of a class clown, who was always seeking attention from other students. The only difference between him, and a true class clown was his *genuine intelligence*. Rudy was really smart; he just never showed it. He never played high school sports, or participated in any after school activities. He liked to read though, and spent most of his time reading spy novels and thrillers. "How about, a good friend will always help you move some furniture, but a best friend will always help you move a dead body," I said and waited for his response. At first, he seemed reluctant to say a word. Probably because he wasn't sure what his folks would say, if they perused his yearbook and found my comment. His parents weren't thrilled about him spending most of his time reading spy novels. They had even mentioned their concern; telling him he needed to focus on attending college and stop thinking about espionage. They never realized, but Rudy also thought a lot about *females* and *beer*. Finally, he muttered, "Okay. If that's what you wanna write."

"You said you wanted me to write something funny, didn't you?"

"Yeah, yeah. Anyway, it's all good! Write what you were going to write." He handed me his yearbook and I put my thoughtful quote near my photo. While I wrote the quote, he asked me what my plans were, now that I had graduated high school? I finished the quote, signed my name and said, "I'm looking at joining the marines."

"The marines! The *military marines*?" he asked, seeking clarification.

"Yeah, why?"

"Sebastien, I never thought of you as a marine."

"Well, that's my plan. I'm gonna join the marines, see the world and go to college afterwards. What are *your* plans, now that you graduated?" I asked him. Figuring he'd be thinking of joining the military too, because he loved to read action thrillers and novels that involved government conspiracy. "I'll be going off to college soon."

"What college?"

"Florida State University, where the temperature is warm and the girls are warmer," he chuckled.

"I can see what you're major is going to be..."

"You know it – *babes* and *beer*!"

"I'm thinking of having the marines pay my way through college, with the G.I. Bill when I get out."

"Don't you mean, if you get out?" he offered, teasing me.

"I figure four years active and four years in active reserve. Besides, I want to give back to this country for allowing me to become a citizen. I've benefitted a lot and this is my way of returning the favor."

"I get ya, it's all good. When you get out, look me up, okay?"

"I'll do that, if I'm ever down in Florida," I replied. Rudy had a weakness for beautiful females. His attention was distracted by two stunning beauties. He rushed off to ask them to sign his stomach, instead of his yearbook. I smiled, thinking he was never going to grow up.

"I got a surprise for you," said Jimmie. I turned and faced him.

"What kind of surprise?" I thought he and my mom had either arranged to take me out to dinner, or he planned on taking me axe throwing again. He had gotten me addicted to throwing knives and axes – and I was very good at it. Jimmie just looked at me, with an expressionless face. I was beginning to think something wasn't right, when suddenly, he raised his right hand and showed me a pair of dangling car keys. "You know how you always ask me, when am I gonna cover my 1966 Chevy Impala?" He told me to put my hand out, with my palm facing up. Then he dropped the keys into my hand and said, "Well, it's yours now. So, if I were you, I'd do an online search for a car cover to fit it."

"This is a joke, *right*?"

"Not at all, Sebastien. You worked hard. You overcame a lot. You turned out better than I expected. I know how you love the car; I see it every time you get in. You deserve it – it's yours now. Do me a favor though."

"Anything!"

"Take really good care of it and maybe when you're not too busy, you can take me for a ride, now and then."

"You bet I will, and anytime you want to go cruising, just let me know."

"After you get back from the marines," he reminded me.

"That's right."

"You're always welcome to come over and use it, while he's away, Jimmie," said my mom.

"Yeah, it's gonna need to be driven, while I'm away."

"Don't worry about that, I'll work out the details with your mom," he offered. "What do you say, we take your classic car for a ride? Your mom's invited me out for dinner and since it's your graduation and you're going to be a marine, I figured it would be my treat. You have any place in mind?" he asked me. I told him I knew the perfect restaurant; it was one my mom always talked about, but she could never afford.

SEVEN

To say the training to become a Force Recon Marine was intensely difficult, demanding, stressful and arduous was putting it *mildly*. It began in three distinct phases. First phase, was four weeks long and focused on individual physical skills; such as running, high repetition PT, obstacle courses and special skills, involving land navigation, helicopter rope suspension training, communications and arms support. Second phase, was three weeks long, consisting of training on small unit tactics and mission planning – along with team; open-ocean amphibious skills. Third phase was two weeks long and involved team communications and patrolling skills. Part of my training involved mountaineering equipment and the proper use of knots and how to tie every single useful knot, known-to-man. Advanced water survival was extremely difficult and several of the cadets I got to know, weren't up for the challenge. They wound up quitting and returning to their originally assigned MOS, also known as Military Occupational Specialty. On average it takes a year and a half, to two years to become a full-fledged FORECON. I had received additional training in force recon sniper school and was attached to the 1st Recon Battalion, stationed at Camp Pendleton, California. I was deployed three times, for eight months at a time, over to the Middle-East. I was part of a six-man team and our mission was highly classified. We didn't know much of the details of the job, only that it involved targeting and eliminating a Middle-Eastern Taliban leader who went rogue, after the US government helped establish and fund him, with taxpayer dollars. On August 8th, 2008, near the village of Shewan in the Bala Buluk district, Farah Province; Afghanistan. US and coalition forces encountered up to 350 insurgents. Our mission suddenly changed from seeking a known Taliban leader to conducting a clearing operation of the village. After about 8 hours of grueling combat, we were able to defeat the Taliban fighters. Force Recon helped in opening up route 517, which was the main supply route – opening the route was key to continuing combat operations in the area. My team was deployed in other operations around the world, we even helped the CIA, MOSSAD and MI6 with some of their black ops, including destabilizing other countries, for the purpose of regime change and to ensure British dominance, around the world.

Every sniper I knew, including myself kept a mental score card of all the successful kills. While in the Force Recon, I managed 3,703 confirmed kills. These were men who didn't deserve to breathe, let alone continue to harm others. My service in Force Recon, changed me from the inside out. When I returned to the states, I was feeling hollow inside, like something was missing. The adrenaline that used to course its way through my veins, was no longer stimulating me. I felt like a lost vessel at sea, wandering *aimlessly*. There was only one person I was certain, who would understand how I was feeling and could possibly help me navigate through my *depression*, so I went to see Jimmie. His grandpa, Lloyd at the convenience store, told me Jimmie was involved in a shooting, while following up on a domestic. Apparently, the boyfriend of the victim, didn't want his girlfriend talking to the police. He threatened her with violence and a struggle ensued. She managed to get away and call 9-1-1. Jimmie was one of the first responders, and was shot twice – once in the torso, where the bullet penetrated the abdomen. The other bullet, struck him in the neck – missing his right carotid artery. He managed to returned fire, killing the assailant. He was taken to Northwestern Memorial Hospital and placed in critical, but stable condition. I rushed over to the hospital, unconcerned about my own safety; driving fast and passing slower moving traffic. When I got to the hospital, I parked out near the main-entrance and rushed inside. I was told he was in the MICU located on the ninth-floor of the Feinberg and Galter pavilions.

"I'm here to see Jimmie Derenis! How is he?" I asked one of the nurses at the nursing station. I noticed her name, Carla Huntington on her employee ID, attached to her uniform. She looked up at me and said, "Are you a family member?" For a moment, I was unsure how to answer her question. I realized if I said I wasn't, I probably would not be allowed to see him. However, if I lied and said I was, and the hospital found out, I might be barred from visiting. I remembered Jimmie calling me *son*, at my graduation, and that was enough to solidify my confidence. I answered, "Yes, I'm a family member."

"Mr. Derenis was in surgery yesterday, to remove a bullet from his abdomen," she explained.

"I heard he was shot twice."

"He was. Once in the stomach and the other bullet passed through his neck. Luckily for him, it missed his carotid artery by three millimeters."

"Can I see him?"

"He might not be awake, but I can certainly show you to his room and let you visit," Carla said, leaving her chair and taking me to his room. As I entered the room, I noticed the lights were off and there was patient monitoring equipment measuring his vitals. I saw him in a supine position, with his eyes closed. He looked comfortable for someone having gone through surgery. Carla directed my attention to the chair at the corner of the room, facing his bed. "You can sit there."

"Thank you."

"Would you like water, or coffee?" she asked me.

"No, I'm good. Thanks."

"If you need anything, I'll be at the nurse's station."

"Okay," I replied. She left the room, allowing me privacy. I went over to his bedside and I reached out, took hold of his hand. "Jimmie, this is Sebastien here. I'm back from active duty. I have so much I want to tell you about my deployments overseas, when you wake of course. Your grandpa told me what happened. He's worried about you too! You're pretty fortunate, you know? Your guardian angel was watching over you. Nurse Carla told me the bullet to your neck, missed your carotid artery by three millimeters. That's extremely close. Later on, I'm thinking of contacting your girlfriend, Vicky and letting her know what happened, assuming she hasn't already heard. You know, when I heard you were shot, I have to admit I was a little surprised? I say that because you're so knowledgeable and careful. How did you manage to get shot in the stomach? I can understand the neck, but the stomach? Weren't you wearing a vest? You couldn't have been, otherwise the bullet wouldn't have found its way into your stomach. I never thought you'd wind up here. Times have changed. The streets are getting more dangerous by the day. I'm sure you have your stories you know, it just dawned on me, all the time I've known you, you've never once told me about your police experiences. When you wake, I'm gonna ask you. I wanna hear all the stories, especially the details concerning how you got shot? What was going through your mind, when you heard the 9-1-1 call? Did the guy who shot you, try to reason with you? Or did he just shoot you? And when you got shot, were you scared? Were you scared of *dying*? A couple of guys I knew in the marines got shot. One named Tex, he was real stoic...pain never seemed to faze him. There was another guy, we called, Hollywood, because after the corps he was planning to become an actor or go into doing television commercials for a living. He got shot too and he complained and complained. My time over there made me realize; pain is simply a state of mind. You can overcome it, as long as you don't dwell on it. Anyway, I wanna hear it all when you wake." I looked over at one of the monitors, measuring his heart and blood pressure. "I gotta admit, I feel helpless. I wish there was something I could do to fix this. You hear about stuff like this happening all the time, you never really think about it, until it hits home. Now I understand how others feel, when they lose a loved one to gun violence. We always hear how something has to be done, yet nothing ever changes. The media blames guns for the violence, not the broken homes where single moms are forced to raise their children, without a father. Everything begins at home. If we really want to stop gun violence, senseless school shootings and other violent crimes, we need to focus on the family. I remember you saying, 'Guns don't kill people, people kill people. If it wasn't a gun, it would be a knife or something else.' Remember? Anyway, I'm gonna sit over here, and keep you company for a little while."

EIGHT

I went to the hospital every day that week, to see how Jimmie was doing, hoping he would be awake so we could talk and he could tell me exactly what happened. I arrived just as the nursing staff did a shift change. I was hoping nurse Carla would have something new to tell me about his status. I found her leaving his room. "How's Jimmie doing?" I asked.

"He's awake. He woke earlier this morning. He just asked me to get him some pain killer, I told him I'd have to speak to the attending physician, about it."

"Is it alright if I go in and visit?"

"Absolutely! I'm sure he'll be happy to see you," she replied kindly, before returning to the nursing station. As I went into Jimmie's room, I felt anxious to see him – I wanted to hear his voice again. "There he is!" I beamed, as I approached him. He was lying in the Fowler's position, which is about a forty-five-degree angle and he looked comfortable. "God, I'm glad to see you're awake! How do you feel?" I stopped at the side of his bed.

"I got a little bit of pain. I asked the nurse if she could gimme some pain killer, she told me she'd have to talk to the doctor about it. Anyway, I'm really glad to see you *too*? You on leave, or something?"

"*No*, I'm semi-separated from the corp."

"How so?"

"I'm finished with my active-duty obligation, now I just have to complete my inactive reserves."

"And what does that involve?" he asked, sounding genuinely interested.

"I was told it involves doing drills, one weekend a month two weeks a year."

"That isn't bad."

"Enough about me, I wanna know what happened with you?"

He rolled his eyes and said, "All I remember is I went to a domestic and found myself looking down the barrel of a gun."

"I heard you got shot in the stomach."

"Yeah."

"How did that happen, weren't you wearing a vest?"

"No, I'm a detective now. I know that's not an excuse. I really should have been wearing under armor, but like they say, hindsight is *twenty-twenty*; my bad. So, now that you are home, what have you got planned?"

"I'm thinking of either taking the civil service exam for the fire department, or police...maybe *both* and see what happens."

"You wanna be a *cop*?"

"Yeah, why not?"

"And wind up like *me*, laying here after being shot twice."

He took one hand and placed it on the bandage along his neck. "I was told I was really fortunate, because the bullet could have struck my carotid artery or *worse*, got me in the head. You want my advice concerning the job?" he repositioned himself in bed, he was now in a sitting position looking straight at me.

"Sure."

"Chicago streets are getting worse. It's like cops have a huge target on their backs. What happened to going to college after the marines, like you told your mom?"

"I don't know, maybe – I just have been through a lot. I guess I'm looking for something with a little excitement. Something to help get my adrenaline flowing again."

"Trust me, being a cop aint what it used to be." I watched as he shifted in bed, and reached for the newspaper on the overbed table. He managed to grab the paper without too much effort. He opened the paper to where he had read an article earlier. "Listen to this, before you decide a career as a cop, here in the windy city. Early Tuesday afternoon, a nun on her way to St. Angela's School was accosted by five teenagers. She was taken by van to a building in an abandoned location, where she was gang raped and beat to death, before her body was set on fire. All five teens were taken into custody and when asked why they did such a horrendous crime. One teen, whose identity could not be disclosed said, 'Why did we do it? 'Cuz it was something to do. We burned her body, to get rid of the evidence.' Little did the teens know, the authorities would be comparing dental records, in which they were able to identify the nun, and locate where she was that day. CCTV was able to record the encounter, the van and license-plate and the teens were picked up shortly afterwards. However, due to Chicago's lenient District Attorney Solomon Harari, the teens won't be charged for murder. Instead, they will face six years' probation. And you know what, because they're all juvies, their files are sealed. That means they can apply for a job, and their employer will never know. You can't even get their names released – isn't that justice! Can you imagine that, a nun who has done nothing to those little creeps, gets kidnapped then raped? Those punks aren't satisfied with just raping her...*no* they have to burn her body, thinking that'll prevent them from being identified. I'll tell ya', my whole outlook on this city has changed *completely*. If that was me on the scene, I'd drop those punks in a heartbeat – I would just shoot them right there! You know why, because the nun aint gonna see justice, so why should they?" Jimmie looked away from the newspaper and said, "You wanna see stuff like that?" I didn't answer right away, so I guess he felt it was necessary to read more about the crime in the city. He turned a few more pages and came to another article in the same newspaper. "Here's another one, it's a real gem. Police serve a warrant; they find more than they bargained for when Sgt. Anthony Harris of the Chicago Police Department, and his team served a warrant at," he said the address. "Sgt. Harris is shocked at what he finds! Apparently, the homeowner, a woman by the name of Amanda Cooper has been prostituting her three young daughters, ranging in age from nine to fifteen years old. The girls' father, Deon Cooper, a well-known drug dealer was also involved in arranging clients to not only buy drugs off him, but sell the services of his three daughters to men who were willing to pay the five hundred dollars for sexual intercourse. Sgt. Harris said, the three girls were tied to their beds and forced to allow many different age men, perform ungodly things to them – including *anal*, *oral* and *vaginal sex*. The oldest daughter; who was fifteen had become pregnant, and Deon helped her through the delivery, before killing the baby and disposing of it in the garbage." Jimmie looked up at me. "You want to bring stuff like this home with you?"

"*No*. It's disgusting! And it's making me angry!"

"It should make you very angry, because the parents who did this to their daughters; will probably only receive a slap on the wrist. You know why? Because first of all, justice is blind; especially if you have the money to afford a good lawyer, or you fit into a protected category, where the district attorney doesn't feel the need to prosecute you. And atop of that pile, you really think the system wants crime to end? You think judges want to sit around twiddling their fingers with nothing to do? No, they want crime! They need crime to keep the system going. It's like a finely oiled wheel, and the public is the ones getting hosed by it. Those three young girls are the victims here, and ironically, they won't really see justice. And the pigs who violated them; they'll never see the inside of a jail cell. If it were up to me, and someone was charged with a sex crime, like this, I'd have their genitals removed, plain and simple. Why is it okay to encourage teens to get life altering sex reassignment operations? But we don't do the same to the criminals, who commit sex crimes? This country is upside down and the lunatics are in charge of running the system; it's a real clown show!"

"Why doesn't the legal system do something about it then?" I asked, looking him directly in the eyes. He just chuckled at my naiveté. "Because the system is malleable. If you're powerful and you have an agenda, you're above the law. On the other hand, if there's a purpose to exploit you, may be for political reasons, then you're also protected by the law. It's unfair to say the least."

"Well, something should be done about it then!"

"Like what? Vote in another weak-minded district attorney, so they can promise to clean up the city, only to turn their back on the problem?"

"*No*. I mean really do something about it! Meet with the mayor, or governor and ask them what are they doing about the crime rate?"

"Let me save you the hassle. I'll tell you what they would say to you. If you were to go see either the mayor or governor, they would say, 'thank you for coming. I will look into your concerns and make sure it is addressed before the next selection...*I mean election.* And on your way out of the mayor's office, he would mentally give you the middle finger, and tell you to go screw yourself! You say, go see the *mayor* or *governor* – haven't you been listening? The entire system is rigged – it's nothing but a dog and pony show. We are allowed to vote, with the illusion of actually voting for a candidate – it helps numb the public's awareness. It allows us to believe we have a voice in this country. Meanwhile, the robber barons who have stolen everything from us for generations, keep feeding us lies! Just vote if you want to see change – yeah, forget that stupidity! Nothing is ever going to change, until the public wakes up and actually holds these son of a bitches' feet to the fire. Excuse my language, but I'm pissed! I'm pissed at my taxes being wasted on useless projects that go nowhere. I'm pissed when I see combat veterans coming home disabled and their own government can't be bothered to help them. No, the government expects charities to pick up the slack. I'm also pissed when I read about how the crime in this city is increasing, and those responsible to control it, can't be bothered! Well, hell with that, it's wrong! The whole thing is a disaster, because of selfish idiots in Washington."

"I agree. What did you mean when you mentioned the word, *selection*?"

"You really think the mayor or governor has any say in what happens in the community?" he said to me.

"Yeah, that's why we elected them."

"All I'll say to that is, that's what the powers that be, want you to think. The ones who manipulate the financial market and dictate what you can do, they think differently. They've been ruling the world for centuries. The bigs get richer, and the poor get to pay for it all."

"Well, something has to be done."

"I agree. So, what are you gonna do about it? You gonna contact the *mayor*? If you do, tell him I think he's a real jackass – give him my name too! Tell him, Jimmie Derenis thinks he's a real idiot," he said. His question concerning what do I plan to do? Left a sour taste in the pit of my stomach, because I knew every word, he spoke was true. The system was broken and something needed to be done. I felt helpless, like when I was a child and my father was abusive. I made a promise that day; I promised to do something. Something to make a difference, and something to remove this awful feeling of helplessness. I'd be lying if I said, I knew one day I would meet my high school friend, Rudy Brennan again. It's funny how fate, or Divine Providence has a way of bringing people back into our lives, especially after several years. I was on my way out of the hospital, when I ran into Rudy. I have a photographic memory, so I knew it was him. "Rudy!" I said, as he entered the main entrance.

"Is that who I think it is? Hey, Sebastien! How the hell are you?" he squawked, facing me.

"I'm good. What brings you here?" I asked, curious. I saw he had his left arm up against his chest, like he had injured it and was intentionally trying not to move it. He looked healthy, like he was taking good care of himself. He was also dressed in fine threads. His slacks looked expensive, and he was wearing a designer shirt that fit him well. His expensive looking shoes reminded me of the stranger in my parent's basement – the one my old man had murdered with a hammer, and went to prison for it.

"I hurt my wrist," he replied, raising his arm just a little to show me. "Actually, Renée is the one who hurt my wrist. She managed to convince me to spar with her. She wound up hurting me pretty good. I'm on my way into the ER."

"Renée?" It had me wondering if he was married, and he was referring to her as his spouse. Before I could ask, he said, "Yeah, her name is Renée Abrio. She works for me – it's all business."

"Works for you? What do you do? If you don't mind me asking?" He didn't answer right away; it seemed he really just wanted to be seen for his wrist injury, and not mention Renée anymore, which I totally understood. I would probably have behaved the same; if I were in his shoes. However, it appeared as if he was thinking about the best way to describe what he did for a living. Finally, he offered, "I work for a very wealthy man; a billionaire."

"Oh yeah, how did you get that gig?"

"Believe it or not, I found him on the dark web. He calls himself Prometheus, because he considers himself the protector of mankind. I've never met him. We correspond through snail mail."

"What kind of work do you do for him?" I asked, thinking he probably wouldn't tell me, because it was associated with the dark web. He paused again, this time he looked around to be sure no one was within hearing distance and whispered, "I wish I could tell you, but I can't. Not unless you want to work for me?"

"Doing what?"

"Again, I'm not at liberty to mention what I do. Weren't you supposed to join the marines?" he asked, seeming like he was trying to change the subject. "I did. I spent four years with Force Recon. I'm officially semi-separated from the marines, I still have to do four years, inactive reserves, which means showing up one weekend a month, to do drills."

"Sounds fun," he bellowed. "So, what are you doing for a living? Besides, the reserves?"

"Honestly, I'm looking for work. I've been seriously thinking of taking the civil service exam for the fire department, or police. I haven't yet decided if I should take the one for the police. Seeing how this city is becoming worse every day; I don't know if it would be wise to be a cop now. I mean I do want to make a difference and clean up the streets, but I don't want to wind up getting shot, only to have the criminal or criminals walk," I responded, remembering the two newspaper articles Jimmie read to me earlier.

"No, you don't want to do that. Why don't you come work for me?"

"You won't tell me what you do?"

"I'll just say this much, I could use someone with your skills. You have the background for the work and it pays extremely well. In fact, you could pretty much name your price."

"Name my price?"

"Yeah."

"You work for a man who calls himself Prometheus. You have an employee named Renée and you say, my background is exactly what you are looking for. What am I missing?"

"A great opportunity!"

"You're not going to tell me, are you?"

"Okay, okay. You don't have to twist my arm. Here's the deal. If I tell you what I do, you have to promise me never to mention it to another person. Promise?"

"I promise."

"Prometheus sends me dossiers on criminals, who have managed to evade the justice system. He sends these dossiers through the mail. First, he sends me a simple text message, that reads, *the garden is ripe for picking*. He then sends me the location of where the package will be delivered and it's my job to pick it up. He has a letter carrier, who works for the post office. It's one of his confidential inside men. The package is always taped to the underside of mail drop boxes. Once I get the package, I open it and give Renée the files of criminals who Prometheus wants brought to justice."

"You only have Renée, doing this work for you?"

"Yeah. That's why I think we could both benefit tremendously. I could use another cleaner, especially one with your expertise and I'm sure you could use the money. Right now, Renée is making twenty-thousand dollars, per file."

"What does the job entail?"

"Whatever Prometheus thinks is appropriate justice. It could be anything from removing the genitals of a perp, to killing the guy, but leaving no evidence that it was murder."

"That kind of work is very risky. It's worth more than twenty-thousand dollars, per dossier."

"Understood. So, since you seem interested, what's your asking wage?"

"Triple that."

"Sixty-thousand? I kinda thought you'd ask for more."

"No, you're right. Eighty-thousand."

"Wow! You know how difficult it is to arrange getting messages to Prometheus? I can't just send him a text, telling him about you, your experience and that I think you'd make a great fit for the job. From the beginning he made it very clear that he wants to remain anonymous. If I jeopardize that by contacting him with a text message, he would cease to do anymore business with me."

"Well, contact him through the dark web then."

"I can't contact him. I have to contact someone who claims to be an associate of his. I'll contact his associate and get back to you. How can I get a hold of you?" Rudy asked.

I gave him my contact information. I was expecting him to shake my hand and tell me he would be in touch, when he said, "Oh, by the way, Carolyn is looking for you."

"Carolyn? *Carolyn who?*"

"Carolyn from high school. Apparently, she's been trying to find you to tell you, you have a daughter."

"A what?!"

"You heard me. You have a four-year-old little girl."

"You saw her?"

"Oh yeah! Beautiful kid, just like her mom."

"Do you have Carolyn's contact info., like a cell-phone number or work number?"

"I have her home number," he said. He told me the number and I immediately saved it in my cell-phone, under contacts. I thanked him for the heads up and we parted. While walking out to my vehicle, I decided to call Carolyn's number, and I waited to hear her answer. The phone rang three times, before I heard it connect. A female voice answered, "Hello." The voice was soft and sounded very pleasant.

"Is this Carolyn?" I wasn't sure, because I forgot what her voice sounded like.

"Yes. Who is this?"

"Sebastien."

"Sebastien!" she repeated.

"Yeah. How are you?"

"I'm okay. Are you still in the service?"

"*No.* I mean I am, and I'm not."

"What is that supposed to mean?"

"I finished my four-year active obligation. I still have the reserves to do, but I'm home now," I explained. "I heard you've been looking for me."

"I have. You're very difficult to find. I attempted to reach you via the military and that wasn't very successful. I wanted to tell you that you have a daughter."

"Yes, I know. Can we meet for coffee or something?"

"Sure, we can meet for coffee. When and where?" she asked. I told her I was flexible with my schedule, whatever was convenient for her. She took a moment and then told me she could meet tomorrow around 1 p.m. I told her that would be great! I would be there. She then said, goodbye, before I could say another word. She gave me the impression, that she was harboring ill feelings toward me. I was sure those ill feeling stemmed from the frustration of not being able to locate me; and tell me I had a daughter.

TEN YEARS LATER

NINE

I've been working for Rudy for ten years now. I didn't get the eighty-thousand dollars per dossier; I had to settle for $50,000 per file. I've managed to squirrel away enough money to afford a palatial pad, fine threads, including several very expensive Italian shoes. I've learned over the years, to avoid developing consistent behaviors; better known as behavioral patterns, because it leaves the possibility of becoming vulnerable – not just to the authorities, but to the criminal element as well. I must admit, it has been a struggle for me to avoid the pattern of having my morning coffee, just after my morning shower. I finish rinsing off the soap, and I turn with my back to the shower head. There are times when I enjoy just standing in the shower, with the pulsating stream of water massaging my neck and back. I turned off the shower, stepped out onto the tiled bathroom floor and grabbed the towel hanging nearby. I patted myself down, including my hair. I turned on the bathroom ceiling's exhaust fan, to help get rid of the accumulated steam. After about a minute or so, the bathroom mirror began to clear and I could see myself, enough to begin shaving. Finally, I was ready to leave the bathroom and I noticed; Dakota wasn't whimpering at the door. Every morning, she waits for me, just outside the door. The average person probably wouldn't notice, but this immediately alarmed me. I returned to the bathroom sink where I keep a knife underneath. I reached underneath and found the handle. I pulled it out from its sheath and went back over to the door. I stepped off to the side, just in case someone was out in the hall, pointing a gun at the door. I reached for the door handle with one hand, while firmly holding the dagger in the other hand – I was prepared to throw the knife at my target. I quietly turned the doorknob and gently pulled the bathroom door toward me. I peeked out through the opening and saw that the hallway was clear. I continued to be as quiet as humanly possible. I quickly wrapped the bath towel around my waist and left the bathroom.

Out in the hallway, I heard the coffee maker turn on as usual. I had set the timer to start before taking my shower. Other than the coffee maker; I heard nothing, not even Dakota, my four-year-old female German Shepherd. I carefully go downstairs, half-expecting to find someone in my home. I imagined the worst, concerning Dakota, because by now she should be rushing up the stairs to greet me, yet she wasn't. I stopped at the landing; there I peeked over the wooden balusters and to my surprise! I saw Mr. Li Wong sitting on the couch, with Dakota, resting beside him, with her head lying on his lap. "Zaoshang hao, Sai ba si di an xiansheng," Mr. Li Wong said. "Good morning, Li," I replied, coming down the rest of the stairs. "I just got out of the shower."

"Yes, Wo dongle."

"Li, could you please either speak *English* or *French*? You know I have trouble understanding you when you speak Chinese."

"Sorry, not comfortable with your languages; better with mine. Still learning *English* and I sorry, but *French* not for me... sorry. Attempting to learn both, is mind aching!"

"I understand. Anyway, I would have gotten dressed, but I thought something was wrong, when Dakota didn't scratch at the bathroom door."

"I see. What it is, in your hand?" he asked. I looked down and saw that I was still holding the dagger in my hand. "Oh, I wasn't sure if I was alone."

"That is how you greet guest?" he teased. "You are dangerous man, Mr. Sebastien...you know?"

"Why do you say that?"

"You are only man I know whom has weapon stashed around home."

"I have learned from experience it's better to be safe than sorry."

"I see."

"Let me go back upstairs and get dressed." I was about to walk off, when I realized Li got in my home, without a key and he managed to sneak around my home security system; not to mention my dog. I turned so I was now facing him, "Li, how did you get in here? I mean how did you get past my home security system? And I don't mean Dakota..."

"Locks meant to keep honest people good."

"You're not going to tell me, are you?"

"Does flower blossom near volcano?"

"What does that have to do with my home security system?"

"Do squirrel forage at night?"

"Never mind. I'll be calling the company to let them know, a good friend of mine, managed to get around their, *so called* home security system. Li, I do want to thank you, because if you can get through it, so can others. So, I'll be definitely getting a better home security system now."

"Much glad to help," Li said, before patting Dakota on her head.

I went back upstairs to get dressed. When I returned, I found Dakota still resting on Li's lap. Li's a good man and I trust him with my life. I know he trusts me as well. I've known him for eight years now. He's a neighbor, and he lives next door. He was kind enough to help me with my furniture, when I moved in, including the couch, which he appears to enjoy sitting on. There's only a few select people I confide in about what I do, and Li is one of them.

"So, how's everything been, Li?" I asked him.

"Been keeping self-busy as usual, with morning meditating routine, among others. What say you, Mr. Sebastien? You do still work modern self-defense, Jiu-Jitsu and Muay-Thai?"

"Yes."

"To do how, all that you do and still practice?" Mr. Li looked directly at me, with a very serious expression on his face.

"I keep myself motivated, because I need to have my skills up to par."

"I see. Look you not happy, these days. Amiss something is? Feel you wrong about what you do?"

"No, it has nothing to do with work."

"I'm all *eyes* and *ears*."

"You mean, *you're all ears*," I said, smiling.

"Yes. Something bothering you, friend?"

"Yeah. It's my daughter and her mother."

"I not know you were married!"

"I'm not. It's complicated."

"I see. Go forth…"

"I think you mean go on. I guess I'll call her my ex. Several years back, we moved in together. I wanted to be a part of my daughter's life. I even considered tying the knot with my ex. We bought a beautiful house and things were going great, for about a year and a half. Then everything came apart. She was no longer interested in getting married, hell, she didn't even want to live together anymore. She said, she didn't like secrets and wanted to know what I do for a living. I told her, it was impossible for me to disclose what I do with her. It was for her own good – her safety."

"I see. Go on."

"I feel like she's making me pay for choosing my job over her. I feel like that's what she thinks and she's using our daughter as a tool against me. She's even tried to convince my daughter that she shouldn't spend any time with me. It's not right and that's what's been bothering me. Sometimes, I just want to get away from all this craziness and start a new life."

"The soul is meant to be free. You are like bird, never meant to cage."

"What do you mean?"

"Careful to be. One day you might get caught. Might you be put in confined area. How you say, pri-son?"

"It's called prison and Li, no worries. I don't take chances. Every job I take, I do extensive research on. I never leave evidence behind; I'm meticulous about what I do."

"You true friend...*decent man*. I think I know you do what you do."

"Why?" I asked. I was curious what he thought.

"Man, you work for wants justice – you also want to make difference. You know law system is broken and feel Sebastien have knowledge and ability to be justice for those who weak or defenseless."

"You make me sound like a *vigilante*."

"You are."

"Maybe you're right. When I began I did it for the money. Now I do it because I feel bad for the victims."

"Their voice are you."

"There's nothing wrong with that," I said.

"No. Very noble to want to help mankind. I have high regard, Mr. Sebastien. You are wise warrior. I believe, you want to help others see this world, the way you see."

"Maybe. Yeah, maybe you're right."

"Careful to be, my friend is all."

* * *

I was standing facing this quite large and very long mirror, looking at my lean muscular physique. I was proud of all the hard work I had been doing to stay *exceptionally healthy* and in great shape! God knew it wasn't easy; not with all the television ads pushing junk food, along with high calorie sugar filled drinks. If that wasn't bad enough, fast food ads pushed supersized meals, which was why I hadn't had a fast-food meal ever since I was a teenager. I had to watch everything I ate and I couldn't let my guard down concerning any type of junk food, even though I had been thinking about stopping off at the supermarket to get a small bag of potato chips. The thought was only temporary, because I knew if I did that, I would inevitably purchase soda and most likely a few other items which weren't good for me. I had to be vigilant about keeping in shape, primarily because my job required it. I had been here in the gym for over an hour and I still had another hour to go, before I could feel satisfied that I had put in a day's worth of exercise. I worked out six days a week, doing a split-training routine; consisting primarily of weight-lifting, along with an aggressive cardio program. The past hour I had been doing mainly weight-lifting and toning. The next hour, I planned on working my abdominals, and doing at least 45 minutes of running on the treadmill. I didn't walk the treadmill, because I trained for real world possibilities. Besides, I had managed to build up plenty of endurance, and today I planned to push the limit, by running even faster. I figured while I was on the treadmill, I could listen to either some classical music or smooth jazz, and hopefully the tunes would help clear my mind of everything, including work. Who was I kidding? I wouldn't be able to stop obsessing about the next jobs, not until after I completed them, and only then, would I file them away in my mind under the heading; finished. Every job I did; I always walked through what I was doing – even while in the act – so I could remember where everything was, that way I wouldn't leave any evidence behind. However, there was always a first, in this line of work, and I hoped that wouldn't happen to me. The last thing I wanted was to be arrested, convicted and sentenced to life in prison; like my old man. *Or worse*, the death penalty! For the past ten years Rudy had been giving me a couple of files each month. It was my job to look over the files, and choose which ones took precedence. I looked at everything, from the actual crime to the history of the criminal, and I even did a little extra research to be sure the individual was in fact, as bad as their file claimed. So far, every file I had been given was accurate. The convicts were the real deal, they were the type that stalked old couples and beat them to death, for their Social Security money. All of them had extensive criminal records, of violent crimes. Prometheus was the one who chose the punishment that fit the crime, to make the perp never forget what pain they had caused. For some it was merely too lenient to just put a bullet in their head; Prometheus wanted them to live in misery, and hell. So, if the file involved a rapist, especially of young children, I was told to remove the genitals, with a pair of dull garden shears, so the cutting wasn't quick, and the pain would be excruciating! On jobs like that, I used two pairs of disposable latex gloves. There were times when the pedophile would go into shock and when he did, I made every attempt to revive him, because I wanted the sick bastard to recognize what he did was despicable, and socially unacceptable!

Every job was different and I never knew what to expect.

Rudy had asked me to call him so we could meet and I could pick up the next set of files. He never told me much about any of the dossiers, over the phone. I guess that was wise, especially with technology the way it was and how Uncle Sam was surveilling average, everyday Americans.

I could only wonder what the National Security Agency had on me. They probably knew I liked to eat Chinese food and watch TV until about eight p.m.; after that I would go straight to bed. Actually, the thought of being watched by the government angered me, because I enlisted and served to defend America's freedoms. However, I didn't let any of this bother me too much, because I still had ten-miles to run.

I went over to the other end of the gym, where all the treadmills were. I found one that I fancied and just before I could get on and set my workout, I was approached by a rather attractive female. If I had to guess I would say, she was in her mid-to-late twenties, with long brown hair and a very angelic complexion. My initial thought was, she was about to ask me if she could use the treadmill I had chosen. She surprised me when she said, "Hi. My name is Casey. I've seen you here before and I've been meaning to talk to you, but every time I look for you, you're always gone, finished with your workout." She smiled, warmly.

"Really?"

"Yeah. I hope this doesn't sound too forward or desperate of me, but I'm single and I'm very much interested in knowing more about you. Would you be interested in having coffee or maybe dinner with me?" Suddenly, I felt rather uncomfortable, because I wasn't prepared for this. "I appreciate the offer and interest, but I'm really not the type of man you're looking for." I said this, because I was thinking about the type of work I do. The last thing I wanted was to involve myself in a relationship, when I was a *paid assassin*. It was not something you could talk freely about over dinner, or even a cup of coffee for that matter. I knew this from experience, because Carolyn, my ex left me due to my secrets.

"Excuse me!" she replied, sounding as if I had just insulted her. I realized if I was going to minimize the damage that I must have caused to her ego, I needed to say something to imply that it was me, not her. So, I said, "What I mean is, I've just come out of a real devastating relationship, and she really put me through an emotional rollercoaster ride. I'm just not ready yet...I hope you understand, that it's not *you*...it's *me*."

"Where have I heard that excuse before?" she sighed. "You know you could just say I'm not your type? What a creep you are." She walked off angry!

TEN

My core was feeling tight and worked, especially my obliques, after doing those planks. My legs felt awfully weak though, and believe it or not, they were quivering. I thought maybe I might have over done my work out, but even so, I felt alive! Like I had just competed in an Ironman contest! I left the gym and went to my baby, a brand-new Lamborghini Veneno, with its 6.5-liter V12, which delivers 740 hp, surging this monster from 0 to 60 mph in 2.9 seconds. I climbed in and started the engine, it fired up, eager and willing to prove itself. I took a moment to listen to the engine roar! I then casually moved out of the parking area, knowing I didn't have to prove anything. I turned left into traffic and proceeded, intending to take the quickest route home. I came to a complete stop at a red-light and noticed behind me, a patrol car, as it creeped up and stopped inches from my rear bumper. I kept my eyes roaming, first looking up at the light to see if it had turned yet, and then back at the cop, who I could only assume must have been wondering who was driving this nice expensive car? I wouldn't have been surprised if he was running the license plate. I wasn't worried, because everything was legit!

The title was in my name, the insurance was current and I had my wallet with me, to prove I was a licensed driver in the state of Illinois. I looked up at the traffic light and saw it turn green; I was about to remove my foot from the brake pedal, when I heard a siren and then saw the cop's emergency lights moving behind me. For a moment, I thought he must have been on a call, and was trying to get around me, so I moved forward and pulled off to the side only to have the cop follow directly behind me. There had to be a mistake, because I didn't have any outstanding tickets, I had no warrants and I was pretty sure no one had called to complain about me. I put the vehicle in park, allowing the engine to hum. I looked at my driver's side mirror and saw the patrolman, as he exited his patrol car and walked toward my vehicle. I had no idea what to expect and I turned to see him step up to the side of my vehicle. "Sir, turn your engine off please," said the police officer. He looked young, thin and I assumed was probably a *newbie*, straight out of the academy.

"Officer, what's this all about?" I asked.

"Sir, just do what I ask. Turn your vehicle's engine off and hold tight a few minutes." He stared at me with a no-nonsense expression. I really didn't think this was some reality TV show prank, so I did exactly what he requested, and I kill the engine. He looked away and talked into his handheld radio, telling whoever was listening that he had the subject stopped and he gave his location. Now, I was really beginning to wonder, what the hell is going on? I was about to ask if

I could make a phone call to my attorney, when another vehicle pulled up behind us. I noticed that vehicle was an unmarked patrol car, and a brunette stepped out from the driver's side. She walked up to the patrolman who was still standing alongside my vehicle, thanked him and approached me from the passenger's side. In fact, she surprised me, when she opened the passenger's side door and climbed in. While she was doing that, I found myself scoping her out. She had sexy curves, with an hourglass physique. "This is a very nice car! I really like it. It's really sexy! I wish I could afford wheels like this on my salary. Not gonna happen though, not anytime soon." I noticed she was looking around at the dashboard, console and then the backseat. She then turned and looked over at me, "Sebastien, this must have cost you a small fortune. What? Did you win the lottery? I admit I buy a ticket now and then. I also am aware of every winner, and to my knowledge you were not in the paper for winning any money. Doesn't that puzzle *you*? It puzzles *me*? How you can afford such an expensive vehicle? It's a shame you seem to favor this vehicle over the other one you have. The other vehicle you have it's a classic, right? A 1966 Chevy Impala?" she said, keeping her eyes trained on me. I couldn't help but notice how attractive she was for a member of law enforcement. I have a rule, never date a lawyer, cop or judge, because it has the potential to be very dangerous! "How do you know my name? And how do you know about my Chevy Impala? I've never been arrested, and I haven't broken any laws."

"Please, don't insult my intelligence, I know more about you then you realize. Do you mind if I call you Sebastien? Or would you prefer, I call you, *Mr. Laurent*?" she asked, looking over at me, with those piercing eyes.

"Sebastien, is fine."

"You and your mother, Mia immigrated here, from France. She divorced your father, Leo Dubois, after he was charged with multiple murders. She then changed her name and yours, back to her maiden name."

"What is this supposed to be, a history lesson?" I said, intentionally being terse. "No sir. I'm sure you're wondering why you were stopped?" she said, smiling. I'll admit, she had a lovely smile and if I didn't feel like I was about to be arrested for something, I'd feel comfortable looking at her pearly whites and perfect lips. "Yeah, I'm sure my lawyer would like to know too," I said, rather sarcastically. I watched as she moved in the seat, so she was now almost facing me. "You don't have to go there," she said and I noticed the patrol car move off into traffic. "You're not under arrest."

"Well then what the hell's going on here? Because I was just stopped and illegally detained for no reason!" I demanded an answer, and was prepared to politely tell her to get out of my vehicle, but for some reason I didn't. I guess I wanted her to explain herself and why she felt it was necessary to detain me in the first place. "I asked patrolman Cayden to stop you, because I need to talk to you for a moment," she said, looking less like a member of law enforcement and more like an average, everyday female. I could see in her behavior; she had a vulnerability about her. It was a learned habit; she probably wasn't aware of. "About what?" I asked.

"My name is Olivia."

I interrupted her, "What no last name? You know mine." I could tell she was contemplating whether or not to reveal her last name. I guess she didn't find me that much of a potential threat, because she went on to say, "My last name is Bartlett. I'm a narcotics detective, with the city. I see a lot and I know who's who?"

"I don't understand what you're getting at," I replied, intentionally acting ignorant.

"Don't play dumb with me. I know what you do for a living."

"What I do, is my business."

"I need your help!" I heard her say, with a sincere voice.

"Excuse me!"

"You heard me, I need your help," she repeated herself. My first impression was, this must be a setup, "What is this some sort of a setup?" I found myself looking in the rear-view mirror, half-expecting another patrol car to pull up to assist this detective, named Olivia. I wasn't even sure I believed her, when she said that was her name. Although, she did look like an Olivia. "No! I'm being upfront with you. Don't even think of me as a detective right now. In fact, everything we talk about right now, is between you and I. It's totally off the record, I promise." I told her I need to check her for a wire. She smiled, "*A wire?* Why would I be wearing a wire?"

"I either check you for a wire, or you leave my vehicle."

"*Fine.*" She unbuttoned the first two buttons of her blouse. I saw her cleavage and her olive-colored skin.

"I'm gonna have to search."

"I'm warning you; you better not touch my breasts or I'm gonna slap you!"

"I won't touch your breasts." I carefully moved her blouse aside, with just the tip of my fingers; mindful not to even rub up against her chest. She wasn't wearing a wire, just a bra. I let her blouse go and said, "You're not wearing a wire. So, we're good."

"What? You aren't going to ask me if you can check *my panties?*"

"*No.*"

"I know what you do," she said. "You're a professional killer. *A cleaner, a hitman* for the right price." She said it with such confidence, like she knew me better than I knew myself. I didn't dispute her claim, because after all I knew she was right. Also, I knew she knew she was correct. She went on and said, "I need your help, because the dirtbag lowlife who killed my daughter, after raping her, is walking the streets as we speak; free as a bird. His lawyer is claiming the circumstantial evidence we had on him was planted, to get a conviction. And also, he was targeted, because he's an immigrant, which is complete nonsense! He's a criminal and a very ruthless one at that."

"I have a question?"

"What?"

"Was any evidence planted on him?"

"No. That bastard raped and strangled my twelve-year-old daughter."

"What's your daughter's name?"

"Hannah," Olivia replied.

"Her full name?" I asked by habit. I visibly see her body language change, as if she's over thinking the question. She then replied, "Hannah E. Bartlett. The E is for Esther. And to add insult to injury, he wasn't satisfied with raping and strangling her, no he had to burn her body, expecting that would prevent him from being caught...well it didn't. Forensics found fibers from his jean jacket he wore. He claimed the jacket wasn't his, he had picked it up at the city mission, where he was staying the night before. However, that was a lie. It was his jacket and he had purchased it new a week earlier and we were able to connect him with the purchase."

"What about DNA evidence?" I asked, expecting her to mention she had that also.

"*No*, he used a condom, and there were no fluids that passed from his filthy body, to hers."

"How can you be sure, he's your guy then? Besides, the circumstantial evidence of the jean jacket?"

"He confessed, that's how? Also, he knew things about

my daughter, that couldn't have been known, unless he was the perp. I figure he must have been watching her for some time, because he knew her daily routine and even admitted following her from school."

"Okay, so where does this leave me?" I'm sure I must have looked a little confused. She took a moment, turned away from me and looked over the dashboard of my vehicle. I noticed she was struggling to try and explain herself, and that was when she turned back and looked directly into my eyes and said, "I want you to kill him for me!" She spoke with such conviction, that I didn't have to ask her if she was serious; I knew she wasn't kidding. I could also see the hurt in her expression, and the loss in her eyes. Either the loss of her daughter lingered with her memories, or she was obviously one damn good, convincing liar.

"Kill him?" I repeated!

"That's right. How much will it cost me?" She said, without hesitation.

"Let's assume this isn't some kind of a police sting, and you're not joking. Why don't you just do it yourself?" The question was too obvious and I was wondering how she would respond, when she said, "That would be an obvious paper trail, because the dirt bag killed my daughter. His name is Miguel del Rosario."

"*The Miguel del Rosario?* The one affiliated with the Mexican drug cartel?" I repeated.

"Yes, that's correct. He was arrested five times before, for other offenses, like assault with a deadly weapon. Possession of an illegal firearm. Possession of narcotics and human-trafficking. Each time he was released, because Chicago's a sanctuary city for criminals like him. Believe me I would love to go find him and put a bullet in his crotch and then another in his stinking head, but I really don't want to face jail myself – not for that dirtbag. And I don't want to know that he's in prison, working-out, watching TV, and spending the rest of the time sleeping in his cell. No, I want my pound of flesh from him! I want him dead."

"You're serious, aren't you?" I commented.

"Absolutely!"

"Can you give me the particulars on him? His file, photo and current address?" I asked.

"I can get you what we have on him."

"If you can get all that stuff, I'll consider doing it for *a hundred grand.*"

"*A hundred-thousand-dollars*?!" Her voice and expression changed.

"Yeah. And it has to be in cash. *Small, unmarked bills. Nothing over a fifty.*"

"That's more than I was expecting to pay," she answered glumly.

"I don't know what you were expecting, but killing someone is not like going to the store and picking out something off the shelf, on a grocery aisle." I watched her turn away, and I could tell she was disappointed. She was probably wondering what to do next? For some reason, I was feeling generous. Maybe that was because this creep she mentioned was the kind of filth, this city didn't need around anymore. With that in mind, I said, "I'll do it without charge...well, without money. I will still expect something for it," I said assertively!

"Look, I don't know what you think of me, but I'm not that kind of woman! And even suggesting that, is solicitation and that's a crime!" Her comment, alerted me that she was suggesting I had made some kind of sexual proposition. My initial response was to defend myself! "Oh, I'm not suggesting that! I'm looking for someone I can trust, on the inside of the Chicago PD, someone who can warn me and even help me on other jobs."

"Are you suggesting *partners*?" Her voice and expression changed. She appeared a bit more perky. "No, not at all. I have two rules: first, no children are ever to be a target. Second, I work alone; *no exceptions*," I said, intentionally misleading her, because I didn't want her knowing, I work with both, Rudy and Renée.

"Okay. Does that mean we have a deal?"

"When can you get me the file on him?"

"I'll have it for you tomorrow," she replied. "I can call you, and we can set up a neutral location to meet. What's the best number I can reach you at?" she asked and I gave her the number to my cell-phone. "Alright, are we done here? Because I have a full day a head of me."

"Yes. Thank you."

"For what? I haven't done anything yet."

"I know. I just feel you will. I know when you see the particulars on this bum, you'll agree he needs to die. And I hope you kill him slowly – torture the bastard!"

"If he did what you claim he's done, don't worry I will see to it that he regrets ever targeting your daughter."

"Good, I needed to hear that."

Very little was said after that and she left my vehicle. I remained parked, watching her walk to her unmarked patrol car. She got in and drove off, passing me as if nothing had happened. I took a moment, remaining there in the driver's seat, looking over the dashboard, wondering if she was being honest with me? I wanted to believe her, because of the story about her daughter, but I couldn't allow myself to be entrapped. The only logical thing to do was to walk softly, cautiously, and have a plan b, just in case this was a setup, and Chicago's finest had me in their sights.

ELEVEN

I returned home to find a few messages on my answering machine. I could tell one was from Rudy, two were from telemarketers, and the last message was from my daughter Amanda. I knew this because of caller ID. I played the first message, to hear Rudy announce he had several more files for me to look over, he gave the location, where he and Renée would be waiting. The next two telemarketing messages, asked if I wanted to save money on my phone bill? The first tele message was so long that the answering machine ended the call. The same marketer had to call back to finish his sales pitch. I immediately erased the two telemarketing messages. Finally, I heard my daughter's message and how she wanted to come and visit me this week. I figured I'd call her after I saw Rudy, to find out what she had planned? She usually had these grand ideas, like she wanted to go to the Brookfield Zoo, or Chicago's Sky Deck, which we haven't done yet. I've tried to convince her in the past; to come with me and see Frank Lloyd Wright's home, and studio, but she'd rather go to Lincoln Park Zoo, or LEGOLAND. Before I leave, I have to feed Dakota, then shower and shave. I figured afterwards,

I'd call Rudy and Renée to let them know I'm on my way. I turned away from the answering machine and I was about to go off toward the kitchen, when Dakota came trotting down the stairs, obviously to greet me. She rushed over to me and I patted her on the top of her head, as we both entered the kitchen. It's amazing how the kitchen turned out; considering what this part of the interior looked like when I first saw it. I opened the refrigerator and took out yesterday's roast beef, still packaged in its store wrapping. I unzipped it and removed enough to satiate Dakota's appetite, adding a little dry dog food on top. I knew from experience, she wouldn't eat the dry dog food, without a little roast beef persuasion. I leaned over to add the food to her bowl and watched for just a second, as she devoured it! I'll never get tired of admiring the finished work in the kitchen, not to mention the rest of this place. When I first looked at this kitchen, there was no center island with a beautiful marble top, along with the hanging copper pots and pans directly over it. No, from what I remembered, it looked like the place had been left abandoned for decades. There were cobwebs everywhere. I had consulted with a knowledgeable and very reputable designer and she helped liven up the place. Of course, the final decisions were left up to me and I think I chose wisely; right down to the appliances which were all modern and state-of-the-art. The refrigerator had smart technology built into it; which notified me on my cell-phone, when items needed replacing – I could even access photos of what was inside my refrigerator. In my opinion, today's technology was both a blessing as well as a curse; because I realized with all this convenience came a price – that price was privacy. I had several safe-guards to protect my identity, but there was always room for error; if a potential intruder became a problem. I didn't really worry much about being hacked by criminal types; as I did about government types; looking for information to build a criminal case against me.

I had a habit of emptying my pockets out and leaving the contents on the island counter top – it was where I usually left my keys. I left the kitchen and went down the short hallway to where the living room was located. I vividly remembered how everything here was also in shambles; needing to be gutted and restored. It was a 19th century Victorian brownstone row-house, located along Lake Park Avenue. According to my real estate agent, the fixer upper was originally built in the early eighteen hundreds. I had all the modern amenities; including a large screen TV in the living room, which was built into the ceiling and came down with the push of a button. I also enjoyed music and had a beautiful grand piano, in the color of black onyx over near the fireplace. On weekends, I spent the entire morning playing my favorites: everything from *blues* and *jazz*, to *classical* and *contemporary*. I also had a hidden room; which I paid plenty to have constructed; it was behind the bookshelves. (The second book from the Bible which was also colored red; was a false novel. It was attached to a lever and when pulled out, quickly released a locking mechanism, opening it, and exposing the room behind it.) The room was exactly thirty by thirty feet, with no windows and it was where I kept all my equipment. I had dozens of blades for specific purposes; which involved getting close to the subject and usually cutting their throat. I also had many types of firearms; from small hand guns to rifles and fully-automatics, all equipped with silencers. There was a workbench in the center of that room, that was where I assembled what I needed. Off to the right, was a file cabinet; with all my current false documents. I had driver's licenses I used; issued to look like it was from the state I was working in. I also had false *passports, birth certificates*, and whatever I didn't have I knew Rudy would be able to get.

I passed through the living room, climbed the stairs and entered the bathroom with the intention of taking a hot shower. It wasn't long before I was lathering up my armpits, thinking about what I'd need from my secret vault for the job I had agreed to do for the narcotics detective. Olivia wanted the individual who killed her daughter to die. I on the other hand; wanted him to realize what he did by raping and burning her daughter, was something a monster would do, and the only way to deal with a monster of his kind, was to treat him like one. I figured I would need those pruning shears, to remove his manhood. If and when he waked after succumbing to shock; I would have another surprise for him, and it would involve one of those combat knives I used for jobs like this. I rinsed the soap off, only to remember Olivia still had to get me the particulars on Miguel. I needed to know exactly how deep his crimes went? I already knew he was connected to the cartel; and I would have to be extremely careful. The last thing I wanted, was the cartel with a vendetta against me. That's one reason why I've been extremely cautious about my relationship with my daughter; I was the one who thought Amanda would be safer living with her mother. If she were living with me; I would constantly be worried that one day I would come home to find her either dead; as payback, or kidnapped; to torture me. At least this way, I get to spend time with her and I know she's going to be fine, because Carolyn is a good mother.

I stepped out of the shower, towel dried myself and shaved before leaving the bathroom. The pleasant warm weather had me thinking; maybe I should dress in a pair of blue jean shorts; with a comfortable form fitted white t-shirt. After dressing, I called Rudy and told him I was on my way. The last thing I had to do was grab myself a cold bottle of mineral water. I've been consciously making an effort to drink more water, because I heard about how important and beneficial it was for the body. I reached in the refrigerator, grabbed a bottle of water, then looked over at the kitchen island countertop, where my keys were and I grabbed them, before patting Dakota on the head and telling her, "Daddy will be back later." My building had a rather sizable vestibule, it was where my mailbox was located. I would have checked my box, but I knew the mailman wouldn't be here for another two hours. He was pretty reliable when it came to delivering the mail after three p.m. I took my time while in the vestibule; looking past the door and beyond the glass, to see if anyone suspicious was hanging around. When I felt confident that I was not going to be surprised; I opened the door and went out onto the concrete steps. My building had a long narrow concrete walkway, leading over to the street. The building was surrounded by a black iron fence, and it was exactly waist high. I had an old car parked out front, that I used to travel over to the storage place, where I kept both my Lamborghini; and my classic 1966 Chevy Impala. I would love to have a garage here, but it was just not possible. I had my vehicles parked at a place called, Trey's Safe-Storage, where I rented two, 10 X 20 storage units, monthly at a very reasonable price. I drove over there to park this heap and picked up the Lamborghini. Rudy asked me to meet him at the Millennium Park. Sometimes we meet at the Jay Pritzker Pavilion; other times at the Lurie Garden which was a beautiful 3.5-acre urban sanctuary. Today he's asked me to meet him at the Charles Fennimore Exhibition. I'm not sure why he wanted to meet there, I assumed maybe he wanted to see some of the exhibits. Rudy loved tangible artwork, whereas I preferred music; and looked forward to a few of the concerts coming up this summer. The park was located at 201 E. Randolph St. I turned onto South Columbus Drive, to find parking at Millennium Park Garage. While at the parking garage, I decided to call Rudy, to find out exactly where he and Renée were? I had his number, as one of my contacts, and I just needed to ask Siri to call him, which I did. "Siri."

"Yes, Sebastien. How can I help you?"

"Call Rudy."

"Okay." my phone replied. Siri then said, "Calling Rudy Brennan." Rudy answered, on the second ring, "Hello!"

"Where are you?"

"Renée and I are standing in front of the largest exhibit, and that's all I'm going to tell you."

"Well, that helps, thanks. I'll find you." It wasn't long before I saw him standing, where he said he would be, right in front of a huge bronze exhibit. An exhibit that resembled a half-eaten donut. That pointless image, was replaced by the large envelope Rudy had in his hand. I fixed my eyes on it, wondering what Prometheus had for us this week.

"How many jobs this week?" I asked, stopping and facing him. I looked over at Renée, she was standing at his right side. I've always been impressed to see her, because she's the quintessential independent woman, with beauty, brains and class. She's so resourceful and refined; that she can attend opera with you and afterwards go to dinner and look you in the eyes to discuss philosophy, psychology, or any other topic; including your financial portfolio, before cutting your throat.

"Six," he replied, handing me the envelope. I opened it and looked at the first delinquent named, Dr. Harold Peterson. I carefully looked over the newspaper article that mentioned him; along with other pieces of evidence, suggesting his

M.O. is to lure children both *boys* and *girls*, into his home where he tranquilizes them before either molesting or raping them. I quickly looked over his past record and how the local authorities didn't have enough evidence to charge him. This information caused me to ask, "I'm a little confused. If he gives these kids tranquilizers and violates them; what more evidence would you need for a conviction?"

"Read on. He's never been convicted of a crime," said, Renée. It was obvious she wasn't happy about this individual and his crimes. I continued to read; how he had never been convicted of anything, not even a traffic violation. This immediately ignited a fuse inside me, and it caused me to want to bring this animal to justice. I looked up at her and said, "Because he's obviously careful and he knows people. People in high places. His last victim he drugged so much, that the district attorney thought the victim's testimony wouldn't hold water in court. Mainly, because she couldn't remember exactly what happened." I then perused the next character; and his paperwork showed that he had a number of run-ins with the law. He went by the nick name, *Murderous*. He was a gang member and apparently, he had been recently released, after the courts decided the circumstantial evidence the Chicago police had on him; was allegedly tampered with. That was his lawyer's argument. "*Murderous*. Nice name," I said.

"Be careful with him," Rudy suggested.

"Why?" Renée inquired.

"He's a *cop killer*! And amazingly he was released *yesterday*."

"I see that," I replied, looking over the newspaper article. The article claimed he shot a Chicago patrolman point blank in the face. His lawyer Peter Fink, argued that his client was framed for the crime, because the weapon used was never directly linked to *Murderous*. In fact, defense counselor Evans, claimed the police were illegally targeting his client, because of his involvement in a gang. The lawyer went on and claimed in the newspaper article that his client was singled out, not just because he allegedly belonged to a gang, but more importantly, according to him, because his client was an African-American; that's why the counselor was such an advocate for the African-American community. "This is a good example why so many people think the system is broken," I said sarcastically. "I don't think the legal system is broken at all," Rudy commented. "I think it's just a reflection of the times we're living in."

"True," I replied.

"Read on, look at the other files," Renée explained. I looked over the next file which involved a mother by the name of Sylvia Wixx. Sylvia was 21 years old, when she met her future husband, Nick Bozzelli. The two moved in together and decided to marry and start a family. Shortly after marrying Nick, Sylvia told him about her involvement in the Church of Satan. She wanted him to become an active member, which he rightly declined. She continued to try and persuade him and after the birth of their first son, Lucus she went to see a lawyer; seeking a divorce from Nick. Mr. Bozzelli was reluctant at first, because he was concerned about their son growing up in a home without two parents. However, later he accepted and sued for *primary parental rights*; due to Sylvia being a horrible influence. Nick claimed, Sylvia conjured up demons and practiced satanism and even did annual animal sacrifices on Halloween. The judge who oversaw this case, denied him full custody and later Sylvia issued a restraining order against him. A year later, police found Lucus's body in the woods, six miles from his home. Investigators believed Lucus was the victim of a satanic ritual. Nick went on the record, claiming his ex-wife was somehow involved, because she was an active member of the local church of Satan. Authorities claim they were left with nothing to go on; and the case went into a dead file. "Unbelievable! It seems pretty obvious to me, Sylvia had to be involved," I remarked.

"I agree, but the police did all they could," Renée explained.

"I know. I realize ritual killings are difficult to solve," I said, remembering a true story I heard about on a podcast. I read the fourth file, which concerned a male by the name of Ian Verlice. Apparently, Ian worked as a broker in Manhattan, where he stole over a 150 million dollars from investors. Many of his victims were left *penniless*, and a few even committed suicide, due to his actions. Ian Verlice, decided to leave NYC and moved to Chicago, to start fresh. The next file involved a male, by the name of Ricky St. James, 23 years old. Apparently, Ricky liked to follow elderly people home from the

bank and rob them; before beating them to death. He had six
prior arrests as a juvenile and recently was arrested for armed
robbery and assault of an elderly couple. He followed Mr. and
Mrs. Corelli home; where he robbed and brutally beat both
of them. Both Mr. and Mrs. Corelli were taken to a hospital,
where they were treated for extensive injuries. Mr. Corelli's
injuries, included a broken rib and wrist. His wife, sustained
multiple fractures; including blunt head trauma. "This guy,
Ricky is a real winner," I commented. "Tell me about it,"
Renée said. "A real lowlife." The last file I read, involved a
serial rapist, by the name of Tyler Mason. Tyler's M.O. was
to follow single women home from the subway system and
when the female target recognized she's being followed, she
immediately searched for a crowd; or an individual to protect her. Knowing this, Tyler had a male accomplice waiting
down the street. Eventually his accomplice showed himself
as someone who could protect her. Once the female trusted
the accomplice, she allowed him to walk her home, or to
her vehicle; where she was accosted by both Tyler and his
accomplice. The two then brutally raped their female target
and warn her if she went to the police, they would return
to kill her. Sometimes Tyler worked alone; and posed as a
delivery man and was allowed into the target's apartment
building, where he gained entry into their apartment, raped
the victim and threatened her with violence or death if she
told anyone about what happened. CCTV footage showed
he had been to dozens of women's apartments throughout

the city of Chicago, but only one victim was brave enough to come forward. However, when she was told she'd have to testify in court, in front of her attacker, she declined to go any further and Tyler was released. Nowhere in the file, named Tyler's accomplice. "Great."

"What?" said Rudy.

"Tyler's accomplice, there's no mention of his name. Probably because he wasn't arrested."

"Yep. If you can't find the accomplice don't worry, because he wasn't listed in the file as a subject."

"Yeah, I know. I just would like to kill two birds with one stone; so-to-speak."

"I'm sure Prometheus will eventually get the details on him and when he does, you'll be able to set the record straight and get rid of the trash."

"I look forward to it." I looked over additional information concerning the last known addresses of everyone listed as a subject, "Are these addresses current?"

"To the best of my knowledge."

"Rudy, how much am I getting for these?"

"As usual, fifty-thousand in cash and all expenses," he replied, before he handed me two large gym bags, with cash inside; along with documents. "There's a key fob in the blue gym bag; it's to a car rental. You or Renée can pick it up any time before seven p.m. at Hertz, over on Canal Street, because the car rental closes at that time. I have it under a pair of bogus names, but don't worry; all the paperwork is legit if you're ever stopped for speeding. I've included as usual another driver's license." I opened the blue gym bag and peeked in; I saw the items all bunched together. I reached in to sort things out and see the Illinois license he's mentioned. I looked at the name he had chosen for me. Supposedly, he thought I looked like a Robert Emery.

"Robert Emery, huh?" I said, and looked over at him. "Now I have three licenses. My real license, another license with the name: Michael Richardson; and now Robert Emery."

"Robert Emery is only temporary?" he said. "Besides, you look more like a Robert then a Michael." I knew he was only teasing me, but I was just not feeling it today; not after running into Detective Olivia Bartlett. "Whatever."

"You seem like you have a bee in your bonnet," Renée noticed, something was bothering me. "No, I don't want to give Chicago's finest a reason to arrest me. Earlier today, I was stopped by a narcotics detective named, Olivia Bartlett."

"What? *Narcotics?* What were you doing? Smoking funky cigarettes?" she commented, coming to that conclusion, even though she should know better, because I don't touch marijuana. I assumed she was just teasing me. "No. I had just come from working out. This Detective Olivia has me in her sights."

"Why do you say that?" Rudy asked, sounding concerned.

"Because she knows what I do for a living. She knows I'm a *professional cleaner.*"

"Really! Maybe we should notify Prometheus and let him

know the heat may be on?" Renée said, sounding worried about the real possibility of getting arrested.

"No! We don't need to do that – at least not yet. All she wants from me is to find Miguel del Rosario and kill him for her."

"Are you serious?" both Renée and Rudy say, *almost simultaneously.*

"You know who Rosario is?" Rudy asked me, with a troubled expression written all over his face. It's an expression I've only seen once and that was when he thought his wife was going to have a miscarriage.

"Of course! He's affiliated with the drug cartel."

"*Exactly*! That's one can of worms you don't want to go and open up, my friend."

"I'm not gonna let it bother me," I said. "I'll put Olivia on the back burner, because we have jobs to do."

"You're not concerned that Miguel is part of the cartel?" Renée said. I could tell Rudy was thinking the same question.

"No, he's like any other job."

"Well, you better be extra careful then!" Rudy replied.

"I always am," I said to him, before turning my attention to Renée: "Which files do you want to work on with me?"

"You know I can't stand pedophiles, so I'll take the Sylvia one, the Tyler one and the broker from New York City; Ian Verlice. I figure I can get really close to all of them; without any of them suspecting anything. Then I'll text you, to let you know the fruit has been picked."

"Sounds good." I gave her the files she requested. "Be very careful of Tyler Mason," I said to her. I must admit she's a tough female, because she just said, "Why's that?"

"Because he might be with his accomplice and we have no idea who that guy is."

"Believe me, if Tyler or his *accomplice* try anything, I'll be ready and they'll be sorry, because I'll slice first and ask questions afterwards."

"I wouldn't worry about you so much, if you carried a gun," I said to her.

"You of all people should know a knife is just as deadly. It allows you to get right up to your subject and quietly eliminate him."

"You have a point."

"Do you need me to watch Amanda, while you're out?" Rudy asked, breaking the tension between Renée and I. He was referring to my fourteen-year-old daughter. "I'm sure my daughter Brittney, wouldn't mind having her over for the week."

"I'll have to ask her. She called me earlier and it sounds like she's looking forward to doing things with me for the week. I don't know how I'm going to tell her I won't be able to, because I have to work."

"Yikes...well, I'm here if you need me. I'm sure my wife Kelly wouldn't mind."

"I'm sure. I appreciate the offer; I just don't know if she'll go for it. I think when I tell her I have to work, she's going to wanna just stay with her mother and she'll be angry with me again."

"She'll get over it. She's a strong little girl," said Renée.

"She always does. I better call her, and tell her the bad news. Can you guys hang around for just a moment, because I want to ask her if she's willing to stay with Rudy, so she can spend time with your daughter Brittney, and I'll still be able to see her? I just can't spend the entire week with her."

"Yeah, sure. Call!" both Rudy and Renée said. I had my daughter's name as one of my iPhone contacts. I just asked Siri to call that number and waited for Amanda; or her mother to answer. The phone rang a few times, and I was half-expecting it would go to her voicemail. I realized; she would need to call me back so I could tell her I wouldn't be able to spend the whole week with her. I was thinking all this, when suddenly I heard Amanda's voice, "Hello, Daddy!"

"Hey sweetie! How are you?" I asked, then I looked over at Rudy and saw him making a cringing face.

"I'm okay. Did you get my message I left on your answering machine?"

"I sure did!"

"I've been talking to mom about all the stuff I want to do. She told me I should also agree to do stuff you want too. I told her I would think about it!"

"You did!"

"Just kidding. I agreed with her, we'll do stuff you want too. So, will you be coming to get me, or does mom have to bring me?" Her mother lived in Peoria, it was exactly a two-and-a-half-hour drive from where I resided. In the past, I usually drove to get Amanda. Her voice seemed so excited; the thought of telling her I wouldn't be able to spend the week with her, had me believing this would surely crush her. She was getting older now, and she was liable to take things more personal. "Daddy, are you there?" she asked, because I've temporarily zoned out of our conversation. My mind was on work, thinking about the narcotics detective, with her request to kill a very well-known member of the cartel. I quickly returned to the conversation, after she said: *Daddy, are you there?*

"I'm here sweetie."

"So, are you coming to get me, or should I tell mom to bring me to you?"

"I'll come and get you," I succumbed to strong parental feelings. For the first time ever, I was breaking one of my cardinal rules. I decided to allow her to stay with me, while I worked. It was going to make things much more difficult, because not only would I have to worry for her safety, but also, I couldn't have her know what I did for a living!

"When? When?" she said, excited!

"I'll be leaving soon. So, figure I should be there in a couple of hours, okay?"

"Awesome! I just gotta pack. I'll be waiting." She hung up the phone and I put my phone away. I looked over at Rudy and Renée, "What did I just do?" I couldn't help but feel like I just backed myself into a corner.

"You just did the fatherly thing. Don't forget the car rental," Rudy reminded me.

"I know. Would either of you be interested in taking a ride to Peoria, with me?" I asked them. "It's only a two-hour ride, if I drive fast."

"Nah, I think you and Amanda need to spend the time together. I wouldn't want her distracted with me, being a third-wheel," claimed Rudy.

"I agree," said Renée.

"A moment ago, you said you're there for me," I smiled, because I was joking with him.

"That was then buddy; you're on your own now," he replied, with a whimsical, light-hearted expression, suggesting he was joking too.

"I sure could use a vacation," I said to Rudy, because I was feeling a little stressed.

"What? And leave all this excitement?"

"Honestly, I could use a week alone, just by myself. Some place quiet, with a beach front."

"Well, don't forget Prometheus wants us to travel over to Europe next year. There are some high-profile people over there he wants taken care of. That can be considered, a partial vacation...*right*?"

"*Wrong*! Rudy, I've been working with you for ten years, and not once have I asked for time off. *Not once*."

"I know."

"Well, I need a little time off."

"Okay, I'll make a deal with you."

"What's that?"

"I'll let Prometheus know you want to take some time off... how much are you asking? And be serious, because this is a business, Sebastien. Every day you don't work, its money lost!"

"I'm just asking for a week. *One full week*!"

"You do realize that's quite a bit of money gone?" Rudy replied. His comment had me thinking: I began to imagine all the gears and wheels turning inside his head, as he tried to account for the fifty-thousand dollars I wouldn't receive for each file, and the money he and Renée would lose. It was then I realized, Rudy would make a great investment broker, if or when he retired from this lifestyle.

"Rudy, it's not going to kill you," I protested!

"Yeah, let's just hope that Prometheus, doesn't find another agent. Someone who doesn't require a vacation."

"You're terrible at times! You know that? You're worried about that?"

"Yeah. It's a real possibility!"

"No. He gets us for a good deal, considering what we do. We've always done good by him; he obviously trusts us and knows we get the job done. And he never has to worry about being implicated, in any way. Besides, you still have Renée, who would be working."

"True."

"Hey, maybe I'd like some time off too!" Renée sneered.

"See what you've started!" Rudy said. "Now, Renée wants time off."

"I wouldn't if I were getting fifty-grand a file!"

"Hey, you agreed to twenty. You could have asked for more. Besides, I've been thinking about asking Prometheus to give you a bump up in pay, because you're worth it."

"Thank you!" she said, excitedly! Rudy turned toward me and proceeded, "You'd come back, right? I mean you've told me and Renée, that you've managed to save enough money that you really don't need to be doing this anymore."

"Is that what you're really worried about? You think if I go on vacation, I may decide never to return?"

"*Honestly*?"

"*Yeah*," I replied.

"The thought has crossed my mind."

"Rudy, first of all, I wouldn't do that to you. I know your wife's been spending a lot of what you get. You have a mortgage to pay off, not to mention college for Brittney and that new car you purchased. Besides, I'm not ready to call it *quits*, there's too much cleaning to be done."

"Now you're talking!" Renée exclaimed! I looked over and saw her smiling. "Gentleman, let's stop talking about quitting and get to work. Chicago aint gonna clean itself."

"You know she's right," Rudy hinted, nudging me.

"Yeah, I know."

TWELVE

The rental was a dark gray, 2019 Chevy Suburban; with all the bells & whistles, including light-brown leather seats and keyless *entry* and *start*. I was on I-180 cruising at a comfortable speed of 70 mph; traveling behind a group of other vehicles, and I had two other cars behind me. I assumed it was safer to travel in a pack, because it was less likely the highway patrol would stop all of us, that's when my cell-phone rang and Siri didn't announce the caller. I was reluctant to answer, because the last thing I needed was to have a telemarketer trying to sell me something. On the other hand, it could be Detective Olivia Bartlett; because she has my cell-number and was supposed to be calling me sometime this week, concerning the file I needed on the perp, who raped and murdered her daughter.

I had my phone in the center console; with the screen up, so I could view it while driving. I saw the number and had to make a split-second decision, either answer it or let it go to voicemail. I decided to answer it. I reached over and touched the screen, allowing the call to be answered. "Hello!" I uttered. I didn't waste time redirecting my attention; I just remained focused on the Jeep Grand Cherokee in front of me. There was a moment of interference, before I heard a female voice, "Sebastien, is that you?"

"Yes, who is this?"

"Detective Olivia Bartlett."

"Oh, hey!"

"Are you busy?"

"Well, I'm driving right now. I'm on the Interstate, going to meet someone," I replied, and I intentionally, left out any mention of Amanda. I've conditioned myself not to volunteer information, especially about my private life or my daughter.

"Are you on a job right now?" Olivia pressed me for more information.

"No." I was beginning to feel like she had me under a microscope; and if she continued to ask me questions about what I was doing, I promised myself I would tell her it was none of her business and I wasn't going to say it politely either. I really didn't care that she was a member of law enforcement. I didn't appreciate her asking me so many questions, because I knew from experience, you can wind up painting yourself into a corner; one that may have devastating consequences.

"Good. The reason I'm calling is to tell you I have the file on *Rosario*."

"Great! Does that include his *interview*?"

"*What interview*?" she asked, sounding confused.

"You must have interviewed him, after you arrested him."

"Oh, yeah. That I can't get," she said rather bluntly.

"Why?"

"As it is, I have given you enough confidential information."

"I don't play like that detective."

"Excuse me!"

"You heard me. It sounds like you're worried about trusting me with departmental information."

"I'm not going to lie, it's a concern."

"Well, let me ask you this, is Miguel's interview available to you?"

She hesitated before she said, "Honestly, I'm not comfortable taking a chance, and having someone in the department request it for review and it's not there. Especially, if his attorney wants to see it again for some reason."

"I see your point. And I agree."

"I have everything but the interview; all I need to know now is *when* and *where* to meet? So, I can give you, his file? I was hoping to call you earlier and give you his file today, but I've been busy up to my neck."

"Understandable," I replied. Call it instincts; or just simply a gut feeling, but for some reason, I felt the need to be extra careful when dealing with Olivia. Maybe that was just because she was a cop, or maybe it was because she was making it very difficult for me to believe her. I decided to tell her I need a little time to think about a place to meet. Her immediate response was, *why?* She also asked, if we could meet now, since I wasn't working? In which I mentioned once again, that I was on the Interstate, on my way to meet someone and right now was not a good time. She finally gave up and told me to call her when I could; I told her I'll do that and we both ended the call, almost simultaneously.

When I finally reached the McCluggage Bridge leading into Peoria; I glanced down at the vehicle's clock radio and saw that I had arrived sooner than expected. I would be at my destination in about twenty minutes. Carolyn resided in North Knoxville, Peoria, at Winkler Lofts. It had several residential units, with private parking for tenants and visitors. Her loft was a one-bedroom, with an additional guest room, which Amanda used. I must admit, I was a little jealous, because her apartment had oversized windows, hickory floors, exposed brick walls and a vaulted ceiling; with that coveted industrial feel and appearance. The city had a different milieu in the late evening; compared to what I was used to back in Chicago. It had an assortment of colorful city lights, reflecting off the confluent waters, of the Illinois River. My eyes were fixed on the car ahead of me, when my phone rang again. Immediately, I assumed it was Detective Olivia Bartlett; calling to tell me maybe she could get the interview of Miguel after all. With that in mind, I answered my phone, before Siri could announce the caller. "So, you changed your mind, right? You can get the tape of that interview after all?" I concluded, without looking at the phone number to see who was calling? "Sebastien, it's me Carolyn." I quickly glanced over at my phone; I saw the screen with her name and number. Realizing I should have let Siri announce the incoming call, I said, "Oh hi. I should be there soon."

"Can you give Amanda a little more time?"

"Sure, why?"

"Felix ran away again," she said, rather sadly. Felix was our daughter's cat. Carolyn went on and said, "He's probably over at the house." The moment she mentioned the old place; it immediately brought back fond memories of when we began living together. "I've found him over there twice now," she explained.

"Really."

"Yeah. Anyway, Amanda is so upset that she hasn't yet packed and I'm afraid to go looking for Felix at this hour. Is it possible that you could swing by our old house and check to see if he's around? If he went there, he'll probably be sitting up on the porch."

"Does anyone live there?"

"Yes, an elderly couple. I've met them once. Very nice people. Don't go up to the door or anything, just drive over there and see if Felix is there in view. If you can't find him, I'll have to look for him tomorrow, while Amanda is away with you."

"Maybe it's not such a good idea for her to be leaving now for the week, you know? Not with Felix missing."

"Sebastien, she's looking forward to spending the week with you!"

"I'm only saying, I'm thinking about how she's going to feel, missing Felix."

"Can you just swing by the old house, please?"

"Yeah, sure. No problem."

"I'll let her know you are looking for Felix and I'll call you when she calms down and gets packed."

"Okay." I ended the call and drove on, headed to a very familiar location. It wasn't long before I arrived at what was once our first home. I began to reminisce again, remembering pleasant things that happened, while we were living here. I wished it weren't so dark, because I could see the place better and see if there were any changes. I knew the exterior had been painted at least once. The last time I passed by, there was a dumpster in the driveway and roofers working on re-shingling the roof. There was also a very nice gazebo off along the side. However, it wasn't very visible – not at this hour of the evening. I parked the Suburban directly across the street. I figured this was the best location to see the front porch. If Felix was around, I would see him. The porch had two wooden rocking chairs; they both looked new. Those chairs weren't there the last time I drove through town. I remembered mowing that lawn every summer. I glanced up at the second-floor window; it was the one to the master bedroom. For a moment, I recalled the day we were deciding if we were going to purchase the house. We had been shown everything, including the garage. It wasn't until the realtor showed us the master bedroom, with its two skylights and all the closet space, not to mention the beautiful hot tub. Carolyn and I were both taken by surprise; we both agreed this was the house for us. The following year, she was so excited to tell me she was pregnant again, that she came rushing in and leaped right onto me, while I was still lying-in bed. We spent weeks, every night, before going to bed talking about what to name our next child, depending on whether it was a boy? Or a girl? Unfortunately, we didn't have to decide on a baby name, because Carolyn miscarried, three months later. I looked down at the living room window and remembered how we had furnished the place. I still vividly recalled our first Christmas, with Amanda. Carolyn and I spent a whole weekend finding the perfect tree, bringing it home and setting it up right in front of that window. We decorated it with a bunch of lights, ornaments and angel hair, even our neighbors commented at the time, telling Carolyn it looked so nice from outside. The porch reminded me of Halloween, I guess because it was late and I recalled keeping that overhead porch light on, for trick-or-treaters. We spent the evening watching horror movies and sipping hot-coco. That weekend, Amanda got sick with such a severe fever, that we had to take her to the hospital. I had to carry her down those stairs, and rush her over to where the car was parked, in front of the garage. Directly in the back, was where the kitchen was located. I had no idea if the back deck was still there or not. Hopefully it was, because Carolyn and I spent a whole summer building it; and we didn't use treated lumber

either. We paid a lot more for cedar and the outcome was
well worth it. The dining room was opposite the kitchen and
I remembered helping Carolyn with our first Thanksgiving
dinner. We had invited her parents, my mother and a few
close friends. She was funny, scrambling to prepare everything
and ordering me around, like a drill sergeant. Well, maybe
not a drill sergeant, but still quite demanding. I can't blame
her, she wanted everything to be perfect, all I wanted to do
was eat. I think part of the reason we decided to part and
go our separate ways, was because she wanted everything to
be perfect, *always*. That's just not realistic. It wasn't realistic
then and it's not realistic to think that now. Every couple goes
through what I called, *relationship dynamics;* it was a constant
give and *take*. Many times, I had to choose your battles. All-
in-all, I can say without hesitation I was glad Carolyn and
I bought the house and tried to build a life together. Even
though it didn't work out, we had Amanda and I wouldn't
change that for anything. While remembering all this, I heard
my phone, it brought me back to the present. I looked down
at the screen and saw it was Carolyn calling. Next, I heard
Siri announce the name of the caller. I answered, "Hello!"

"Hi. Did you find Felix?" Just as she asked me that question, I saw him sitting on the front porch among the shadows.

"Yeah, I see him."

"Oh good. I packed for Amanda. I'll tell her you found
Felix; that should cheer her up immensely! Thank you."

"You're welcome. So, should I head over now?"

"Yeah."

"Okay."

"Bye," she said.

"Bye." I ended the call and got out of the rental. I walked toward our old house. Felix noticed me and I guess he was comfortable enough to come over. I reached down and picked him up. I carried him back to the Suburban, put him inside and got in myself. I took one last look at the old house, before starting the SUV and putting the rental in drive. I drove away, eager to see the expression on Amanda's face, when I showed up with Felix in my arms. I was certain she was going to have a smile on her face, the length of the Mississippi River. Felix was probably going to be the subject of our conversation, on the return trip to Chicago.

THIRTEEN

I woke feeling *refreshed* and *rejuvenated* from a very restful sleep, with only one intention; to make breakfast for my daughter and Dakota. I pushed the bedcovers aside and sat up, with my feet off the side of the bed. My actions caused Dakota to become curious, and she left her dog bed and came over to me, sat directly in front of me and began to pant and wag her tail, *incessantly*. I figured that could only mean a couple of possibilities; she either wanted me to feed her, walk her or *both*!

"Hey girl! You ready for breakfast?"

Dakota pawed me with her front paw, telling me in no uncertain terms that in fact she was hungry. I was dressed in just my pajama pants, and my bedroom slippers were nearby. I slipped my feet into each slipper and snapped my fingers; triggering a response for her to follow me, as I opened the bedroom door and went out into the hallway. The guest bedroom was the first door on the right and the door on the left was the bathroom. I stopped in front of the guest's bedroom door and tapped a few times; hoping my daughter was awake and would hear me. Lately it's been difficult to accept the fact that Amanda is growing up, but I've come to realize it's a process that is beyond my control. With maturity comes independence; and she's going to want more space and I'm going to become less and less important in her life. It's a process all teenagers go through; even I rebelled as a teen. My hope was that her mother and I had taught her well, and due to her upbringing, she wouldn't grow too far from us – or become too independent that she wouldn't tell us when something was bothering her. She would definitely have her independence; yet feel comfortable knowing we were always there for her; no matter what curveballs life threw at her.

Tap.

Tap.

Tap.

"Come in!" I heard my daughter shout! I reached for the doorknob; turned it and pushed the door open. I looked in and saw her still in bed, with the bedcovers completely over her head; and her feet exposed to the sun's light shining in through the partially open blinds. "Hey sweetie, what would you like for breakfast?"

"*Sleep*!" she replied, weakly. It was obvious she was exhausted. However, I was persistent, "No really," I said, and I watched as she pushed the covers off from over her head; exposing her tangled messy hair. Amanda reminded me of an older Punky Brewster – same hair color, only longer. My daughter also had that distinguishable young-looking face; with rosy cheeks and a healthy complexion.

"You want cold cereal, hot oatmeal or pancakes; with bacon and eggs," I asked.

"I'm tired, dad! Really tired!"

"Honey, you gotta eat breakfast."

"I promise I'll get up for lunch!"

"Nope. Young lady, you don't want me to have to take drastic measures, do you? Like maybe pouring ice cold water on you?" I said, hoping she would get up and rush off the bed, but she remained lying there, like she didn't think I could ever do such a thing. She knew me well, because I couldn't do that to her.

"Dad!"

"What?"

"This is Saturday morning; couldn't we have breakfast a little later? Maybe have breakfast for lunch and lunch for dinner. I was up late last night; worrying about Felix."

"I know, and reading too." I told her I saw her bedroom light on and peeked in, figuring she was either on the computer, reading or on her cellphone.

"How did you know that?" she sat up.

"Have you forgotten, I'm your dad. I know everything," I boasted, smiling. "Now, what about breakfast? What do you want?"

"Not oatmeal, *yuck*!"

"You used to like oatmeal."

"Yeah, when I was like *five*. What are you havin'?" she asked, looking directly at me.

"I'm thinkin' pancakes, with delicious crispy bacon and fluffy scrambled eggs...that's what I'm going to make for myself. Does that sound like something you'd like for breakfast?"

"How many calories are in crispy fat bacon?" she asked, with an odd expression on her face, like she was deciding if she even wanted to entertain the thought of such fat producing; artery clogging food.

"Oh, I don't know. I wouldn't worry sweetie one piece of bacon won't hurt you."

"Yeah, but I don't want to get fat dad."

"Sweetie you won't. Tell you what, after breakfast I'll teach you how to play piano."

"No. You already tried and I suck at it!"

"What?! Why would you say that?"

"Because it's true; I stink at piano. It's too difficult! You make it look so simple, like you were born to play."

"That's because I practice a lot sweetie. I think if you really give it a shot, you might like it."

"Maybe tomorrow."

"I don't know what you'll be doing after breakfast, but I'll be playing the piano." I turned to leave the room, because I had to use the bathroom before I going downstairs. My daughter saw this and jumped out of bed, "Wait!"

"Sweetie, take Dakota downstairs because I have to use the bathroom."

"So do I!" she cried out. "Let me go first!"

"Alright, but be quick, okay?"

"Yeah."

After breakfast I began playing a few of Frederic Chopin's classic Sonatas, Etudes and a Nocturne. I was still thinking about Carolyn; even though I knew she wasn't right for me and in my state of mind: longing for something more than superficial one-night stands, I chose to play the song *Romance*. I sat facing the keys, with my back straight and my hands out ready to exercise each finger. It amazed me how these same hands could play such beautiful music; yet were still *capable* and *responsible* for the murders of too many criminals to mention. My fingers began to move by muscle memory, while my mind wandered again. This time I started to ponder my association with Detective Olivia Bartlett, and I recalled her getting in my vehicle. My mind was like a recording device, with the proficiency to play back what had happened in the past few months. I also had the ability to cognitively rewind and examine each and every word someone said to me. While playing *Romance*, I began thinking about what Olivia said; and her reasons why she couldn't kill Miguel herself. As a professional, I was quite pessimistic, because I didn't believe Olivia when she claimed there would be a paper trail leading back to her; because there are many ways to kill someone, and not worry about evidence. Olivia should know this, which has me wondering what her real intention is? I also didn't trust her trying to relate to me, like we were on the same team, which was anything but true. She was supposed to be a member of law enforcement, while I knew where my loyalty was, and it was far from being lawful.

I was right in the middle of playing Chopin's, *Romance*, when I heard the phone ring. It rang again and again, before my daughter cried out that she was going to answer it! I heard her from behind me, which meant she must have been standing and watching me play. I hoped, my love for classical music would eventually rub off on her and she would grow to appreciate its fine qualities. I tried never to end a melody by interruption, so I continued playing. While my fingers were moving, I heard my daughter, as she approached me from behind, "Dad, it's your friend Rudy!"

"Ask him what he wants?" I played unaffected, even with the distraction behind me. I heard her ask him my question. It wasn't long before I had the answer. She replied saying, "He wants to know if you want him to bring Brittany over?"

"Tell him yes!"

I heard her tell him, *yes!* Then all I could hear was the melody, that I continued playing; as my eyes followed each line of sheet music in front of me. My fingers were moving in precise unison, with the rest of the melody; like a well-choreographed performance.

"Dad!"

"Yeah."

"Rudy said, he'll be over within the hour!"

"Okay."

"What are you playing?" she asked, coming up beside me with the phone still in her hand.

"Frederic Chopin's, *Romance*." I played right up to the end.

"That was nice."

"Thank you, sweetie."

***

Honestly, I saw the Harold Washington Library as a rather large cubed shaped building, made of *stone* and *mortar*, with those massive arch-shaped, dome-style windows; along each side of its boxed appearance. I was there to do research on *Dr. Feelgood*, because I chose him as my first job. I used the library, because it offered anonymity. For instance, I had a bogus account and I researched under a different name. In the event my research is identified, by the IP address; it allowed me time to make tracks, which wouldn't be possible if I were working from home. I had grown to know the library well and could find my way around quite easily. The library staff knew me as Michael Richardson. If only they knew the real reason, I used the library; I wondered what they'd think of me then? That thought was only brief, because I didn't care what they thought of me. Business was business, and it was impossible to make friends. The few acquaintances, I had acquired over the years at the library, were *obtuse* and rather *myopic*; when it came to real life and the social culture that took place outside the library walls. I saw them for whom they really were, which was intolerant of ignorance and believed literature was somehow their safe room, or default key. When things went wrong for them in life; they most likely found solace in between the pages of a good book; preferably a classic. They were rather imbecilic of such things as going out on a Friday night to have a drink and socialize; or dance for that matter. The library employees I knew, believed such behavior was *ritualistic* and *unbecoming*. They were the same people who were the first to criticize the average working person; because he or she wanted to socialize in a bar with a beer, watching the game. I read microfilm, and researched news articles about Dr. Peterson; from his graduating class to when he was first suspected of sexually abusing children. I researched even further, by going and finding a computer that wasn't being used. I intended to dig and uncover everything I could find about this man. I had the means and the ways of surfing the dark web, using software called, "The Onion." It had links to places on the internet called: *The Private Path* and *Paradise Lost*. The Private Path allowed me access into his personal life. I would be able to surf his grades in college and see whether or not he was a good student. Did he receive financial aid? Or did his folks pay his way through school? I also had access to the deed to his home and could tell if he was still making mortgage payments or not? With the link, Paradise Lost, that allowed me access to his credit card purchases, and would let me know if he had made any sleazy downloads of kiddy porn. My intention was to turn his world completely upside down, shake it thoroughly, like a cosmopolitan, and see what fell out. I managed to gather extensive information about the *good doctor*. Including his Social Security number, new home address and weekly planner, with his schedule. The doctor seemed rather obsessive and compulsive, when it came to planning his day. The afternoon, he planned on going over to Chicago's Riverfront, under the heading: *extra-curricular activities*. For all I knew, that could mean he was intending to have an affair. I decided to find out what his extra-curricular activities were, and left the library, headed for the riverfront. Chicago's Riverfront was very nice during the summer. There were plenty of things to do, including boarding the riverfront boat and taking in some of the sights. I wondered if he planned to take a river cruise? I was glad it was Saturday, because the weekly grind of traffic wasn't so intense, this allowed me to get over to the riverfront much sooner than if it were the beginning of a work week. When I arrived at the riverfront, I saw there were plenty of activities going on, including family fit day. Family fit activities involved stretching, jogging in place and doing pushups and sit-ups along with leg lifts. I scanned the crowd to see if Dr. Peterson was around. I really wasn't surprised to see him standing in the front of the crowd; staring at the children, like some pervert with only one intention in mind. I moved effortlessly through the crowd, moving closer to my subject. I intended to get very close, without him suspecting I'm following him. Prometheus only requested one thing; and that was to torture this monster. I assumed he didn't care if I murdered him or not. I agreed with Prometheus thinking that the proper punishment should be the removal of his manhood. As I moved even closer, I saw the expression of delight all over Dr. Peterson's face. I attempted to try and see what he was looking at, which child had caught his interest. I viewed the area he was looking at and saw a young girl, exercising alone. I was almost certain her parents probably just stepped away for a moment; to get food at one of the many vendors. It was obvious, Dr. Peterson saw this as an opportunity to get closer to the girl. I was prepared to stop him by claiming I know him from college. I was confident I could convince him that I knew him, because I had retained so much knowledge about him, even what classes and grades he got back in college. With so much going on and people distracted; Peterson moved on impulse. He broke free from the crowd and went over to the little girl. I moved on this; and intercepted him before he could even introduce himself to the child. "Harold is that you? Harold Peterson? You son of a gun!" I said, reaching out and putting myself in his path. He looked disappointed and surprised! He was definitely disappointed that I had interrupted his conquest and probably surprised, because I knew his name; yet it was obvious he had no idea who I was.

"Who are you?" he asked, and looked confused.

"It's me, Ryan." Ryan was the first name that came to mind. "Ryan Frates!" The last name Frates was a name I recalled seeing, while doing my research. I was hoping it was a name he might vaguely remember; which would offer me a little cover. I saw he still had no clue, so I add, "We went to the same university! Remember, Professor Grayson?"

"Oh yeah! How could I forget him!" He voluntarily mentioned another professor, "What about Professor Mehlman? You remember him?" Honestly, I couldn't place the name, but I remained confident and undeterred. "Yeah, he was a character. I hated his weekly quizzes and super difficult tests."

"Oh, believe me I know, tell me about it!" I replied, and tried to appear as if I was in complete agreement. "I remember you got very good grades," I said, hoping he wouldn't ask me how I knew?

"Yeah. I considered myself an average student. Glad those days are over, right?"

"Absolutely! I can't complain though, I had some good times."

"Oh, I'm sure. So, did I. We're you in a *frat*?"

"Yeah," I replied. I told him the name of the fraternity and I even elaborated a little from what I remembered reading. It's times like these when research pays off in huge dividends, because not only did he appear to believe me; he even contributed some of his own experiences of what he remembered. He told me how his initiation into the fraternity almost got him killed; and how he wound up in the ER on a Friday night and didn't get to leave the hospital, until the following morning. He talked even more about past experiences and we wind up gabbing for a little over an hour, before he asked if I'd like to have a beer with him? I told him I didn't drink, but wouldn't mind getting something to eat. He suggested a place that I wasn't aware of and we walked off, leaving the riverfront. I figured before I torture this monster, I wanted to pick his brains. I wanted to know why he did this to children? Even if it meant having lunch with this animal! We walked over to the Bridge House Tavern, where I ordered a hamburger with a salad. The so-called, *good doctor* ordered a draft beer and a hamburger, as well. We agreed eating outside on the patio would be better on such a nice day. He took a seat under the canopy and I sat directly facing him. "So, are you in medicine too?" he asked me. His question only momentarily caught me off guard. I recovered quickly, so he wouldn't suspect anything odd in my behavior, as I replied, "No. I wound up changing my major."

"Maybe that's why I don't remember you. So, what is it that you do for a living?"

"I work with people."

"What? Like public relations?"

"Yeah, *exactly*! I have my own business," I offered, confidently.

"So, what does someone in public relations do?" he asked. "I assume you must work with celebrities, like *actors and musicians*?"

"Yes, that's exactly what I do."

"Sounds exciting!"

"It can be."

"So how many celebrity clients do you have?"

"All I can say is a few. I'm under contract not to go into any details about who they are, or what they do when they're not in the public eye."

"Understandable." He took a sip from his beer and said, "You ever get invited to those wild celebrity parties, everyone hears about?"

"I have."

"Have you been to the Playboy Mansion? Tell me you have!" he practically begged, like a pervert would.

"Unfortunately, I haven't."

"Oh well, that's one party I'd love to be at!"

"I'm sure," I said, with a fake smile. "It would be nice."

"Oh, hell yeah! Seeing all that titty and ass. Has me wishing I was in public relations now," he chuckled at his comment. While I just continued my friendly façade. We then talked about his practice and I got him to subconsciously give me more valuable information; about who he was and what made him tick. I began to see a better mental picture of this monster, which allowed me the opportunity to take a peek directly into how he thinks in public; which was his cover and how he dealt with society in general. I knew he had a dark monstrous side, which I wasn't anticipating. I first wanted to understand *Dr. Jekyll*, before I questioned, *Mr. Hyde*.

FOURTEEN

When I arrived at Dr. Harold's residential address; it was a
little after eight thirty p.m., and I found the perfect spot to
park. I had managed to memorize his schedule, so I knew
he was going to be home. I could only imagine what he was
up to? What perverse things he must have been thinking?
Watching? Or doing? I knew the layout of his security system. It was a respectable company, with only one fatal flaw.
The entire system was wired hot to the main panel; and
with the pull of the meter, everything including the security system would surely go out. That wouldn't have been a
problem; if the system notified the security company of the
breach, but instead when it lost power, it failed miserably,
unable to inform the command center that this house was
now unprotected! Also, by the time anyone monitoring the
home; became aware of the problem, it would be too late,
because I would be gone. I walked around the rear of the
house, where I saw Dr. Peterson watching kiddy porn. He
was *shamelessly* enjoying himself. The image of him pleasuring
himself was disgusting! I wanted nothing more than to kill

the power, and interrupt the pervert, so I quickly left where I was standing and went in search of the electrical meter. When I found it, I put on my black leather gloves and pulled off the strap that was attached to the meter hub. I then quickly and carefully removed the meter, pulling it out towards me; and shutting off all the power to Dr. Peterson's home. I put the electrical meter down near a pair of Azalea bushes. I quickly moved to the back of the home where the deck was located. I maneuvered myself so I was able to quickly climb over the railing, and onto the surface of the deck. I had already made a key to the rear door. I quickly unlocked it and went inside. I heard Harold in what I assumed was the living room. He was stumbling around in the dark! I began to hear curse words! I used the high-powered flashlight I had brought with me, to illuminate my path. As I turned the corner, I saw him over near the couch. I blasted him with the full strength of the beam of light. It was impossible for him to see me. "Hey! Who are you?!" he said, looking over in my direction, "and what are you doing in my house?"

"How are you feeling Harold? Maybe a little *vulnerable*?" I moved closer.

"How am I feeling? How do you know my name? Who are you? What the hell is going on here?" he demanded, putting up his hands in front of his face; in a poor attempt to block the bright blinding light. "I'm here to see the *good* doctor," I replied, as I grabbed him by the hair and pulled him down to the floor; so, he was on his knees. "Kiddy porn, if only your neighbors knew what a freak you really are. You think any of your neighbors know the real doctor? The real pervert!"

"Get your hands off me!"

"*How many*?" I asked.

"How many, what?" he repeated.

"How many innocent children have you hurt? You bastard!"

"I don't know what you're talking about."

"Don't even go there! You know exactly what I'm talking about. I'll ask you again, how many little children have you molested, or raped?" I removed his hands from in front of his face, so he couldn't protect his eyes from the light. "I don't know who you are? But I'm warning you, get the hell out of my house! I have no idea what you're talking about; concerning molesting or raping any children. I don't do that. Only pedophiles do such things and I'm not a pedophile."

"Is that right? You're *not* a pedophile?"

"*No*. I think you have confused me with someone else. My name is Harold Peterson. Doctor Harold Peterson."

"I know exactly who you are! You don't remember me, do you?" I knew he couldn't see my face, but I thought maybe he could recognize my voice. Apparently, he didn't recognize my voice. "No, who are you?"

"That's irrelevant! The fact is, I've done a lot of research on you and I know exactly what you've done. You are a pedophile, only you haven't been charged with it, because the legal system can't seem to make anything stick on you; because you're like *Teflon*. Why is that, Harry? Do you have any idea? I think I have a pretty good idea, and it involves the powerful people you know. The same ones who helped you to evade the authorities, the last time you molested a child, you fuckin' pig!"

"Molested a child! I have no idea what you're talking about; and there's no need to use obscene language."

"You of all people telling me not to use obscene language. That's hilarious coming from a pervert like you."

"I'm not a pervert. I happen to be a very well-known dentist."

"I know all about your oral exams." I removed some newspaper clippings from my coat pocket. I had memorized the names of the victims and their stories. I threw the first article at him and it struck him in the face. I watched as he picked it up off the floor and looked at the heading. "Maybe that will help jog your memory. Remember, Elizabeth Blakely? Seven years old." I watched as his expression changed and he appeared more serious – more nervous. I continued to mention children's names. "What about Megan Philips? You remember her? Or Jennifer Owens, she had just had her fifth birthday, the year you molested her. Let's not forget about Amy Rodgers...you remember her? You repeatedly molested her over a five-year time span. Remember what happened when she turned thirteen?"

"I don't know any of these children and I have no idea what you're talking about!"

"What are *you* talking about? Look at the name in those articles; it mentions you liar!"

"It could be another doctor named Harold Peterson. I'm not the only one with that name!" he attempted to play dumb, and that only infuriated me! "Now doctor, that is a boldfaced lie! You know it, I can see it in your face. You know it's true what they say about the eyes; they really are the windows to the soul. Your eyes say volumes about what a foul pervert you are. On Amy Rodgers thirteenth birthday, she hung herself in her bedroom closet. She left a suicide note...did you know that? Look at me when I'm talking to you! DID YOU KNOW THAT?!"

"There's no reason to yell! I'm right here. Yes, I remember reading about her death in the paper. It was very unfortunate. She was a lovely girl."

"She was a lovely girl, so you finally admit to knowing her? Now we're beginning to make a little progress. Do you feel you and I are making progress?"

"Sure. I suppose."

"Good! Anyway, she had mentioned that she was repeatedly sexually abused by someone she knew and was so embarrassed about it, that she didn't want to mention his name, or what he did for a living. Sound about right, doc?"

"No, it's not me! If it was me, she would have mentioned me. After all I do recall taking care of her dental needs."

"Her dental needs! What the hell was her dental needs... did that include oral sex you pig?"

"Absolutely not!"

"She had confided in one of her closest friends at school. A girl named Bridgette Meyers. Bridgette did claim Amy was referring to you, however, when the police questioned her, she changed her story...probably out of fear. Were you molesting Bridgette too?!"

"Go to hell!"

"Did you threaten her?"

"Who are you? And what do you want? I have money, I can pay you."

"I'm not here for your filthy money, you degenerate. I'm here to serve up a little justice. Something that should have been done a long time ago."

"What the hell are you going to do?!"

"I'm here to see to it that you don't hurt anymore children again. See, I could give you the easy way out, by putting a bullet right in your stinking head; but at this point, I don't think I'm going to do that. Instead, I'm thinking about doing something more appropriate...something that's going to make you suffer, for the rest of your filthy life. I want you to never forget what you did to those kids, that you molested. Before I do that, I want a reason."

"What are you talking about?"

"For my own curiosity, I want to know what turned you into the monster you are. *The sexual predator you are*?"

"Go drop dead!"

"In time I will, but right now you better start talking,

because my patience is wearing thin with you. In fact, you have less than three minutes to convince me, that I'm wrong about you. If you can do that, I'll just remove your testicles. If you fail to convince me, I'll remove everything, including your manhood. I can't imagine how you're going to pee with no penis."

"What?! You're insane!"

"Maybe, so you really should listen to what I'm saying then."

"What do you wanna know?"

"I want to know why you felt it was necessary to hurt so many kids? Were you a victim of sexual abuse?" I asked.

"I don't have to answer that. You're not a cop? Or a judge."

"Tick-tock. Tick-tock. Tick..."

"You're not going to touch me."

"Is that so? Why is that doc?" I shined the light right into his eyes.

"Because I didn't do anything wrong and I know very important people! Very important!"

I chuckled and mocked his comment, "I'm sure you do, you filthy pig! That's why you haven't been formally charge in a court of law. I can tell you a dozen more names of children, I recall reading about, who were victims of your sick behavior. You traumatized them for life, and you either don't realize that, or you just don't care."

"*Alleged victims*...I read the articles too! None of them

ever proved anything. Besides, if their stories were so truthful, why wasn't I ever charged?"

"I already told you, because you're like *Teflon*. You know certain people, that's obvious. But your luck has run out, the bill is due, the dance is over and I'm here to collect."

"I want you to take your hands off me and leave my home, before I call the police and have you arrested for breaking and entering, as well as trespass." When I heard, he was going to call the police I said, "Where's your phone?" He grabbed it off the coffee table; next to him. "It's right here!"

"Gimme it! Then put your hands together on the floor in front of you." I watched as he handed me his phone, before putting his hands down on the floor and placing one on top of the other. I then stepped forward placing my foot on his hands, keeping them down and in place; while I scrolled through his phone. First, I went and looked at his phone's photos. I recognized as I was scrolling, two public officials. One was the mayor of Chicago; and the other was Senator Louie Mendelson. As I scrolled further, I came across naked photos of children and porn videos that he downloaded from the dark web. I showed him one of the pictures on his phone of a naked child. "I think the police would like to see this. It's evidence they can use against you."

"You put that on my phone! After you broke in and assaulted me!"

"I didn't break-in, I had a key. As far as assaulting you... can you be more specific? Did I do something like this," I lunged my fist forward, hitting him in the face. He cried out, yelling for me to stop! "Please don't hit me anymore!" He folded over, while I still had his hands under my foot.

"You have a low tolerance for pain, don't you?"

"Yes, my hands are hurting. Please stop!"

"I'll tell you something about me...I welcome pain. Actually, I embrace it. I have to...you know why?"

"No, why?"

"Because this job requires it. I deal with scum like you, on a regular basis. Sometimes the animal fights back...but not you. You fold like a cheap suit at even the thought of pain." I stepped off his hands; letting him go and allowing the blood to return to his fingers again.

"I need to stand up."

"You can stand up after you tell me what the hell happened to you? You obviously weren't born a monster!"

"What are you some sort of *criminal psychologist*?" the doctor said, sarcastically.

"*No*. Someone very close to me, taught me about the criminal mind. He knows criminal behavior, very well. He's delt with scum like you on a regular basis." I stopped short of mentioning Jimmie's name. I left the beam from my flashlight focused right on his face. He looked down at the floor, trying to avoid the intensity of the light. I saw a change in his demeanor as he said, "No, I wasn't. Honestly, I don't know what drove me to act like this, because I was never abused. Maybe I was born this way?"

"Maybe so. Whatever the reason, it ends now," I said. His expression changed again, this time he appeared scared and I thought he knew I was serious about what I intended to do.

"But I told you what you wanted to hear."

"*No*, I wanted a valid *reason*, not an *excuse*."

"And I told *you* I was probably born this way."

"So, you're saying it's in your *DNA*?"

"*Yes*! It is and you can't blame me for that. It's not my fault. Those children needed me as much as I needed them. They wanted me to be a father figure to them. You know I asked them to call me daddy and they did?"

"You're a sick fuck! They trusted you." I then removed the dull cutting shears from my coat pocket. The tool fit right in the palm of my hand and was large enough to do the job. I put the shears up in front of his face, so he knew what to expect next. "Come on, I can stop!"

"Maybe you can, but I can't. I'm under contract and I'm not leaving here without a picture of you, along with your family ornaments in a shoe box. And *yes*, I brought the box with me. You wanna hear something funny?"

"What?"

"Tomorrow, I'll be giving the box to a friend, who'll wind up mailing it with everything you remember about your manhood. The individual I work for requires proof. When he gets the box with your junk in it, you know what he'll probably do after he sees the photo of you on the burner phone; the one I'm going to use to take the photo?"

"No, what?"

"Something, I'd do myself."

"Really? What's that?" he asked, looking up at me.

"He's gonna *burn it*!" I said, referring to Harold's family jewels. On the way home, I called Rudy to tell him I had the cellphone he gave me. The one Prometheus wanted, so he could view the evidence; ensuring that Dr. Harold Peterson wouldn't be hurting anymore children. I told him, both the *phone* and *physical evidence* would be in the shoe box; and I would have it wrapped and ready to go in the morning. He told me he would be over first thing in the morning to get it and we chatted for just a few minutes. I asked about how my daughter was doing? He told me, she had been asking about me, and seemed a little homesick. When I arrived home, I parked the rental right out in the street, in front of my residence. I immediately noticed the living room lights on; meaning only one thing, my daughter was home. I walked up the stoop and into my building's front entrance, where my mailbox was. I gathered today's mail and went to my apartment door, pulled out the key I needed to get inside and as soon as I entered, I saw Detective Olivia Bartlett, sitting on the couch, facing me. "You have a very lovely place here. Very warm and cozy," she said, looking at the piano and then back at me. I closed the door behind me, just as she said, "Do you play? That's one thing I regret when I was young, I never thought about music or taking piano lessons. Probably if I had, today I'd be some famous musician, instead of a narcotics detective. Oh well, it is what it is. What's in the box?" she asked me, referring to the shoe box I was holding with Dr. Peterson's junk inside. "A new pair of sneakers. How did you get in here? Past my home security system?" I'm also thinking how did she get past Dakota?

"I have my ways. Look who I'm telling that to!"

"Where's my dog?"

"Upstairs. He's really not that friendly."

"My shepherd is a *she*. Did you hurt her?"

"No. Well, *not really.*"

"What do you mean, *not really*? You better not have hurt her!"

"Settle down, I didn't hurt her. I carry a dog whistle for times like this. It has a certain pitch that dogs hate. Especially, *aggressive dogs*. When I heard her barking, I took out my whistle and well, it wasn't long before she was upstairs. I managed to locate her in – I think it's your bedroom. When I saw her in there, I just shut the door and that was that."

"What do you want?"

"You want to hear something really funny? I have been stressing over giving you Miguel del Rosario's file. You've either been too busy, or I haven't been able to get a hold of you, for one reason or another. Remember *Miguel*?"

"Yes, how could I forget?"

"Well, it seems I've temporarily misplaced his file. Don't worry, I will find it. If, however I am not successful, I promise I will get you copies of everything."

147

"Fine."

"I hate when I'm feeling stressed. My job adds plenty of stress to my life, so when I'm feeling stressed, especially like now, I tend to misplace things or forget stuff. It can be a pain at times...and I've even heard it's not good for my health. So, were you out working?" she asked, with a whimsical, almost odd tone, changing the topic instantly.

"Yes, I was."

"You must feel stressed at times too, *right*?"

"Honestly, *not really*. I have techniques I use to avoid becoming over stressed about anything."

"Really, that must be quite beneficial."

"It is."

"Well, when I get you his file, you will find time to work on it and put an end to him breathing? Right?"

"I work according to my timeline, that way I don't over commit myself, it's one way I avoid stress. And like I told you; I have prior commitments."

"Don't get so defensive. I realize you have other obligations. However, know this...I'm a member of law-enforcement...I can either be *beneficial*, or quite a *nuisance*."

"Are you threatening me?"

"*No*, just pointing out the obvious. Sometimes, we forget and we need a little reminder, that's all." She got up and walked directly over to the piano, touched the keys, before looking at me. "You're a parent, I'm sure you can understand where I'm coming from."

"I do understand and when you get me his file, I will let you know when I can start working on it. I have several other projects, I will be working on soon, which I need to finish, before I can even consider looking at Miguel's file."

"Understood. I will be sure to find his file and contact you as soon as I do. Know this, I want his head...*literally*!"

"I'm sure you do."

"*No*, I'm serious. I want proof, so I want you to remove his head and gimme it. I can even supply the leather bag I'm thinking of putting it in."

"*What*? You don't trust me?"

"It's not *you*. I don't trust *anyone*. This job turns most into cynics," she said, calmly.

"I can get you his head, but why? Usually, I just take a photo," I said, lying and feeling bad about doing it, but in her case, telling her the truth could have detrimental consequences for me. I found her request rather odd. "You and I both know photos can be faked," she said with a subtle, yet devilish grin. "Now you're insulting me, implying that I don't do my job." My expression remained obstinate. "Oh no, I know you're a *professional*. Believe me, I'm not questioning that at all. It's just I want more than a photo of that bastard! Think of it as I want a souvenir of sorts...something I can show my friends."

"Your friends? You wanna show his head to your friends?"

"Why not?"

"Nice friends."

"Exactly! They want him dead too, especially after what I told them about what he did to my daughter."

"I get it. I want you to know one thing though."

"What's that?"

"If you get caught in possession of Miguel's head, you didn't get it from me, is that clear?" I said, firmly.

"Sure," she said, with such a nonchalant reply. "You seem awfully tense. What? Did you have a bad day?"

"No, it was going fine, up until now," I intentionally said, rather coldly.

"*Ouch.* It's getting rather *cold* in here. I better get going. I'll be in touch."

"Next time, *call.*"

"That's one of my bad habits, I tend to just drop in." She lets herself out. I went over to the living room window and peeked out through the curtains. I watched as she stopped and looked at the only vehicle parked in front of my residence. I figured she would eventually run the license plate and see that it was a rental and she would probably become confused by the name it was under. I assumed it wouldn't take long for her to realize; I was using it under a fake name. However, I could care less – she's just as dirty as I am. I continued to watch as she went over to her unmarked patrol car, got in and drove away.

FIFTEEN

I was on my way over to see Jimmie, because he called earlier
and told me he wasn't feeling *well*. It's been difficult for him;
since his grandparents passed away. Their death, forced him
to relocate, because he couldn't keep up the building – due
to his disability. The Derenis convenience store had to be
sold, and Jimmie took that money and mortgaged the condo
he lived in, on North Olmstead Avenue. The place was in a
good neighborhood, with plenty to do and everything was
within walking distance, even the grocery store was nearby.
His condo was located on the second-floor. It was a little
over 1,100 square feet, with one bedroom and one bath. It
had a beautiful fireplace, private fenced patio with sliding
glass doors and a gorgeous marble kitchen countertop. The
exterior of the complex appeared to be well-maintained, with
a manicured lawn and signs of a new coat of paint *here* and
there. The interior of his condo would be more appealing to
the eye, if it weren't painted *primarily white*. Everything from
the living room and kitchen to the bathroom and bedroom,
was the color *white*. The kitchen offered a little contrast, with
some newer amenities, including a stainless-steel refrigerator.

151

I had a key to the lobby, which allowed me to get in without buzzing Jimmie's condo. I wished he gave me a key to the condo itself, so I wouldn't have to knock and wait for him to answer, especially in a real emergency! I climbed the flight of stairs and turned right at the top. His place was the third door on the left. The building complex was relatively quiet which was a good thing, because he had no one to complain about. When I reached his door, I instinctively stepped off to the side; it was out of habit – something I've learned over the years. I knocked at the door and waited for him to answer. I heard groaning, as he made his way to the door. "Who is it?" he said, with a weak sounding voice.

"It's me, *Sebastien*!"

"Hold on!" He then fiddled with the locks and finally opened the door. He peeked his pale face out through the doors opening. He looked rough! Like he hadn't slept in a week. He was wearing just his bathrobe. I was quite surprised at how unhealthy he looked, considering he didn't look this bad only a few months ago! It was obvious he had been spending all his time indoors and would benefit from getting some fresh air and much needed sunlight. "Get dressed, you're going out for a walk!" I said, while looking at the dark colored bags under his eyes. "You my friend need some sun, not to mention some fresh air."

"No. I don't feel like going out right now, maybe later." He invited me inside.

"So, what's this about you having pain in your stomach?"

I asked, as I followed him into the kitchen, where he claimed to have coffee brewing. He turned to me and said, "I just need some Pepto-Bismol. I ran out of it, last night. The pain kept me up most of the night."

"How much of that stuff are you taking?"

"I take it as needed."

"You seeing your doctor about the pain?"

"What for?"

"*What for*?" I repeated, because I thought his answer was rather odd. "For one thing, *your stomach*!"

"You know what he's gonna tell me? Nothing I already don't know, and there's nothing that can be done about it either." He turned away and continued to walk toward the kitchen. He stopped at the kitchen counter, where the coffee maker had just stopped brewing. "You want a coffee?"

"Sure. So, what aren't you telling me?" I asked, entering the kitchen.

"My stomach is the least of my worries," he said, grabbing two coffee cups from an overhead cabinet. He began to pour coffee for both cups. I was even more curious to hear his answer as to what was wrong with him? "Oh yeah, why? Jimmie what aren't you telling me?" He paused for a moment. I could see the mental anguish written all over his face; it was like his personal business card that he carried around with him. "I was diagnosed with advanced liver cancer...probably has already spread to my other vital organs. I've been coughing up blood for the past two weeks now."

"And you're just telling me *now*! Jimmie what the *hell*! How come you didn't tell me this two weeks ago?"

"And have you worry? You don't need to be worrying about me kid. You still have a full life ahead of you." He began to sound melodramatic. I could sense the melancholy in his voice and body language and figured he must have been struggling with the fact that he was facing something that could kill him relatively soon.

"So, what does your doctor say about all this?"

"What exactly are you asking? You wanna know if he gave me a time frame, when I should expect to leave this earth?"

"To be honest, *yeah*. I'd like to know."

"All I can say is sooner than I would like." He went over to the refrigerator and grabbed a container of coffee creamer from the top shelf. He then poured the creamer into his coffee cup and asked me to help myself to cream and sugar. "Isn't there something that can be done? *A liver transplant...? Chemo...? Anything?*"

"Sebastien..."

"What?"

"It would only prolong the inevitable, including my *suffering*."

"So, that's it?! You've given up? What does your girlfriend Vicky, think about that? Is she okay with you giving up?"

"We're not together anymore."

"What?! When did this happen?"

"Does it matter?"

"No, I guess not. You know, I don't hear from you for months at a time and when I do, you usually just call and talk a few minutes before telling me you have to go. Now out of the blue, you call to tell me your stomach is hurting. I'm thinking it's due to you being shot...ten years ago, but then it had me thinking, why haven't you complained about your stomach before? *Why now*? When I get here, you unload this on me; telling me you have advanced *liver cancer* which just might have spread. Let me tell you something Jimmie... you may not give a damn about yourself, but I care about you! I never told you this, but you've been like a father to me; I mean a real dad! You helped me through high school. You attended my high school graduation. You even gave me your classic car. You taught me self-defense. You even taught me the methods and motivations of the criminal mind. You wanna know why I joined the marines? It wasn't just because I wanted to give back to this country for accepting me as an immigrant. I had another reason. The other reason was I wanted you to be proud of me!"

"I am proud of you! And to be totally honest, ever since your high school graduation, I've thought of you like a son."

"Really?"

"Yeah."

"I guess I'm being selfish."

"Why do you say that?" he said.

"Because I don't want to see you go that's why?"

"Come here." He came over and gave me a great big hug

and said, "I'm gonna be alright. I just need you to go get me some Pepto-Bismol." As soon as I heard him say that, I immediately let go and pushed him away. I could feel anger, as it coursed its way through my veins and even though I knew I would be justified, I suppressed that emotion. Instead, I said, "You called me all the way over here, just so I'd go get you some *Pepto-Bismol*?"

"Well, I can't really go out like this, can I?"

"You're impossible," I said. I watched as he smiled, and at that moment I knew I couldn't be upset with him, and for some reason it made me feel better.

SIXTEEN

The material on Murderous read like a portfolio of who's who in the criminal world. His crimes were nothing but *atrocious*, to say the least. His career began at the ripe old age of seven-years-old. Most seven-year-olds were playing either cops and robbers, riding their bikes, or simply hanging out with friends, while playing video games. Murderous on the other hand, enjoyed stealing, robbing other children and getting into street fights. When he was sixteen, he committed grand-larceny in an attempt to be accepted into a neighborhood gang. At the age of seventeen, he committed his first murder. His lawyer claimed it was in self-defense, which allowed him to skate on the charges. Between the age of 19 and 24, he was suspected of several drive by shootings, including killing a nine-year-old little girl, while she was walking; on her way home from school.

Now at the age of 33, he had been released after shooting one of Chicago's finest.

His local hangout was a nightclub called, *Ace of Spades*. It was a nightclub known for being in the newspaper for fights and the occasional assault with a deadly weapon. I wasn't concerned with the nightclub's negative publicity, because I was confident, I could handle myself. I entered on the south end of the building, avoiding the cameras. Immediately, my auditory senses were bombarded by the sounds of intense rap music. I had in my possession a current photo of what Murderous looked like, so I immediately began looking around at all the unfamiliar faces. I received more than a few stares, and even a few racist comments concerning the color of my skin. I had another rule, which was I didn't listen to rude comments. On the other hand, if those comments were followed by a violent attack, I responded immediately! I never allowed anyone to enter my personal space; especially if it was going to explode into a physical altercation, or conflict. "You're in the wrong place, white bread!" I heard someone say behind me. I ignore the comment and continued moving through the crowd. "Hey cracker, you in the wrong place boy!" said another fool. "He aint in the wrong place, he just has a death wish!" said another individual. Finally, I saw Murderous and he wasn't alone. He had three females at his table; along with another black male. I went over, knowing exactly what I was going to say. "Murderous, you are one lucky son of a gun, you know that?"

"What?" said the other black male. "Who the hell are you, honky?" He then turned to Murderous, "You know Casper? I sure as hell don't!" I looked directly at Murderous and said, "I know Murderous. He's the dirtbag lowlife who was recently released after killing a cop. Aint that right Murderous?"

"Man, I can't believe he just called you a dirtbag!" said Murderess's friend.

"I would call anyone with his background a dirtbag? White, black...hell even an Indian chief. Color and race are irrelevant. It's the crime and Murderous is a number one dirtbag in my opinion." Murderous looked surprised! Almost shocked that a white guy would have the gaul to come into his playground and make snide comments. "You better be walking, while you still can. You get my drift white bread?"

"No, I actually like the vibes in this place. You think the D.J. would mind if I asked him to play a little Beethoven? You can get the modern version with violin."

"Very funny. You know who I am? *Really*?"

"Yeah, I know exactly who you are. You're a stupid ass-hole gang member, called *Murderous*. You have an I.Q. of a vegetable and you're taking Viagra, because your impotent. Am I right?"

"Boy, you are one cocky bastard! I gotta give you credit though...coming in here with an attitude, knowing that you aint walking outta here *now*!"

"Well, I'm not ready to leave just yet."

"You poked the bear, now you dead, *homey*!" said the other black male. He tried to leave his seat and that was when I moved quickly to stop him. I hit him right in the throat, causing him to go from *kinetic* to *flaccid*, in just a few seconds! He sat there in his seat, coughing and holding his throat with both hands. I could tell by his body language that he wasn't about to challenge me again. "Hey, what the hell?" said Murderous! He was about to pull a weapon when I moved closer, grabbed him by the back of the head and forced it down onto the table top, with a rapid strike. I simultaneously pulled his head up and looked directly into his eyes. The girls at the table rushed off. "You ever pull a weapon out on me again; I will use it to bash your fuckin' head in! Is that clear?" I immediately sensed others coming up behind me. Two were bouncers and I quickly reacted, stopping them dead in their tracks by kicking out their knee caps! Another five guys, who looked like regular nightclub goers decided to assist the bouncers and I disabled them as well; one at a time in what looked like a choreographic fight. No one else seemed to want to challenge me and that was when I excused myself to a group of onlookers, who couldn't believe what they just witnessed! I pulled Murderous out from the table he was at. "Who the hell are you?" he cried out! "Don't worry about that," I said and pulled him along. He continued to struggle, until finally I couldn't take it, so I did a wristlock maneuver on him; placing my arm between his armpit and twisting his wrist until he complied. With the lock in position, and the pain showing on his face, he was no longer willing to resist. At that point, I was able to usher him out of the night club quite peacefully. I escorted him outside, over to the rental and told him to cooperate, or I would end his life right here; with a single bullet to the side of his head. I then cuffed him and gave him a thorough pat down, searching for any weapons on his person. I found the gun he was planning to use on me, along with a wad of hundred-dollar bills. "Hey man, that's my money! You can have it though, if you just let me go and walk away."

"Just like that, *huh*?"

"Just like what?"

"You're gonna gimme all this money; just to let you go?"

"Yeah, honest!"

"How much is this?" I showed him the wad of money.

"Five grand."

"That won't even cover my property tax. I'll pass."

"Wait man!"

"Get in!" I opened the passenger's side door and helped him inside, before shutting the door and going around to the driver's side and getting in. I quickly scanned the parking lot, hoping no one was using their cellphone to take video footage. Everyone was inside the night club. "Who are you and what the hell is goin' on here man?!" he demanded to know, looking genuinely confused. "I've never seen you before in my life. How did you know I just got out of jail? Who told you? Am I being set up, man? You gotta be a cop! Can you take off these handcuffs?" I looked over and put my first finger up to my lips and responded with, "Shhhh."

"You a cop? Cops aint supposed to do stuff like this!"

"I'm not a cop."

"I don't know what this is about man, but I know people... important people. *Gangstas*!"

"You know how many times I hear that?"

"Nah man, how many?"

"Too many to remember! Everybody claims to know somebody important, when it's their ass on the line." I put the key into the ignition and started the rental. I put the vehicle in drive and just as I was about to drive off, he began to talk again. He became adamant about knowing who I was? "Man, kill me if you want, but do the honorable thang and at least tell me who the hell you are?! I mean you aint just no white boy, not wit' the shit you pulled back there inside. You took on seven guys homey! *Seven*! Who does that shit? Besides someone like Bruce Lee, Chuck Norris or Steven Seagal. You like MMA'd the shit out of them. You ever been an MMA fighter?"

"No. I'm just here to set things right," I said, tapping the gas pedal with my foot.

"What?" Murderous replied. "What the hell are you talkin' about?"

"I'm talking about your history...and how you like to commit crime. You know that cop you shot in the face?"

"Yeah, so what!? He was a pig, man!" he said, unrepentantly. "He always bothered me in the hood. Me and my homeys finally got sick and tired of his shit! Tailing us for driving the speed limit. Pulling us over, because of our gang colors! You don't know how it is in the hood man. Cops be messin' wit' us day in and day out! They think we all bad news..."

"No, cops don't think that. They just know you and your so-called homeys are *deviants*."

"What's that?"

"Criminal types."

"Nah man. That's stereotyping, and it's *racist*!"

"Racist, huh?"

"Yeah, when it involves the hood, man."

"You left his wife a widow, having to take care of three children. Two boys and a baby girl. Did you know that? Or do you even care?" I asked, looking over.

"He got what he deserved man. And no, I don't care about the cracker's kids or his whore wife!"

"Oh really?" I put my foot on the brake, rapidly slowing the vehicle to a standstill. "Show a little respect or I'll make you eat those words, right here and right now!"

"Okay, I take it back, but I aint sorry for what I did and if given the opportunity I'd do it again man."

"I figured that. So did the man who hired me, to find you and kill you," I said, turning away and putting my foot on the gas pedal again.

"Kill me! Kill me for what?"

"You haven't been listening, have you? I'm here because of your criminal background. You are a menace to Chicago and a very important individual who is funding my work, has hired me to see to it that you disappear."

"I can do that!" he howled, sounding serious. " I have relatives in Los Angeles. I can fly out first thing tomorrow."

"No, that's not going to happen."

"What do you mean? You want me to disappear!"

"My contact, the person I work for wants evidence that you're no longer here, among the living."

"What?"

"You heard me."

"Where are you taking me?"

"Some place quiet."

"Is this about money, because I can give you an easy hundred grand!" he claimed, looking over. The amount was tempting, but I wasn't going to accept another offer. Primarily, because I had already been contracted to fulfill my end of the agreement. Besides, I didn't believe Murderous was being honest with me. I didn't think he could come up with that amount of cash on such a short notice. "Save your breath," I grumbled.

"Man, I got a little sister who needs me. She's like diabetic and all. In fact, she's all handicap and shit. No joke! She's like in a wheelchair and walks with a limp. In fact, I should be home with her right now seeing how she's doing and giving her, her meds."

"Really? Walks with a limp and in a wheelchair? That's one I haven't heard. As for her meds, what would they be?"

"They're meds, you know stuff the doctor ordered." He looked over at me, like I should know what he was trying to say.

"Name *one* med."

"She's got too many to name man! She's like a walking pharmacy...like a fuckin' Walgreens dude."

"Can't even name one, *can you?*"

"I know one is for her sugar...the name I honestly don't remember."

"*Insulin*," I said, calmly.

"Yeah, that's it! I gotta be sure she gets her insulin. So, you better let me off at the corner. I'll catch a cab. It's been real man."

"Nah, I don't think so. Nothing you say now will change your outcome. You're gonna die tonight, by your own hand."

"Wait a minute!"

"What?"

"My own hand?" he smirked, sounding confused.

"That's right, you're gonna kill yourself."

I took Murderous to my planned location, which was an old warehouse building, near the river. I left the pair of handcuffs on him, so he wouldn't try to run. I drove up to the building's double doors, parked right in front. I exited the vehicle, casually went around to the passenger's side and opened the door, pulling him from the seat.

"Is this necessary!" I heard him say.

"Just shut up and move!"

"Man, you don't need to be doing this."

"Why?" I replied, pushing him along, over to the entrance door and pressing his face forward, so he wouldn't dart on me.

"Because I got family man. I got a wife and kid at home." He managed to speak out of the side of his mouth, with half of his face against the mortared brick. I removed the key from my inside pocket, unlocked the building's door and pulled him away from the brick, and said, "Your married? With a kid?"

"Yeah man. Newborn too."

"Wow! How did you pull that off?"

"What do you mean?"

"There's no record of you being married, or having a kid; at least not one you know about, right?"

"Since you're gonna waste me man, what's your name?"

"Sebastien, why?"

"Yeah, right! And my name is Santa Claus. What is it really?"

"I just told you." I pulled him inside, closing the door behind us. The inside had overhead fluorescent lights set on motion detection. They were lit and I pulled him farther inside the warehouse; over to the opposite end of the building, where I had set up a chair along with some equipment, I used for jobs like this. "Can I talk to this guy whose hired you?" he asked me, just as we reached his final destination.

"No, I don't even have that opportunity, and I work for him."

"I just wanted to tell him; he doesn't need you to do this."

"Is that so? And why is that?"

"Because I'm a business man. We can work something out, you know? I believe in spreading the wealth. I have plenty of cash and I'm willing to make a deal! Cash is king man; we can make a deal? I know we can!"

"Nah, that's not going to happen. What is going to happen is, you're going to go over to that chair over there and sit down." I pulled him, so he was not trailing behind me. "And see that gun, near the chair?" I had rigged the gun's trigger with thick string, so when he sat down, his weight would cause a reaction behind the chair, dropping a small weight and tugging on the string, causing the trigger to be pulled and the gun to be fired.

"Man, you got that shit rigged up," he said, looking at the chair.

"*Congratulations*! You're not that fuckin' stupid after all." I pushed him over towards the plastic sheeting. I laid out 6 mil poly for this purpose, so when he sat down and the gun fired, there wouldn't be much of a mess to clean up. The chair was directly centered on the plastic. "Come on man, I can't do that!" He was showing signs of being reluctant to move any further, which I completely understood; I would have been behaving the same way if I were in his shoes.

"It's either that, or I come up with something more drastic."

"Like what?"

"Well, I could start by cutting your fingers off. I have a cordless circular saw in the vehicle. You want me to run out and get that?"

"No. Come on man, we can't figure something out? I can pay you and for evidence, you can take a picture of me, with my iPhone. We can go to the supermarket, buy some ketchup and pour it on me and I'll lay on the floor like I was shot. Is that cool?"

"Let me think about that. You mean you'll pay me that hundred grand you mentioned, and we'll get some store brand ketchup, I'll pour it on you and that'll prove you were killed, right?"

"Exactly! It's all good. You get paid, your friend gets what he wants and I get to go home and see my little sister."

"Murderous, you know when you start lying, people begin not to believe anything you say, that's what my dad used to tell me and he was right."

"*Lying*! I aint lying man!"

"Well, you are. You don't have a little sister at home. In fact, my research on you revealed you're an only child. Now how do you think that makes you look?" I said looking straight at him. He immediately turned away, "How do you know that?" He finally mustered up the courage to look at me again, knowing he had been caught lying.

"I do my homework, asshole," I said rather bluntly!

"I see that. Even though I lied about having a little sister, can we still work something out? I'm good for the cash man, that's a promise man. I'm a well-known gangsta. If we can make a deal and agree on a price, it's yours no questions asked."

"Agree on a price? I thought you said you were good for a hundred grand."

"Come on man! How about we say ten grand? Take the five, and I'll owe you five. I'm good for it."

"You'll owe me five? What an awesome deal that is?"

"I know, right! So, we good?"

"No, I was being sarcastic asshole."

"Come on man, I'll do *twenty*! Five now and I'll get you the rest tomorrow, I promise!"

"You promise?"

"Yeah man!"

"After telling me all kinds of lies. Now you expect me to believe you?"

"Man, I was scared!"

"Now you're just wasting my time. I have other business to tend to. Sit down now!"

"Nah man, I really can't do that!"

"Listen to me asshole! You either sit down or I'll have to go back outside and get the cordless saw. You know cordless circular saws have a tendency to bind up, especially if the battery is low. It'll take a lot more effort and time to make exact cuts, by then I'll be really pressed for time, so I'll just start cutting shit wherever I see fit. I'm thinking the fingers first, followed by the feet, so you better remove your shoes."

"Look I'm begging you, gimme a break here!"

"Really! A guy like you, with your tough reputation as a gangster is going to beg?"

"I aint that tough."

"I see that. I have a simple question for you?"

"What's that?"

"When you were in court, being sentenced for the murder of that police officer you shot in the face, did you happen to get a good look at his wife and three children?"

"Yeah, why?"

"Good! Because I'm going to make you a deal of a lifetime. One that you'll never get again, ever! So, listen carefully, okay?"

"Yeah."

"I'll let you go *free*, if you can answer one question..."

"You'll really let me go?!"

"Yeah, I'm a man of my word."

"What about the evidence you said you'd need of me being dead?"

"That idea of ketchup works for me."

"Cool!"

"Don't get your hopes up yet! I managed to follow your case when you were in court. I watched it on television. I was really surprised, no make that shocked! I was shocked, to hear that you were being released from jail. It's amazing how upside-down things are in this world. You can shoot a police officer directly in the face, and walk, without serving your sentence. It's quite unbelievable. Now if I were the judge, I would have sentenced you to death."

"Well, I guess I'm lucky."

"We'll see how lucky you are answering this simple question. Do you remember that day? The day you were in court, waiting to hear your sentence?"

"Yeah."

"Take a moment and think about that day. Make sure it's really clear."

"I remember it!"

"Good. Now, if you can tell me what Amy and her three children were wearing, I will un-cuff you and we'll go to the store to buy that ketchup for a convincing photo."

"Who's Amy?"

"She's the wife of the police officer you shot."

"Oh."

I looked down at my wristwatch. "You have exactly five minutes starting now."

"You just want to know what they were wearing?"

"Yeah. Just tell me what her and her three children were wearing that day?"

"Just the clothes? Not like their shoes?"

"Just their clothes," I repeated. I noticed he was visibly struggling to recall. "Times running out here, you now only have four and a half minutes."

"What were they wearing? What were they wearing?" he repeated to himself. It was pretty obvious he didn't recall, but I was still going to give him the benefit of the doubt, even though he didn't deserve it. "I'm sorry, is that a question for me?"

"No. I'm trying to remember correctly!"

"Right. Four minutes."

"Do you know what they were wearing?" he asked me.

"Do I know what they were wearing? Yeah, you know why?"

"Why?"

"Because I could see the grief they were going through, having lost Patrick."

"Was that his name?" Murderous said coldly.

"Yep. You now have three-and-a-half minutes."

"Uh, she..."

"Her name is Amy."

"Amy, was wearing." He closed his eyes, like he was really trying hard to remember. "Something colorful that day."

"Can you be more specific? I mean colorful can mean anything. Hell, you're wearing a colorful shirt."

"Huh." He sounded confused.

"What about the kids? You remember what the kids were wearing?"

"I don't fuckin' remember, man!"

"That's unfortunate for you." I pulled him by the handcuffs over to the chair and forced him to sit down. He struggled a little, before succumbing to my exertive force. I reached out and stopped the string with the weight attached. "You weren't really going to let me go, were you?" he said. In return I answered, "Honestly, I would have, but only if you answered my question. You didn't so, now you're sitting here and you're about to die."

"Can I ask you a question?" he said.

"Yeah."

"*Why?*"

"Why what?"

"Why did you want me to answer your question about what his family was wearing that day in court?"

"Because, it would have meant that there was a tiny shred of humanity inside you. Enough to have me consider giving you a second chance. But since you weren't really concerned about them and what you put them through, it only validates my initial thought of you. You deserve to die. And die the way you killed Patrick, with a bullet in the face." I noticed him looking at the barrel of the gun. "That's a big gun man!"

"Yep. And when I let this string go, it's going to fire a bullet right into your face, just like what you did to Patrick. You ready to see hell?" I released the string and the weight fell to the floor. It was a mess! I figured I would take some photos, before cleaning. I was glad much of the blood splatter was contained on the plastic sheeting. It makes cleaning up a lot more convenient. His body remained slumped over until finally it succumbed to the forces of gravity; and fell to the floor.

Thud!

SEVENTEEN

Rudy recently asked me, if I weren't working with him what else would I be doing? His question caught me off guard, because honestly, I never gave such a question any thought. I think what he meant to say was; what did I intend to do growing up? The events of my childhood were responsible for shaping my personality and making me the person I am today. If I were asked by one of my grade school teachers, 'what my plans were for the future?' I wouldn't have said, excitedly, "I plan to be a hired assassin!" I wouldn't have even known what the word meant, or what that job title entailed? The memories I did have of my childhood, revolved around the mental and physical abuse I had endured by the actions of my father. The rest of my childhood was vague and typical of boys that age. I somewhat recalled wanting to be a fireman, until I saw firsthand a neighbor's home go up in flames! I also wanted to be an astronaut, until one of my teachers explained how difficult it was to become one. I toyed with the idea of becoming Prime Minister of France, but that plan only lasted for about two weeks. Believe it or not, I even wanted to be a member of Interpol: *how ironic*. Lately, I have been pondering the idea of what drives me to continue doing this type of work? It wasn't the money, although I'll be the first to admit, the income is nice. My guess was this motivation had deep roots. Roots that traveled far back into my youth, when I was quite impressionable. My father was the type of man who refused to show emotion. He never cried a day in his life. For the longest time, I believed he was somehow superhuman, because nothing fazed him. Honestly, I think he enjoyed punishing me, in a sort of *sadistic ritual*, one he must have learned from his father. Whenever I did anything wrong, he would use a wet leather belt to spank me; driven by a primal rage. A rage to break me down and have me conform to his way of thinking – for my own good, or so he believed. After all, I was forbidden to draw outside the lines and experience failure or disappointment on my terms. He also didn't want me to confide in any of our neighbors. He was adamant about keeping family problems surreptitiously confidential, especially his heavy use of alcohol, which left bruises on me. He was a cruel mean drunk. Eventually, I grew to hate him, with such fervor. I recognized this *sadistic, vicious, heartless trait*, minus the use of alcohol, he had success-fully inculcated in me forging the man I was today. I guess I used this job to vent my anger, somehow believing it was a cathartic way of finding justice for those like me; who were unwittingly brutalized, both *physically* and *mentally*. I found the bullet that had passed through Murderess's skull, and I managed to wrap him up in the same plastic, which was on the floor when he was shot. I ducted taped the seams and made it impossible for any of his blood to leak out. I managed to carry his body out to the SUV and placed him in the back; behind the rear backseat. My intention was to bring him over to a crematorium, where I knew the undertaker, and had been given permission to burn Murderess's dead body into ashes. I locked up the warehouse, returned to the rental and looked once in the rearview mirror, before putting the vehicle in drive and pulling away. I made a conscious effort to remain within the posted speed limit. I finally merged onto the highway and that was when my cellphone rang! The sudden sound startled me! I reached down, turning my phone, so it was now facing me and I could see the number. It was at that point, Siri announced Rudy was calling. I accepted the call. "Hey what's going on Rudy?"

"Not much. How you doing?"

"Just finished meeting with *M*." M stood for the name Murderous. We both knew not to say much over the phone, because the authorities could be listening. So, we were purposely vague and used our own lingo. References to things that only we knew what they meant. "How did that go?" he asked.

"Everything went smoothly."

"That's good. What are you doing now?"

"Just out for a drive. I'll call you later."

"Wait!"

"What?"

"I called, because *R.A.* had an incident earlier this evening," Rudy said, referring to Renée Abrio. I kept my eyes on the cars ahead of me, while being mindful of how fast I was driving. "Should I be concerned?"

He said, "I think so. When you get home, can you give *R.A.* a call?" I answered him without giving it any further thought, "Absolutely! Is everything alright?"

"Just call *R.A.* when you can."

"You want me to call her after I finish the call with you?"

"I don't think that would be wise. You have your hands full, besides *R.A.* just wants to rest and relax."

"Okay. How's *A* doing?" I asked, referring to my daughter.

"Good. *A* had a salad for dinner. *A*'s sleeping right now," he said. Just as he said those words, I saw a bright floodlight off to my left; before I could squint, I saw flashing lights alongside me. Just my luck, the police! I told Rudy I needed to go, because I was being pulled over by a cop. He told me to call him later. I ended the call and began to change lanes, so I could safely pull over to the side of the highway. I fully applied the brakes, coming to a complete stop and I waited inside the rental, hoping the officer wouldn't shine his flashlight in the back and find Murderess's wrapped body. While waiting there, off on the side of the road, I looked at the driver's side mirror and that's when I think I saw Detective Olivia Bartlett. It was dark and the passing traffic, along with the unmarked car's headlights behind me, were obstructing my vision from making any final conclusions. Finally, I got a better view and saw that it was Detective Olivia Bartlett and she was alone. I rolled down my window and waited for her to reach my door. I watched as she walked up alongside the SUV, stopping at the driver's side window. "Good evening, Sebastien. How is everything going?" she said, looking in with her flashlight fixed on my face; momentarily blinding me. I replied, "I don't think I was speeding."

"You weren't. I stopped you because we need to talk."

"You couldn't have called me?"

"Well, it's funny, because I was driving and I noticed you change lanes several miles back, and you didn't use your directional. That's when I saw you Sebastien, and decided to pull you over because we need to talk." I figured she must be lying. I bet she ran the vehicle's plate the night she left my apartment and probably had been tracking me for some time now. I wouldn't put anything past her. She's a desperate woman and desperate people do desperate things. I just hoped she had enough common sense to pull herself together, and get a grip! "This really isn't a good time for me," I said, trying to be polite, yet firm. "Why's that?" she asked, appearing curious. She began to move the flashlight she was holding. I watched helplessly as she probed the front passenger's seat, with a bright powerful beam of intense white light. "Because my daughter is visiting and I'm on my way back to spend time with her. We're going to watch movies and have popcorn."

"Really?"

"Yeah."

"How is that other project of yours coming along? I mean you can't be that busy, if you're going to be watching movies and having popcorn with your daughter, *right*?"

"Well, she's my daughter, you know what I mean? Spending a little time, watching a movie isn't that big of a deal. As far as my other project is concerned, that has been resolved."

"Oh good! If I knew I'd be running into you this evening, I would have brought Miguel's file along with me. I managed to find it, which is good news!"

"Yeah, that's great!"

"You look awfully nervous this evening, compared to the last time I saw you."

"Well, I'm looking forward to spending some time with my daughter and I just wanna get home." Several vehicles pass, one comes dangerously close – Olivia seemed unfazed by the close call. A semi-truck had to change lanes quickly and almost cut off another vehicle. She commented, "Drivers really need to slow down. You'd think they would move over, with my emergency lights flashing. Anyway, is your daughter staying with you? Or are you going to get her?"

"Why?"

"Because if you're heading home, you're going the wrong way. You missed your exit ten minutes ago."

"No, well I'm going to get her. She's with her mother."

"I see. What's your daughter's name? If you don't mind me asking?" Olivia asked. Actually, I did mind her asking. However, she had the upper hand and could make things quite difficult for me if I began to speak out of line, or become rude by telling her it's really none of her business. Instead, I was quite diplomatic and replied, "Her name is Amanda."

"*Amanda*, I gotta remember that. That's a nice name."

"Thank you."

"So, where are you coming from?" she asked, moving her flashlight once again, so the light was now illuminating most of the backseat. I said the first thing that came to mind. "I was out shopping."

"Grocery shopping?" I noticed her look toward the rear of the vehicle. Probably wondering where the groceries were. I quickly replied, "Yes. I bought a few perishables and I need to get them home." I decided to appease her as quickly as possible, before she checked any further and found Murderous. "Can we get together tomorrow and talk about *Miguel?*"

She answered, "Sure. What time? I have tomorrow off?"

"How about *noon*, we'll have lunch? I'll call you and tell you where to meet me."

"Sounds good. Okay, I'll expect to hear from you tomorrow."

"You will. I'll call you before noon," I said. She told me to have a good night and left at that point returning to her vehicle and driving off into traffic. I wasted no time getting back on the road, because the last thing I wanted was to be stopped again, by another member of law-enforcement. I was heading west, hoping I wouldn't get any more phone calls, or traffic stops. It took another hour and forty minutes for me to arrive at my destination. The crematorium was spooky at this time of night. It would be worse if it were Halloween, with all the tombstones off in the distance. Sometimes, the moon's full and there isn't a cloud in the sky. That was how it was this evening. The moonlight was reflecting off the cemetery tombstones, while the crematorium was in direct contrast, with plenty of dark shadows. There was a single dull looking floodlight, directly over the crematorium's entrance. I pulled up close to the bay doors, left the vehicle and went in search of Wilson. Wilson was the undertaker. He had already promised he would know when I arrived, because he would be keeping an eye on the property's cameras. Just as I was about to ring the bell for the rear bay doors, I heard the lock disengage and one of the doors opened inward. Wilson stepped out, with his long-sleeve white shirt on and black tie; with matching slacks. Even his leather shoes were black. He was approximately a foot shorter than me and was about a hundred pounds heavier, with eye-glasses and no facial hair. I on the other hand, had a distinguishable five o'clock shadow coming in. "Where is the package?" he asked me; referring to the body. I answered, "I have it in the vehicle. I could use a hand, he's a big guy. I almost broke my back getting him into the back of the rental."

"Let me get a flat cart."

"Did you remember to delay the cameras?" I asked him, hoping he at least remembered to stop the camera here at the rear doors. He stopped dead in his tracks, turned to me and said, "Yes, of course. That's the first thing I did when I saw your vehicle's headlights."

"Good," I replied. He walked off and brought back what could only be described as a metal gurney. I moved aside to let him pass and I followed him as he walked the gurney over to the rental. We managed to get the body out, on a count of *three* and placed it firmly on the flat cart. From there I followed him back inside and beyond the bay doors. Murderess's ashes would eventually wind up in a freezer Ziploc bag. In the morning, Rudy would send both the bag and an image of Murderous to Prometheus, per his request. I knew from experience, this was going to be a long night and I still had a long drive home, ahead of me. I decided to ask Wilson if he had any fresh coffee available? He told me there was a pot in the breakroom. I left him to tend to his business, while I went in search of caffeine. I guess I was fortunate, because I found the last Styrofoam cup. I poured the coffee into the cup; made it the way I like it with five sugars and two cream. I then went in search of Wilson. I found him exactly where I should have expected he would be. He was loading the cremation casket; which was nothing more than a plywood box. He heard and then saw me enter the basement by way of a single steel door. I approached him, asking if he needed any help? "No. I just have to ignite the pilot and the burners will do the rest," he replied.

"And he should be done in…?" I asked. It had been a while since I used Wilson's services, so I wasn't exactly sure how long this procedure would take. I remembered last time it took a few hours. Wilson replied, "Two hours for the body to be reduced to just bone. From there, we'll have to wait about a half-hour for his bones to cool. Then I'll be placing them into a machine, which will pulverize them into ash. That could take up to an hour or so."

"Then into a Ziploc."

"Yes, then into a Ziploc," Wilson repeated.

EIGHTEEN

The following morning, I returned from the crematorium without having slept; yet not feeling a bit tired, so I could give Rudy the package which was Murderess's ashes in a Ziploc bag, along with a single image of his dead body. I handed Rudy the package and said, "Don't go anywhere! I'll be right back! I want to hear what happened with Renée. First, I gotta go upstairs and check on my daughter; see how she's doing?" I left Rudy in the living room, just as Dakota came trotting past me. When I got upstairs, I peeked in the guest's bedroom and saw Amanda peacefully sleeping. I returned back downstairs, to where Rudy was seated on the couch, with Dakota lying next to him. "So, what's going on with Renée?" I asked.

"I think it would be better if she told you herself."

"*Rudy*! What's this about?" I demanded to know!

"Sebastien, all I can say is she was *severely assaulted.*"

"By who?"

"One of the perps...*Tyler Mason.*"

"Isn't that the *serial rapist*?"

"Yes."

"So, what happened?! When you say *severe*, what are we talking about? Was she raped?" My mind was racing with images of what she must have had to endure. I couldn't help but think all the possibilities, having read Tyler Mason's file and his modus operandi. He was a violent serial rapist, who either brutally beat his victim or tortured them with probing objects.

"No, she wasn't raped. According to her sister, Renée was repeatedly stabbed."

"What?! Is she in the hospital?"

"No. Her sister Remi is taking care of her wounds." Remi used to work for Rudy. She did a little cleaning, to help put her through medical school. She's now a surgeon, with her own practice. "Maybe I should call Remi, to find out how her sister is doing?"

"That probably is a good idea."

"You know what? I think I'll take a drive over and make a call on the way. I wanna see Renée for myself. You wanna join me?"

"I wish I could. I have to get this package of Murderous off to Prometheus. Then my wife needs me to drive her to her doctor's appointment."

"Is she ok?"

"Yeah, it's just a consult. She wants breast implants."

"She wants them? *Or you want her to get them?*"

"You could say, *we're both in agreement.*"

"Okay. I guess, I'll let Renée and Remi know you couldn't

join me. Should I tell them, you'll stop in, later in the week? Maybe tomorrow?"

"Sure. Tell 'em I'll stop by in the morning."

"Okay. Well, I better be off."

"Is Amanda going with you?" I heard Rudy ask. I turned to him and said, "No. She's sound asleep. She probably won't be up for hours. In fact, I'll probably be back, before she wakes."

"Yeah. Let me know how Renée is, okay?" Rudy got up off the couch, patted Dakota and walked with me, as I left the apartment, locking the door behind me. "You know, all of Renée's files are still open, because of this incident." I heard Rudy say, from behind me. I turned and said, "Don't worry, I'll complete them, beginning with Tyler."

"You still have one of your own to finish, *right*?" Rudy asked, referring to the file of 23-year-old, Ricky St. James.

"Yeah, I'll be finishing that sometime this week. I have to meet someone at noon, before I can find Ricky."

"You're meeting someone? Are we talking *romance*?" he asked, following me out to the SUV.

"No. It's *personal* and *business*."

"I see." He didn't press me any further about my appointment. He just reminded me to call him as soon as I finished meeting with Renée and her sister. I told him not to worry, I would definitely reach out, as soon as I knew how she was. We parted at that point and I got in the SUV, started it and drove off, intending to call Remi before I got to the interstate. Just as I changed lanes to merge onto the interstate, the call went through and Remi answered, "Hello." Her voice was smooth with *character*, and had sex appeal; along with tonal vitality. It was actually a pleasure to hear her speak. "Hi, it's me Sebastien," I said.

"Oh hey! How are you?"

"I'm ok. I've been busy."

"Busy is good," she replied.

"I-huh. I heard about what happened to your sister. Is she okay?" I asked, before I put my cellphone on loud speaker and tucked it inside my shirt pocket – this allowed me to keep both hands on the steering wheel, while I talked. "She will be. She was stabbed three times in the torso. Luckily for her it wasn't a chef knife, because if it were; it would have turned out quite differently."

"So, she doesn't have any life-threatening injuries then?"

"*No*, but they are serious and I'm treating them so she doesn't get an infection."

"I see. You mind if I stop in, just to say *hi*?"

"No, I don't mind, I think she'd like that. She's been asking if you called."

"Well, tell her I did and I'm on my way to see her. By the way, how's everything going with *you?*"

"Well, between my schedule at the hospital and private practice, it's difficult to find – *me time*."

"I can imagine. So, you're not working out or boxing anymore?"

"Actually, I find time to work out early in the morning.

The boxing and self-defense though are another story. I haven't been able to find anyone to spar with. It's not like I can ask someone at work if they want to spar? If I did, I'm sure I'd get a blank stare, maybe even a rude comment," she said, exaggerating a little.

"Well, since I'm on my way over, why don't we spar a little, that is if you're up for it?"

"You wanna spar with me? This morning?"

"Yeah. Unless, you're too busy."

"No, I'm game! Are you up for doing some wrist-lock techniques too? I haven't done those in a while and could definitely use some practice," I heard her say.

"Sure, that would be great!"

"Don't forget to bring your gear!" She was referring to my MMA style weighted gloves, with additional wrist protection, mouth guard to protect my teeth and cup to protect me if she kicked me in the groin.

"Too late! I guess I could go back home and get my gear."

"Don't do that! I got some gear you can use."

"You have a cup?!" I asked, surprised!

"No. Don't worry I promise I won't kick you in the balls." Remi lived more than an hour away in a spacious home, with plenty of acreage. There was a long narrow driveway leading up to the house. The property was littered with an abundance of foliage, which was a nice feature, because her place couldn't be seen from the road – offering much needed privacy. At the top of the driveway, near the two-car garage, there was an area for guest parking. Before I made it to the front door, I saw it open and Remi and her sister came out. I was relieved to see Renée walking, without the aid of her sister. "There you are! How are you?" I said, as I approached her. "I'm feeling a little better. Is Rudy with you?" Renée asked.

"No. Unfortunately, he couldn't make it. He told me to tell you he'd stop by tomorrow morning, to see how you're doing."

"Okay. I'm lucky my sister is a surgeon." Renée lifted her shirt, showing me the area of her stomach, where Tyler stabbed her. Her sister had completely wrapped it with medical gauze and bandaging. "Could have been worse," Renée said. "My sister told me you heard what happened."

"Yeah. So, tell me everything! How did he manage to stab you? And how did you get away?" I asked, stopping in front of her and giving her a hug. She told me how she met him. He worked for a 24-hour plumbing service that cleans clogged drains. She searched the internet and found an apartment, where the tenant was away on vacation and the apartment didn't have a security system to worry about. She let herself in and called the plumbing service, *personally requesting Tyler*. "Yeah, then the receptionist asked me for the address. I told her it was a new place, because she couldn't find the previous work order. She then asked me what my old address was? She caught me off guard and my mind went completely blank! I wound up telling her, I've been on pain medication for a back injury and honestly, I couldn't remember."

"And she bought it?" I asked.

"Believe it or not, *yeah*. She told me not to worry. She would send him to my current location and it would be approximately, thirty minutes."

"And then what happened?" I asked.

"Then I waited for him. When he finally arrived, I let him in. I told him the tub was clogged, because I showered earlier and the water wasn't draining like it should. He asked me to show him to the bathroom and I was planning to cut his throat right there in the bathroom, so he'd bleed out in the tub, but he saw me in the mirror and turned around. That's when he grabbed my knife from my hand. I fought him off, but couldn't prevent him from getting me three times. I managed to rush off!"

"What happened to him?" I asked, curious.

"I don't know. I assume he left. When I got to my vehicle, I called Rudy and my sister."

Remi commented, "And I told her to come and see me *immediately*!"

"And I did," Renée added, looking over at her sister.

"I'm going to need whatever information you've compiled on Tyler, because he's going to pay for this," I said. Renée turned to me and said, "Unfortunately, I won't be able to join you," she sounded rather disappointed. "Maybe I can assist?" I heard Remi say. I turned and looked at her, "I wouldn't mind having you join me, you'd just have to let Rudy know."

"You think he'd be okay with having me work with you?" Remi asked, sounding uncertain.

"I don't see why not."

"Remi! Sebastien can handle it; besides you have a full plate with the hospital and your private practice."

"She's right," I added.

"I'm just trying to help."

"I know, but I really don't want to see you get caught up in this way of life again. You built a good stable life for yourself. You don't need to risk losing it," claimed Renée, showing her persona; of being a concerned older sister.

"Don't worry, I can handle it and I promise Tyler will regret ever meeting your sister," I said, in an attempt to reassure both of them that justice would be served.

"I'm sure," Remi said confidently; knowing full-well my capabilities.

"My sister also told me you're here to spar with her."

"Yeah, I called because I wanted to see how you were doing? Remi and I got talking about a few things, and sparring came up in the conversation. I figure she can put me through my paces."

"She's good at that!"

"Believe me, I know. I remember sparring with her. She moves *fast* and hits *hard*!"

"*Yeah, yeah, yeah.* Enough talk, let's gear up and get busy," Remi said. I followed her and Renée inside. We went down into the basement. The entire basement was setup like a gym and boxing arena. She added new features, including a toning station with adjustable weights. Over at the other end of the basement was a large heavy bag for punching. There was also a rowing machine, a stationary bicycle, free weights for lifting and much more.

"Wow! You did a lot down here."

"Yeah, I added a couple of things since the last time you were down here," Remi said, putting on her MMA weighted gloves. She told me there was an extra pair over by the speed bag. Just as I was about to go over and get them, Renée gently reached up, grabbed the pair and tossed them over to me. Remi came over and said, "Now don't hold back, just because I'm a female." She put her hands up and got into a fighting stance. I couldn't help but notice how sexy she looked while in her pose. I've always been attracted to lean, feminine women and I had a special place in my mind for feisty, tone females that were in great shape; with *long legs* and *defined abdominals*.

"Why do you think I'd hold back, just because you're a female?" I replied. Actually, I did plan on holding back, but I didn't want her to know. The last thing I was about to do was go full metal jacket on her beautiful face. I knew I could easily knock her out with just one punch, but I also knew it would take a lot of effort on my part to achieve that. That wasn't my objective, because she was fast, wiry, and not afraid to hit. She wasn't going to allow me an easy opportunity to strike her in the jaw. We began with exchanging jabs. I was pacing myself and I noticed she was already burning pure octane, as she came in closer, using combinations. I moved back, because I didn't want her doing one of her spin kicks or worse, jumping and mounting me around the back of my neck. I knew from experience, that was one of her favorite styles of fighting. If she could mount her opponent, she could use gravity to take that person to the floor, before ending it with a devastating and crippling armbar move. "So, tell me about work?" I said, before I through a jab. She counter acted and punched back. "Are you asking about the hospital? Or at my practice?" she managed to get the words out, while throwing a combination. She hit my glove with the first punch, and the following second punch, almost hit me in the face. "Both," I replied.

"I work at the hospital, in the O.R. two days a week. The other three days, I work at my practice, seeing patients."

"You ever miss working for Rudy?"

"Not at all!" She throws another combination. "I wish my sister would find a better career, while she still can. She probably won't be doing this in another ten years."

"I'm right here! Can we not talk about me, *please*?" Renée said, while watching us spar. Remi stopped dead in her tracks and turned toward her sister. "Renée, you're a very intelligent woman. There's no reason you should be risking your life, working for Rudy. You must have saved up enough money over the years...why don't you invest in your future and start a business or go back to college?"

"What? Like you? Go to medical school?"

"No, not medical school. You like *accounting* and *finance*, why don't you go to college to learn accounting and work in that field?"

"Because I get paid well," Renée bloomed. "In fact, I bet I make more in a month, than most accountants make in a year. You of all people should know how lucrative my work is, you worked with Rudy too, remember?"

"Yeah, I remember, and I took plenty of risks. You get caught; you go away! Rudy walks, only to find someone else to do his dirty work." Remi turned to me and said, "No offense, Sebastien."

"None taken," I replied.

"Remi, you know full well, I don't work for Rudy," Renée wooed, trying to make a point.

"I know, you work for some guy named *Prometheus*," her sister replied.

"Yeah, a very wealthy billionaire, according to Rudy," I heard Renée say. I was about to lower my guard, because the two seem to want to continue verbally sparring. Just as I lowered my hands, Remi saw this and told me to put my guard up we're not done! She then said to her sister, while throwing a few jabs at me, "Renée, what do you know about this *Prometheus*?"

"All I know is he wants to clean up the crime in Chicago and there's nothing wrong with that. God knows the legal system doesn't work."

"It works! It just doesn't work in favor of the average person," Remi said.

"*Exactly*!" Renée exclaimed, sounding vindicated. I continued sparring with Remi for a full hour. After sparring, we did wrist-locks. She began by having me grab her wrist. She quickly lifted the hand I was holding and did a few maneuvers, which ultimately put me at a disadvantage, with her twisting my wrist. She increased the pressure, until I reached my plateau of pain. It's a level I've increased over time, and if I ignored the pain, she could actually dislocate my wrist. I tapped out, hitting my chest twice. "I thought you said, you were out of practice!" I said, remembering our phone conversation.

"And you believed me!"

Now, it was my turn. I asked her to use a different mode. I asked her to throw a punch, which she did and I blocked it, tracked her forearm down to her wrist, where I put her in a lock; one that must have been awfully painful as I increased the pressure. I saw her expression, as she attempted to avoid tapping out. She was tough, but even she had a limit. She quickly tapped out! Complaining of the pain. "I should have stretched my wrists some more," she claimed.

"You ready?" I asked, ready to grab her wrist again.

"No, I want you to throw a punch."

I threw a punch directly at her face, she moved slightly, blocked my punch and tracked my arm doing exactly what I did to her. This time she really torqued my wrist. I surprised her with a release technique, which allowed me to get out of her lock. "Nice!" she said, looking surprised!

"Thanks."

"How's Carolyn and your daughter?" she asked me.

"Amanda is visiting for the week," I said.

"You have anything planned for her visit?"

"Yeah, I have a few ideas in mind."

"Yeah, for her next visit," I heard Renée comment. I turned toward her and said, "What's that supposed to mean?"

"Have you forgotten work? When are you going to find the time this week? Your daughter is only visiting for the week."

"Well, I'll talk to Carolyn and see if I can convince her to allow Amanda to stay another week."

"You really think your ex will go for that?" Renée said, sounding pessimistic.

"She might if I ask, *politely*."

"Don't you mean, *beg*?" Remi said, smiling. She then quickly threw a jab, striking me directly in the face. She hit me hard enough to cause my nose to bleed. She offered me something to help stop the bleeding, which contains *Amylopectin* in it. "Let me get you something to help stop the bleeding."

"I could use a glass of water too," I added.

"I'm gonna have some iced tea, you want some?" Remi asked me.

"Sure!"

"Renée, you want some iced tea?!"

"*Lemon*?" Renée asked.

"Yeah. Freshly squeezed! *And cold*!"

"Sounds great!"

NINETEEN

I was relaxing on the patio, with my iced tea, when Remi asked me if I was going to stay for lunch, which she claimed would be something she planned to have delivered. I was about to ask her the name of the establishment, when I suddenly remembered my appointment with Detective Olivia Bartlett. I told Remi I had to leave, because I had a very important appointment. She didn't ask with whom and I didn't offer a name. I thanked her for sparring with me and having iced tea out on the patio. I turned to Renée and said, "When you get a chance, can you give Rudy the files I gave you. Especially, Tyler Mason's file. I want to get started on his file soon." Renée was reclined on one of the patio chairs, sipping her iced tea. She looked over, "If you walk me out to my car, I can give you the files now. I have all of them."

"Oh good!" I made an effort to assist Renée, putting out my forearm, offering her something to lift herself up from where she's seated. She declined my offer, "I got it."

"Just trying to help."

"I know, but when you're gone, and my sister is busy, I'll have to get around without help," she said, *very independently*.

She managed to push herself up off the chair, complaining only slightly about her wounds. I walked with her out to her vehicle, where she gave me the three files from Prometheus. I thanked her, gave her a subtle, but loving hug and we part ways. She went back inside Remi's home, while I returned to the rental. Inside the rental, I made a call to my daughter, to see if she was up yet and if she needed me to stop in to make her something to eat? I was thinking she was more important to me, than Detective Bartlett's case on Rosario. Besides, Olivia needed my help and services, I didn't need hers. My daughter answered the phone, "Hello." She sounded very unenthused. I knew it took a little while for her to acclimate for the day ahead; after waking and getting out of bed.

"Hey sweetie! Is everything ok?"

"Yeah, I just got up about ten minutes ago. Where are you?"

"I'm visiting a friend."

"A girl?"

"Yeah, why?"

"Does mom know?"

"Sweetie it's not like that. Besides, your mom and I are divorced. You know that."

"Yeah, well it shouldn't be that way!"

"*Sweetie* it is what it is."

"I don't like it though."

"I know. You need me to stop in and make you breakfast?" I asked, knowing it was noon and I really should be asking her if she would like lunch?

"No, I can find something myself."

"Ok. When I get back, I'm probably going to need to lay down for a few hours."

"Yeah so?"

"I'm just saying. Maybe after I take a nap, we can go do something?"

"Like what?"

"I don't know maybe go for ice cream."

"Dad!"

"What?"

"*Ice cream!* Really, I'm not like five years old anymore."

"I know. Well, think about what you'd like to do and we'll do it, ok?"

"Whatever. It doesn't matter anyway; I'm going to visit with Brittney later. I'll do something with her."

"Hey! What's with the sarcasm?"

"You're always busy."

"Hey you're visiting and I'm willing to make time."

"Gee, thanks dad." I heard the dial tone. I couldn't believe she just hung up on me! She was getting more and more rebellious, with each passing year. I could have called back and gave her a piece of my mind, but I figured I would probably have to leave it as a message. I decided a better course of action would be to talk to her later. I would make it clear that I'm her father and she's going to be respectful of that fact. I put my cellphone down in the vehicles cup holder, turned the ignition key and started the engine. I was beginning to feel the effects of not getting any sleep. With the vehicle idling I reached for my phone and dialed another number; this one was to Detective Olivia Bartlett. I was beginning to regret promising to see her for lunch this afternoon, because I would rather be getting much needed sleep. I heard the phone ring twice, before Olivia answered, "Hello."

"Detective!"

There was a moment of silence. "Is this Sebastien?"

"Yes. I'm calling about meeting you for lunch, *remember?*"

"Yeah. Where would you like to meet?" she asks me. I told her of a *quaint* place I knew about, which would offer us plenty of privacy and the food was rather good. She told me she would have Miguel's file with her. The way I was feeling, I couldn't care less if she brought his file or not. I told her I was on my way over to the eatery, and would see her when she got there. I figured on the way; I'd stop off for a coffee, because I needed a little something to get me through lunch with Bartlett.

The coffee seemed to help; I no longer felt mentally *sluggish* or *physically* fatigued. I arrived at the rendezvous, only to see Olivia in her vehicle directly across from me, turning to enter the parking lot. I followed her into the parking area and pulled up next to her vehicle. I looked over to see her staring at me. She smiled and waved like we're friends or something. I left the rental and meet her at the driver's side door of her vehicle.

"Since I got here first, does that mean you're buying lunch?" she asks. I had no idea if she was serious or not. She looked serious, so I say, "Sure, why not?" We went inside, found a place to sit and the waitress brought us menus. I looked over mine, not intending to eat much because I wasn't really that hungry. I just wanted this lunch to end; the sooner the better! I ordered soup. I was half-expecting her to order something similar because she's so thin. I was rather surprised when she ordered enough to feed two people her size. She claimed she ate large meals in the afternoon, and practically nothing in the evening. Honestly, I didn't care when? Or what she ate? While waiting for our orders to arrive, she placed a folder on the table in front of me. She pushed it over toward me and said, "Here's Miguel's file." It was a pretty lengthy file. There was probably fifteen to twenty pieces of paper inside. I opened it to look over the first page rather carefully. The page looked like she just printed it on her home printer, because it was black and white – not color, like I would expect to see. It was his wanted picture and profile. He was accused of more than I expected. I then looked over the next thirteen pages, which documented some of his prior arrests and criminal activities. He was no choir boy. Actually, he could be a candidate for Prometheus's list. I quietly expressed my disgust in Miguel's character and offenses. "Wow!" I heard myself say, with a subtle expression.

"I told you he's a real lowlife!"

"I see that." I read how he was charged for raping a

twelve-year-old and beating her with a steel pipe. The victim reminded me of my daughter's age. I noticed Olivia lean over, probably wondering what page I was reading. I shared with her: his victim was as young as my daughter and he beat her with a metal pipe. "That bastard beat her so bad that her face was unrecognizable."

"So, how soon can you get to work on him?"

"I have something else that's come up; it was unexpected, but I will also work on Miguel's file."

"When you say *work on* – what exactly does that mean?"

"It means researching him thoroughly, knowing exactly what he does day in and day out. I want to know where he goes to get gas for his vehicle? What he eats for lunch? Where he goes to shop for groceries? Does he workout? If he does, does he workout alone? Or with his crew? Is he ever alone? Does he have a routine? If so, does he follow it to the letter? I also wanna know if and when he's alone? How long is he alone? I wanna know when he wakes? When he goes to bed? Who are his closest friends? Does he have family? Does he visit his family? Does he have a girlfriend? Or does he sleep around? What type of female does he like? Etc., etc. You understand?"

"Yes, so how much time are we talking? A ballpark figure? I won't hold you to an exact time."

"In good conscience, I can't even give you an estimation. All I can say is, I will work on it and I will see to it that no rock is left unturned. That's all I can offer you at this time."

It seemed like she was mulling the comment over in her head. She appeared slightly frustrated as she said, "Okay, just keep me in the loop."

"Will do." Our food arrived just in time. I still couldn't get over all the plates of food in front of her, while I had just a bowl of soup in front of me. While eating, Olivia asked me how old was my daughter? I told her. She then had other questions, which concerned me, because that meant she was thinking about little girl. I had a sneaking suspicion; Olivia was gathering intelligence on my daughter. My guess, she wanted to have a bishop or rook in her corner, something she could use against me; in this game of chess, she was playing.

TWENTY

The research required on Miguel, took me in many different directions and I was left to consult with a good friend of mine. A friend who was very familiar with everything that happened on the streets of Chicago. He preferred that I used his most recent street name when making contact, because he was a bit paranoid about the *local* and *federal* authorities listening to his personal phone calls. He had more aliases than everyone who has ever been protected by WITSEC. His birth name was Mathias Cristello, but he wanted me to refer to him as, *Dante*. I suggested we meet in person, and I used old tactics he was familiar with. I suggested a location close to the real place, where I would like us to meet. The place I offered first, seemed to throw him off a bit and he immediately asked me to suggest somewhere else. I guess his level of paranoia was either becoming worse, or he had trouble at that particular location. I suggested two more locations, finally he agreed to meet me at the latter. To be fair, if I were in his shoes, I too would be a little paranoid. Afterall, he had his hands in practically everything that happened on the streets; from *illegal drugs* to *prostitution*, along with many other criminal activities.

When it came to finding out everything there was to know about someone doing criminal activities, Dante was the last word. We met at the Art Institute. I found him staring at one of the Institute's Fine Arts display. He appeared to be almost mesmerized by the piece. I came up from behind and said, "I've been trying to get my daughter to come here, for almost three years." He remained still, with his head facing forward toward the sculpture. He said with a subtle reply, "Youth is wasted on the innocent and young. A day will come when she will regret not having spent those memories with you."

"I can't blame her. I did the same when I was her age."

"Yes, and that proves my point. Most of us are guilty of squandering our youth. Question?"

"Shoot."

"If given the opportunity to know this world, the way it is now, but return to your youth, would you? Would you want to return as a younger man knowing what you know today?"

"Who wouldn't?"

"I'll take that as a *yes*. My thoughts exactly." He then casually walked around the piece of art, with me following. "So, who is it that you need information on?" He stopped about halfway around the object and continued to eye the piece, like he was amazed at its beauty and meaning.

"His name is Miguel del Rosario."

"*The*, Miguel del Rosario?" he repeated!

"Yes. Sounds like you're well aware of him."

"Oh yes, he's quite a character! He's also *extremely* dangerous too!"

"How so?"

"It's well-known on the streets that Miguel is affiliated with the Mexican drug cartel."

"Yes, I know. He's like a runner or mule, right?"

"Oh no. He's no longer a mule. He's a lot further up the food chain than that. No, he's a very, very bad guy. He's not like you. He has *no code*...anyone is game for him. He would kill his only child if he benefitted from it. He's connected with some very powerful people in this country too."

"Like who?"

"Like some of our senators, congressmen and ag."

"The attorney general?"

"Yep. Remember the old phrase, *follow the money?*"

"Sure."

"Why do you think Miguel can do practically whatever he wants? And he never goes away for it?"

"He's been arrested; I have a file on him."

"Arrested yes, but not *convicted*, there's a big difference. You ever wonder why the government claims they want to protect the American people, yet the same people in Congress refuse to do anything with a porous border? You'll understand if you follow the money. Why are you looking into the background of Miguel?"

"Someone I know wants me to find out everything there is to know about him."

"A Client?"

"You could say that. She claims he raped and murdered her daughter, yet I can't find anything in the paper concerning the event or death. I've looked as far back as ten years on micro-film."

"Who's your client?" he asked, putting his hand up to his heart and added, "What you tell me is between you and I. You should know by now; you have my word."

"She's a narcotics detective."

"A detective! Are you saying, Chicago PD?" he sounded surprised, that I would have a member of law enforcement for a client.

"*Yes.* Her name is Olivia Bartlett."

"Oh, Ms. Olivia Harari! You my friend are a lucky man."

"Why do you say that? And why did you call her *Harari*?"

"Because I may have just saved your life and that's her real name. She had it legally changed before joining the Chicago Police Department. See, Olivia is a former Israeli soldier; she worked with *Sayeret Matkal,* an *elite Israeli unit.*"

"Come again?" I was confused.

"Detective Bartlett is really Detective Olivia Harari, a former member of the Israeli special forces and she's a snake!"

"How so?"

"Olivia is a very dirty cop. On the take." He slightly coughed to clear his throat.

"With who?"

"The mob!"

"*The mob*?!"

"Yeah, you know, the *mafia*. Not the ones from Italy either. *The Russian mob*!"

"You're kidding me!"

"I wouldn't do that. Olivia is a real viper. If she's put a contract out on Miguel, it's only because the two are having turf wars and she's using you to do her dirty work."

"Son of a ...!"

"What?" Dante said.

"She's played me. Now, it makes sense. She told me her twelve-year-old daughter was raped, strangled to death and the body burned by Miguel."

"Olivia has a daughter!" He sounded surprised! "That's news to me. The woman is single, never married, and has no children. Check it out, *search her maiden name*, you're the expert in research and public records. Sebastien, take my advice and don't do anymore dealings with that witch. She'll cut your throat while looking right at you, and then tell you, your throat is just sore." Dante looked over at me, my guess he was wondering if I had any more questions? I slipped him a few new hundred-dollar bills for his information and I wished him God's speed. I then left the Art Institute, intending to first get some much-needed rest at home. After that, I would have plenty of work to do, because now I needed to know more about Ms. Olivia Harari. She hadn't been honest with me, so I was not about to ask her to tell me the truth now. I was beginning to feel a little paranoid, as I pondered the possibility that maybe Dante had reasons to want to make false claims about Detective Bartlett, because she may have something on him. Then again, he had never lied to me before. He really had no reason to send me off in a different direction. Finally, he wouldn't have the reputation of being the last word on the street, if he misled people.

TWENTY-ONE

I was thinking of the quote from Sir Walter Scott, "Oh, what a tangled web we weave, when first we practice to deceive." This quote reflected more research I had been doing on Hannah E. Bartlett. I had been surfing several internet search engines, including FamilySearch.org and the Social Security death master file. I honestly wasn't sure if Dante was being honest with me and I wanted to be sure I turned over every stone to find the truth. So far, there was no Hannah E. Bartlett or Hannah E. Harari. Well at least none, matching a twelve-year-old Jewish female, who had been brutally raped and burned to death. I also spent the last five hours visually rescanning old newspaper articles, concerning young girls who were raped and brutally murdered. It was becoming quite evident that Dante was being totally candid, and Detective Bartlett had obvious ulterior motives. However, my efforts hadn't ended up fruitless, because I had managed to find out that Olivia's father, Solomon Harari was the district attorney for Cook County. I also came across articles about him being very lenient, with several suspects believed to have political ties to Russia. One of the suspects, named Tatiana allegedly bribed a Democrat senator with cash, a new luxury car and diamonds worth hundreds of thousands of dollars. Tatiana's lawyer had no comment and Senator Jon Patrick Murphey claimed the allegations were all political, meant to unseat him by his Republican opponent. Sen. Murphey went on the record, stating that the alleged bribery charge would be dismissed, once the truth came out. Olivia's father, Solomon Harari dropped all charges against Tatiana, along with Sen. Jon Murphey, claiming that the FBI intentionally entrapped Tatiana, with intention to build a criminal case against Sen. Murphey, where no case existed. Furthermore, Solomon Harari had received large sums of money from Russian interests, for his reelection campaign. Since I was already in the library doing research on Olivia and her father; I decided to research Tyler Mason, the serial rapist, who stabbed Renée three times. I charted Tyler's daily schedule, including work, time-off and places he went on weekends. Apparently, according to his credit card records, when Tyler wasn't working for the plumbing company, he spent plenty of time at a coffee shop in the city. My initial thought was *why*? Why would he be spending several hours, every weekend in a coffee shop? Was he scoping out the female customers? Then I did a Google Map search of the coffee shop. I scanned other businesses in the area. One business in particular leaped right out at me! It was an aerobics club for women. The coffee shop was directly across the street, offering Tyler the opportunity to watch the female members come and go. It was his way of window shopping, while having his morning coffee. I decided to call Remi and see if she would do me a favor. I logged off the library computer, left my work area and walked toward the lobby exit with my cellphone in my hand. I found Remi's number and pressed the call icon. Just as I was leaving the library, Remi answered, "Hello Sebastien."

"How's Renée?"

"She's doing ok."

"Good. I huh...I could use your help."

"How so?"

"I'd like you to help me lure Tyler Mason, but Renée can't know."

"Okay."

"Are you busy now?"

"I think I can step out, without her knowing."

"Good!" I gave her the address of the coffee shop and told her I was on my way there. I also explained, there was a good chance Tyler Mason would be there, because this was his usual window of opportunity, he used to go to the coffee shop on Saturday's. While driving, I had the radio on and the song playing was from the Rolling Stones called, *Gimme Shelter*. When I got to the coffee shop, I went inside, ordered a small regular coffee with five sugars and two cream. I was tempted to buy a cinnamon donut, but I didn't. Instead, I paid for my order and found a seat, with a bird's eye view of everyone coming and going. I waited and watched for Remi. While waiting, I saw Tyler over by the window, having his coffee. He was watching the aerobics studio across the street. A cement grey colored, Toyota FJ Cruiser caught my eye, because it was a vehicle Remi owned and drove. I watched for a moment, to see where the FJ Cruiser went. It turned at the light and parked across the street. I wasn't the only one who noticed her step out of her vehicle. Tyler saw Remi too. In fact, he watched as she waited for the light to change, so she could safely cross the street. Remi entered the establishment, and noticed me seated at one of the tables. I gave her a hand gesture, one she knew. I used my index finger and ran it across the bottom of my chin, meaning not to approach me. She immediately noticed and went up to the counter to order something, most likely tea, because that was one of her favorite drinks. She received her order, paid by cash and walked directly past me and sat over by the window on a stool, just two empty seats away from Tyler. More customers entered, while a few left. I watched as Remi's body language implied; she was getting nervous. She was either nervous about someone sitting in one of the empty seats, between her and Tyler or she was worried what she may do if he attempted to start a conversation with her. I could only hope she would remain professional and not allow her emotions to cloud her judgment. That's when I noticed Tyler look over at Remi. It appeared he made his decision, concerning the female he had chosen. I left my chair and found a seat closer to both Remi and him, because I wanted to be within hearing distance, to hear everything! "I haven't seen you in here before," Tyler said, looking over at Remi. She looked over and replied, "I'm new to the area."

"New," he repeated, before leaving his seat and sitting at the seat *next to her.* "Where are you from?" he asked. I sensed hesitation in her response, like she was over thinking the question. She took a sip of her drink and said, "I moved here from Boston."

"Never been there," he claimed. "So, how do you like Chicago so far?"

"It's okay. There's a lot I plan to do."

"Oh yeah. Like what?"

"Well, for starters go see a cub's game. Maybe dine out in one of the fancier restaurants," I heard her say. I knew she was baiting him and he bit, just as I expected. "I know a great place if you're up for Italian food."

"Maybe. First, tell me a little about yourself," she said, sounding genuinely interested. The two talked for another twenty minutes, before he invited her to Shedd Aquarium. I overheard him mention the aquarium had live sharks. She turned to me and I quickly nodded my head, implying *yes,* go with him. It was odd for him to want to take her there, but he had his reasons. They walked right past me on their way out. I left my seat and followed. He told her they could take public transportation, because he didn't own a personal vehicle of his own, which was a lie. He owned a sedan which he used for work. He took public transportation in an attempt to confuse his victims, so they didn't have a *clear and concise* mental picture of what took place, before being raped. He also wanted to size her up; to see if he could manipulate her to do what he wanted. It was his way of gauging the amount of effort he would have to exert to get her to listen. If she complied with all his wishes, then he knew she would be an easy target. However, if she resisted because she had a mind of her own, then he would have to resort to other measures; possibly involving his accomplice. "But I have a vehicle," I heard Remi say.

"It such a nice day. I think the walk would do both of us a great deal of good. Especially me, I've been cooped up inside all week at work. Besides, you just moved here and this is a great opportunity to see the city, first hand," he said, trying to convince her to listen and follow his directions. She agreed to take the train and I followed, maintaining a healthy distance – one where I wouldn't be noticed or risk losing sight of them. I managed to follow them on the train to the aquarium. He showed her around, obviously having been there more than once. He probably thought she was going to be a rather easy mark because so far, she agreed to everything he suggested. Afterwards, he posed the question, "Would you like to have dinner with me?"

"Sure."

"What do you say we go to your place?" he asked. He looked anxious, like he was hoping she would agree. Remi saw me over near one of the large aquariums and I nodded yes. She then turned to him and said, "I don't see why not."

"Great!" The two walked off, passed right by me, and that was when I heard Remi say, "I will have to go back to the coffee shop, because I parked my vehicle there."

"I noticed you have a nice vehicle. Is it new?" I heard him say.

"Yes."

"I'm so used to using public transportation. It must be nice to have a vehicle of your own."

"Believe me, it is." Next thing I knew she was texting me. Telling me she was going to pick up her FJ Cruiser, then she was going to head home, because she thought Renée would like a chance to meet Tyler again and this time talk about what he did to her. I looked at the message and immediately I replied: **Are you crazy! I told you I didn't want her knowing**.

She texted me again, this time: **Relax! I'll tell her it was my idea.**

I followed Remi and Tyler back to the coffee shop. I was expecting her to wait for me to get my vehicle, but she didn't. Instead, she drove right past me, with Tyler in the passenger's seat. As soon as I got to my vehicle, I called Renée to let her know her sister was heading back, with Tyler Mason. To my surprise! Renée was thrilled by the idea! I heard her say, "Good, I'll be waiting for him." Before I could reply, I heard her hang up. "Hello!" I said, "Renée! Are you there?" I immediately looked down at my cellphone. I saw the words: call ended. I called back, hoping she would answer, but she didn't. My call went directly to her voicemail. I decided to step on the gas, attempting to catch up to Remi, when I saw a police car off to the shoulder, monitoring traffic. The cop tagged me for speeding and chased me down. I pulled over, and waited for the officer to approach my vehicle. When he did, I gave him a viable reason for speeding. I told him, I had heard my daughter was injured at home and I was trying to get back ASAP. He asked me for my driver's license and vehicle registration. I gave him the rental agreement, along with my license. He looked it over and said, "I'm a parent too, so I'm not gonna ticket you, or delay you any further. Get home to your daughter, but do it safely!" He handed me back my documents. "I will. Thank you." I drove off, mindful of the speed limit. It took me another thirty minutes to get to Remi's home. I pulled into her driveway, seeing her FJ Cruiser parked in front of her garage. I didn't know what to expect as I left the rental and rushed up to the front door. I was about to ring the doorbell, when the door opened and Remi stepped out. "Why didn't you wait for me?" I say, looking directly at her.

"I didn't want Tyler thinking something was wrong."

"Where is he?"

"Inside. Tide up. He won't be hurting anyone anymore," she said.

"Where's Renée?"

"Inside."

"Is she okay?"

"Yeah, I was just coming out to make room in my vehicle for his body."

"Where are you taking him?" I asked, curious.

"I have a few places in mind."

"Since you helped me lure him, do you want me to get rid of him?"

"If you could, that would be great!" she said.

"I will. I need to get a photo first, for Prometheus."

"Of course. I know the routine."

TWENTY-TWO

I arranged another meeting with Dante. This time we met at the Garfield Park Conservatory. The conservatory truly is as it claims, *landscape art under glass*. It boasts about having nearly 120,000 plants representing some 600 species, occupying its 1.6 acres. I must admit I couldn't have picked a better place to meet. I found him quietly admiring some plants. He must have either had a seventh sense or eyes in the back of his head, which weren't visible, because he immediately sensed me approaching. "Olivia must have you running around in circles in your head," I heard him say.

"I'm not here to talk about her. Well, not directly about her."

"I see. Then what can I do for you?"

"What can you tell me about, Mikhail Mogilevich?"

"What can I tell you about, *Mikhail Mogilevich*? I think the appropriate answer to that is, how much time do you have to hear what I know?"

"That much?"

"More than you know. I guess I should start with what do you know about the Russian mob?"

"Not much."

"Mikhail is a Ukrainian boss. *He's known as the destroyer.* He's so evil, Satan worships him. He's so ruthless, he'd have you killed if you looked at him cross eyed. He has turf in Chicago, Boston, New York and Miami. In fact, he's been stepping on the toes of the Aguilera Cartel, here in Chicago. Mikhail has been trying to assert dominance over the Aguilera's and they're not having it. The Aguilera Cartel originated in Honduras. Their leader, Simeon Lopez hates competition and vows to behead Mikhail if given the opportunity, which is highly unlikely, because both bosses are heavily guarded by their foot soldiers. I bet you didn't know, Detective Olivia Bartlett and her father, Solomon Harari are on Mikhail's payroll."

"Olivia's working for the Russian mob?"

"Yep. Her and her old man."

"Question?" I said, looking across at one of the rare mixed Coleus flowers.

"What's your question?"

"Is Miguel del Rosario, affiliated with the Aguilera Cartel?"

"Yes. He's the one responsible for Chicago, and Los Angeles. Simeon Lopez oversees everything else, including: Tucson, Arizona, Brownsville, Texas and Albuquerque."

"So, Detective Olivia Bartlett thought I'd do her dirty work, by getting rid of Miguel, to try and intimidate Mikhail?"

"Getting rid of Miguel would definitely send a strong message to Simeon."

"Well, she's gonna have to find another errand boy, because

I'm not getting involved with a turf war, between the cartel and the Russian mob."

"You may not want to, but believe me, Olivia isn't going to just let you walk away that easy. She has too much to lose. Obviously, she has her mind set on having you get rid of Miguel."

"Yeah, well. Like I said, it aint happening."

"Little word of advice, from William Congreve. You must have heard the proverb, *hell hath no fury, like a woman scorned?*"

"I have."

"It's very good advice when dealing with Olivia. Believe me when I say, she will not be kind when you tell her you're not interested in helping her. She will seek revenge, probably more so against you, then Miguel. She will see you as the reason for the obstacle in her path."

"Well, I guess I'll have to prepare for whatever she decides to do."

"I think that would be wise," he said. We parted ways and I left him at the conservatory. My cellphone rang, just as I reached the rental. I was expecting Siri to announce the caller, and when the caller wasn't announced I reached for my phone and looked at the number. It was Olivia. I answered before it went to voicemail. "Hello."

"Sebastien?"

"Speaking."

"This is Olivia."

"Yes, I know. I have caller ID," I replied, before hearing

an announcement in the background about a plane leaving at gate 11. It sounded like she was at O'Hare International airport. "What can I do for you?"

"I just wanted to let you know I'll be away for a week on business. So, you won't be able to reach me."

"I have a question?"

"What?"

"Are we talking official police business?" I asked.

"I'll contact you when I return."

"Good, because I have a few questions for you?" She immediately went silent. I heard more airport announcements in the background. I knew she was still on the line, because I could hear the background noise. "Olivia! Are you there?"

"I'm here. What questions do you have for me?"

"I don't want you missing your flight. I'll talk to you when you get back."

"Is it important?" she replied, sounding concerned.

"Nothing you have to worry about at this point."

"That sounds very reassuring," she said, sounding a bit sardonic. "Well, like I said I'll reach out to you when I return."

"I realize it's not any of my business, but I am curious; where are you off too?" I asked, feeling a little bold. She answered, "You're right, it's none of your business. I'm sure if you wanted to you could search my name and find what flight I'm on and where I'm going. So, I guess I'll save you the trouble and just tell you I'm off to see someone in Odesa."

"*Odesa*? That city is in what state?" I said, teasing her.

The only Odesa I knew, was in Ukraine. I could tell by her silence that she was up to something nefarious. I heard her say, "You ask a lot of questions."

"It's part of my job."

"As it is, I've told you more than you should know."

"Really? Since I'm working for you, I expect you to be honest with me, honest at all times."

"Now is not the time to discuss this; I have a flight to catch. Have a good weekend and tell your daughter I said hi." She ended the call, before I could respond. I got in the rental, intending to see if I could locate Ricky St. James in real time. I had a tracking app on my phone, that allowed me to pinpoint the location of a target within a few feet. I had already done my research on Ricky and knew more about him, then he knew about himself. I looked over the psychological profile, I had managed to compile on him over the past few days. I also viewed his past record and saw he had been in and out of group homes, since he was a teenager. His birthday was today, and he was now twenty-four years old. Part of me felt pity for him, because there by the grace of God go I. I could have turned out like him, or worse, if it weren't for *Jimmie*. I checked the tracking app on my phone and saw Ricky was still at home. Earlier in the week, I placed a tiny tracking device on his sneakers. They were the only shoes I could find when I entered his apartment, while he was in the shower. I guess I could have put other tracking devices on his other clothes like his jacket, or belt, but I had decided his sneakers were sufficient. Since he was home, this gave me the opportunity to plan a surprise for him. After all, it was his *birthday*! I put the vehicle in drive and headed home.

TWENTY-THREE

On my way home, I began to wonder if my daughter would be there, or if she was with Rudy and his family. It was after 3 p.m. so I assumed my mail must have been delivered. I climbed the stoop, entered the lobby of my apartment building. I opened my mailbox and I wasn't surprised; I had received mostly junk mail. I separated the utility and credit card bills, from the advertising ads. When I got inside my apartment, I was greeted by none other than my most faithful companion; Dakota. She was so happy to see me, she nearly caused me to trip over her. I knew she understood every word I uttered, especially when I mentioned the word, dinner! She became more excited and followed after me, as I went through the living room, headed for the kitchen calling out my daughter's name.

"Amanda!" I cried out twice! The place was totally quiet; all I could hear was Dakota's paws making contact with the wooden floor, as she trotted behind me. My daughter had to be over at Rudy's. I checked the guest's bedroom to be sure. To my surprise, she actually had made the bed! I closed the door and returned to the kitchen, where I found a note stuck to the refrigerator. The note was from Rudy and he mentioned that Amanda was safe. She was with his daughter, and the two planned to go shopping with his wife. He also mentioned additional material Prometheus gave him, and it was on my desk in my study. I figured I would have a thorough look at the paperwork, after I prepared a meal fit for a German Shepard. Over the years, I've managed to spoil Dakota, because she won't eat plain dog food anymore. Whenever I cooked steak, she expected some of the grease to be poured over her food. I cleaned her water bowl and added fresh cold bottled spring water. I left the kitchen, and went directly to my study. I had invested both *money* and *time* in the room. I had a master carpenter and his helper, build me what I can only describe as the most detailed, astonishing looking recessed bookshelves I've ever seen. The only wall that had no books, was the one where my desk was located. That wall had paintings on each side, and the bay window acted as a nice center piece. I purposely had set my desk with my chair to the window. More times than not, I sat kitty corner, between the desk and window, where I could just turn my head and look out at the street. From across the room, I saw the envelope on top of the desk. I went over, pulled out the leather chair and sat. The envelope was thicker than most, which I assumed meant there would be plenty to read. I opened *it*, tearing a straight edge along the top flap. I emptied out the contents on top of the desk. I began carefully looking over each piece of paper. There were multiple newspaper clippings about investors who lost everything, when Ian Verlice tricked them, with his *Ponzi scheme*. I saw that Prometheus had purposely used a dark colored magic marker to conceal the name of a billionaire, who was also a victim. That billionaire investor lost fifty million dollars. There was a typed letter, I assumed it was either from Prometheus or someone who worked for him. It read: **The billionaire mentioned in the newspaper article is *Prometheus*. This material should have been included in Verlices' dossier, so please accept an apology. What Ian Verlice did is quite personal! It is expected Mr. Verlice will not be permitted to do such illegal activities ever again. Do with him as you wish, *an eye for an eye and a tooth for a tooth*.** I then briefly looked over the other articles, claiming some investors lost everything and decided suicide was the only alternative. One man was so distraught, he killed his family because he didn't think they'd survive now, being *broke*! I had many questions for Ian, but right now I needed to concentrate on Ricky St. James. I put all the paperwork back inside the envelope and stuck it inside my desk. The drawer had a four number combination. I mixed up the numbers using my index finger on each dial, so the drawer could only be opened by me. I left the study and went inside my secret vault, where I had a black leather laptop case laid out on the center table – exactly how I left it. I planned to give Ricky an opportunity to redeem himself. However, if he didn't than I planned to use this case to bump into him and inject him with a toxin that would gradually make its way to his spinal cord and render him handicap. Eventually, he wouldn't be able to move his *arms* or *legs*. The toxin was *permanent* and *irreversible*. I had a mini refrigerator where I kept medical specimens, including the *injectable toxin*. I removed the syringe from the refrigerator and I placed it inside the laptop case – in a compartment attached to a trigger located on the case's handle. Once again, I looked at the tracking app on my phone. Ricky was now on the move. He recently left his apartment – the time stamp claimed he had been on the move for ten minutes. I closed the case and took it with me, leaving the vault. I gave Rudy a call on my way out of my apartment. I wanted to find out how Amanda was? When he answered, he explained my daughter was doing fine and would be sleeping over. At that moment, she was helping his wife make dinner. I asked, "Oh yeah, what are you guys having for dinner?"

"Chicken Cacciatore," he explained.

"Sounds good!"

"Oh, believe me, it will be! So, what's going on?"

"Just wanted to check on my daughter, that's all. Oh, I-huh, I looked over the file you left for me, from *P*."

"Yeah. What are we talking, *good* or *bad*?"

"It's only additional material on a topic I'll be covering soon."

"Got it. You know, you're more than welcome to visit for dinner? We have plenty of food here. My wife and daughter would like to see you and I'm sure Amanda would love for you to have dinner with us."

"I would, really! But I have work to do."

"Okay, I just wanted to be sure you know you're always welcome here."

"I appreciate that and the offer. I'll let you know how it goes with *twenty-three*." Rudy knew not to use Ricky's real name over the phone, *just his age*.

"Okay. Have a good night."

"You to buddy. Hey, tell my daughter I love her! Okay?"

"Will do."

The coordinates on my phone, showed Ricky stopped at a nightclub called, Club Eden along north Broadway. The club's hours suggested it would be open at eight p.m. That gave me about an hour to kill. I decided I would stop off for a cup of coffee at a place I knew along the way. While driving, my cellphone rang and Siri answered, "Dante is calling." I looked down into the cup holder and saw his number on the screen. I answered: "What's going on, *Dante*?"

"My friend, how are you?"

"Okay. And you?"

"Things could be better. The reason I'm calling is I may have some valuable information for you; if you're interested? The question is, are you interested?"

"Absolutely!"

"Even if it costs, let's say five grand?"

"That's quite a sum for information!"

"Well, inflation dictates the price, not me. Are you still interested?"

"Maybe. I guess it depends on how important the information is?"

"I would say if I were in your shoes, I'd want to know, because it concerns Olivia."

"Really?"

"Yep."

"Okay, I'll bite. I'm interested."

"Are you busy now? I know you always want to meet in person."

"I can meet you now. However, you do realize I don't have five grand on me?"

"I trust you're good for it. I can meet you at the Long Room." The Long Room was a casual beer & espresso bar, with a patio. It was a nice place for a slice of pizza and a cold glass of beer. I told him, I'd meet him there. "About how long are we talking?" I heard him ask.

"I should be there in fifteen minutes, or so."

"Sounds good." Dante ended the call. It took me nearly twenty minutes to get to the Long Room, because of traffic. I found a place to park and texted Dante, letting him know I had arrived. He returned a text, telling me he was inside, having a beer at the bar. I went inside and sat at a seat to his left. I asked the bartender for a cup of coffee – five sugars and two cream, before I turned my attention to Dante and asked, "So, what can I get for five grand?"

He replied, "You can pay off credit card debt. The average American household owes $15,000 dollars."

"I'm debt free," I replied.

"You can get a cat?"

"I have a dog."

"You can start a business?"

"I already have a job."

"You can donate it to charity..."

"I do that a lot as it is. That's not why I'm here though."

"What I'm about to tell you; didn't come from me. Understand?"

"Yeah," I replied, just as the bartender arrived with my cup of coffee.

"Olivia isn't really working for the Russian mob. I mean she is, but she isn't. The mob is just her cover. She's really working for the *SVR*."

"That used to be called the *KGB*."

"Yes, I know," Dante said. "She's working for a man named, Sergey Naryshkin. My source tells me, he wants her to get detailed information concerning the American electrical grid...for the purpose of *disabling it*, if not *destroying it completely*."

"Who is your source that told you this?" I asked, taking a sip of coffee.

"Sebastien, really? You're really going to question my sources? There's more than just that." Dante finished his beer and asked the bartender for another glass. Same imported beer.

"Go on."

"You recall me telling you about her wanting you to get rid of Miguel?"

"Yeah."

"That's her cover too. She wants you to make it look like a turf war, when in fact, she's really supplying intel to the Chinese – so they can flood the streets with *Fentanyl* – using the Aguilera gang as their drug mule. It's a combined effort on the part of China and Russia, to infiltrate the United States and bring it to its knees. Not to mention the enemies within our federal government, who have slowly weakened us for this purpose."

"What are you suggesting? Are you saying, that China and Russia are playing war games with the United States? And that our own government is complicit?"

"I wouldn't call it a game. I'd say, they're playing for keeps. As far as our so-called government is concerned, Congress was bought and paid for a long time ago, my friend. It's just now, we're beginning to see the extent of the corruption."

"Really? When you say, enemies within our federal government, who in particular are you referring too? Do you have names?"

"Yeah, the *president, congress* – both the *house* and *senate*."

"So, the *entire* government?"

"Follow the money and you'll never be wrong."

"Everyone in congress?"

"Sebastien, it sounds like you doubt what I'm saying.

Believe me when I say, every word I've told you is *accurate*. Nothing I've said has been elaborated."

"I don't know what to say?" I took another couple of sips of coffee.

"You could start with when do you think you'll be able to pay me?"

"I like you Dante, I really do. That's why I'm gonna pay you tomorrow, even though I think you overcharged me."

"*Overcharged you*! I told you inflation dictates my prices."

"Yeah...I know. I'll call you in the morning and set up a time to meet. I'm gonna pay you in cash, so how do you want it?"

"I prefer Benjamins...but I'll take *Grants* and *Andrew Jacksons*."

"Benjamins it is. Talk to you tomorrow," I said. I left my seat at the bar. I tapped Dante on the shoulder, and wished him a good evening, before I left the Long Room.

TWENTY-FOUR

When I finally arrived at Club Eden, I saw people crowding near the entrance to get inside. I left the rental, crossed between oncoming traffic and blended in with the others waiting in line. The bouncer at the door, took one look at me, before waving me inside. The music that played was from the band Depeche Mode, and the song was, *My favorite stranger* and it was loud! The majority of females were scantily clad – to put it mildly. I couldn't help but notice one female, probably in her early twenties, wearing jeans, with two rips right up to her buttocks – showing that she wasn't wearing any panties. I was tempted to approach her and tell her to go home and change; but I didn't. Instead, I went in search of Ricky. I found him at a booth, with a couple of people his age. I assumed they were his friends. I sat at the table across from them, and ordered a chilled bottle of spring water. Even with the loud music, I could hear their conversation, because they had to speak louder than the noise around them. I overheard Ricky tell the others, today was his birthday! And he wanted to get royally messed up! He mentioned going clubbing all night. Hearing this, I looked over and said: "Congratulations!"

"What?" Ricky replied. He looked confused, so I felt it was necessary to repeat myself. "I said, congratulations!" I spoke even louder, so he could hear me. This time he replied, "For what?!"

"I heard you say today is your birthday!"

"Yeah, mind your own business." He went back to talking with his friends. I decided to go over to the booth he was seated at. "Do your friends here, know what you do to elderly people?" I said, and my comment immediately struck a nerve in him. The effects of alcohol hadn't yet surfaced, and I assumed he was still relatively sober. "I don't know who you are *pal*, but if I were you, I'd get outta here! Make tracks fast!" he said, sounding a bit agitated.

"You know it's common knowledge that people who use nonsense words; only do it because they have a limited vocabulary."

"Excuse me!"

"I'm just saying you fit the profile of someone with a limited education, that's all."

"Who are you and what are you talkin' about?" One of Ricky's friends said. I focused my attention on him, when Ricky said, "Look pal, get the hell outta here before I call the bouncer and have him beat your ass outside!"

"I guess I better go then," I said, sarcastically. I had already considered what could happen with the bouncer and if provoked, I had already taken inventory of what I thought were his weak points; so, I didn't feel intimidated by him at all. "One question before I leave."

"What's that?"

"Are you sorry for hurting all those people you *beat* and *robbed*? Some of them have severe disabilities today, because of you. One man by the name of Alex Hutchinson, died from his injuries and if I recall you only got – ten lousy dollars from him."

"My friends know exactly what I do! With that money, I take it and have a good time...like I'm doing *now*! Thing is, you're killing the mood. So, why don't you move along pal."

"One more question..."

"I'm gettin' really tired of your questions man. Who do you think you are? You come over and bother us, on my birthday! First you insult me, now you want to ask me questions. What kinda drugs are you on man?"

"Probably some good stuff!" claimed Ricky's other friend. They all chuckled at the idea that I might be on some mood-altering drug. I remained focused on the task at hand and I said, "How did you convince the judge you weren't guilty?"

"Man, he knew I was *guilty*...he just decided to let me go. See, letting guys like me go, keeps him working. Hell, it keeps the entire system employed!"

"I've heard that before, from a good friend of mine," I said, remembering what Jimmie told me back when he was in the hospital. "So, you have a valid point. However, I think you should have been tried by a jury, maybe the outcome would have been different."

"Yeah, maybe next time."

"There won't be a next time," I said, then I walked away. I decided to wait for Ricky outside. I sat in the rental, watching from across the street. Three solid hours went by and finally he came out with his friends; with the club music still playing loud in the background – another song from Depeche Mode called, *Policy of truth*. He appeared to be intoxicated, but mobile as he hugged his friends and walked off alone in the opposite direction. My first thought was, I guess he decided not to go clubbing after all. I saw this as an opportunity, so I reached down and grabbed the laptop case. I left the rental with the case in hand. I rushed across the street and followed him, as he approached the corner where he had to wait for the traffic light to change. While he waited, I came up directly behind him and bumped into him, pressing the trigger on the laptop handle and pushing the case into his back leg. The syringe did the rest. He obviously felt something, because he reached down and rubbed the back of his pant leg and said, "Watch it man! What the hell are you bumping into me for? You moronic idiot! You're probably drunk too?"

"Excuse me," I replied. He was so drunk that he didn't recognize me. I walked off, taking a detour around the block and returned to where the rental was parked. I got in the rental and thought, in a few days he would feel the full effects of the toxin and probably in a few months; he would be in a nursing home – in a place where he would see plenty of elderly people for the rest of his stinking life. I saw my actions, as *poetic justice*. I started the vehicle, and pulled forward into traffic. While driving, I recorded a message to Prometheus, using a burner phone. **The topic is toxins. Someone is sure to feel the effects, as it begins to coarse throughout his body. Eventually, all limbs will be impeded and immobile. Similar to the effects of advanced multiple sclerosis. Trust me when I say, justice was served and it was served cold.** I continued driving, I was looking for Ricky, because I forgot to get a picture of him on the camera, showing I was in fact in direct contact with the subject. I saw him managing to maintain his balance, as he walked along the sidewalk. I pulled up alongside, rolled down the driver's side window and placed the burner phone so I could get a clear image of him. "Hey!"

He stopped, turned and said to me, "What?"

"Smile!"

He just looked at me and gave me the finger. I took a photo and drove off. I figured tomorrow, before I went to the bank, I'd stop at the post office and deliver this package to Rudy. That way he could get it to Prometheus as soon as possible and my job concerning Ricky was done. Now, I had to concentrate on Ian Verlice the stock peddler, who destroyed so many lives with his *Ponzi scheme*.

TWENTY-FIVE

"There you are!" I heard Rudy say as he entered the vault. My attention was completely focused on the sample of ultra clear PLEXIGLAS. It was exactly three inches thick, with an unbelievable water pressure rating – it could even withstand a bullet. I looked up just as he stopped and stood directly in front of my experiment. "What are you working on?" he asked, with a nerdy expression on his face. I answered, without taking my eyes off the price. "I'm doing a little tweaking. I wanna get the proper amount of C-4, because I only want to crack it, without fully exploding it."

"I see. And this is for?"

"This my friend is for Mr. Verlice."

"*Ian?*"

"Yes," I replied, before I looked back at what I was doing. I took a moment to read my notes again, and saw the adjustments I had written down. I needed to be sure this was going to work, because I had run out of C-4 explosive. While I was cutting the C-4, I heard Rudy say, "I realize you're busy, but could you elaborate?"

"Elaborate on what?"

"What's this going to be used for?"

"Well, I did extensive research on Mr. Verlice. He is a very busy man, so busy that it seems I'll have to go inside his penthouse apartment to have a word with him. Otherwise, I won't get the opportunity until he returns from overseas."

"Overseas?"

"Yes, he spends a lot of time in Europe. I could travel there to his villa and kill him there, but I'm working on a rather short schedule and the faster I can eliminate him, the better. That way I can focus my attention on what I have left to do."

"Yeah, go on..."

"I liked his penthouse so much that I did a 3D search of the layout. Beautiful place – *absolutely stunning!* He has a twenty by forty-foot pool located outside, on the rooftop. With approximately twenty-four thousand gallons of water inside it – weighing nineteen thousand nine hundred and eighty-nine pounds. The building specs on the roof had to be structurally reinforced to allow for the additional weight. If you look at the pool's margin, you can see it has an ultra-clear PLEXIGLAS infinity wall, keeping the water back, while allowing you to swim over to the edge and look down at the city below."

"Wow!"

"Did I mention he lives on the top floor...33 floors up?"

"No, you didn't."

"Can you imagine, going for a swim and swimming over to the side of the building to look down?"

"So, what does any of that have to do with what you're doing?"

"I have a surprise for Mr. Verlice. As you know, I wanna know what makes him tick. Why did he cheat all his investors? What did he do with the money? Etcetera..."

"I still don't follow you."

"Don't worry you will." I put the charge of C-4 on the inside of the PLEXIGLAS and placed it inside the steel bomb proof blast container. I stepped back out of habit, and saw Rudy standing rather close to it. "I'd step back if I were you."

"It's supposed to be blast proof!" he said.

"I've used it a lot. There's no guarantee it will stay intact *forever.*"

"Great! Should I wait outside?"

"Don't you want to see it explode?" I knew I did. The container was approximately four feet high, and resembled a safe. In the front there was an area of blast resistant glass, made of high performance polyvinyl butyral, sandwiched between two panes of shatter proof glass. The viewing window was so durable, it could withstand multiple rounds from an AR-15. I looked over at Rudy and said, "Are you ready?"

"What? To leave?" he replied, sounding a little nervous.

"No, to see it go *boom!*" I purposely used both of my hands to imitate an explosion. He reluctantly agreed to stand over next to me and we waited. I had set the charge on a timer, so it would detonate in 45 seconds. I pressed the start button and the countdown began. "You better cover your ears," I said, just as Dakota came prancing inside, it appeared as if she was looking for me; probably wondering when I was going to take her for a walk. I grabbed her by the collar, just as the C-4 exploded inside the container. The blast was successfully contained, but it was *loud*! I was used to just covering my ears, only this time I didn't, because of Dakota. The blast startled her and she pulled away from me, and rushed out of the vault. "Dakota!" I yelled out, hoping she would return, but she didn't. "That really must have scared her."

"I don't blame her for being scared," Rudy said, and he joined me over near the blast container. We both looked at the viewing area. The glass was smudged with explosive residue. "So much for seeing it explode!" I heard Rudy say, from over my shoulder.

"If Dakota didn't distract us, we would have seen it," I said, before I unlocked the container and reached in for the piece of PLEXIGLAS. "Perfect!" I was absolutely thrilled with the amount of C-4 in the formula, because it was enough to cause spider cracks; yet not too strong to break it into pieces. "I'm still confused," Rudy claimed, touching the sample. "How is it perfect? You managed to cause a ton of cracks."

"It's perfect because I weakened it. See, I know Mr. Verlices' schedule. I'm going to wait until he's away from his apartment. Then I'm going to enter and go to his beautiful pool, where I'm going to attach the proper amount of C-4 to the glass – facing the city below."

"Okay, go on."

"Then when Ian returns and is alone in his pool…"

"How will you know when he's alone? Or if he's in his pool?"

"I guess I'll have to attach a few hidden cameras, to surveil him, that way I'll know for sure."

"Got it!"

"Anyway, I'm planning to get him alone in his pool, so I can ask him some questions, like why did he feel it was okay to steal from so many people? And what did he do with the money the authorities didn't find? And is he sorry for what he did? Does he feel guilty? Is he planning on making restitution? Has he contacted any of his victims and apologized? And does he plan to apologize in the near future? If so, when?"

"Why do you waste your time? Prometheus just wants him dead, not interrogated. What if he tells you to go pound sand; it's none of your business? Or it's my money now and I'm not sorry?" Rudy said, sounding genuinely pessimistic.

"First, if he does that, I plan to detonate the C4 that'll be attached to the PLEXIGLAS of the pool. It should cause spider cracks and severely weaken the glass. With the glass weakened, then I plan to take out the handgun I'll be carrying, with a silencer on it – at which point I will aim the barrel of the gun at the weakened glass and shoot at it."

"Why? Shouldn't you be shooting Verlice?"

"No. That would be too obvious. It would look like he was murdered. And I'd have to go into the pool and retrieve the bullet. See, with the glass of the pool weakened, the bullet

I'll be using to shoot at it, will cause it to break completely. Once the glass is broken, the water will gush out, over the side of the building. I'm hoping the water pressure will be so great that when the glass breaks, and the water starts to leave the pool, it'll ultimately take Mr. Verlice with it – over the side of the building."

"And he'll fall to his death!"

"Now, I think you got it."

"I got it, I just still don't understand why you want to go to all this trouble to kill him. There are a million ways you could kill him and you'd be done, like that!" He snapped his fingers.

"I do what I do; that's all I'm gonna say."

"I realize that. You have your ways, just like *Dexter* had his ways," he said.

"*Dexter*? Who's that?"

"You never saw the television series, *Dexter*?"

"No."

"Well anyway, he kills people too, but in his own way."

"That's good to know. And thanks for sharing that with me."

"Anytime," Rudy ribbed, teasing me.

TWENTY-SIX

It had been four days since I illegally entered Ian Verlices'
penthouse apartment, to setup three very *miniscule* cameras.
One unit was attached to the ceiling – just as he entered the
apartment; with the viewing camera facing the living room's
sliding glass doors. The door was open to the pool; out on the
rooftop. The camera was actually inconspicuously embedded
in what resembled a smoke alarm. I replaced the old smoke
detector with the spy cam. The other two surveillance units
came as faceplates that go over electrical receptacles. I had
decided to place one of the faceplates in the kitchen, with
a pretty good view of the living room and dining area. The
other faceplate was installed outside – *poolside*. The faceplates
allowed Ian to plug a device in, like a radio, without realizing
it was a *spy-cam*. While on my way over to Ian's apartment
building, I was very mindful of what was happening on my
phone. I was using a different *app*, compared to the one I used
to track Ricky St. James. This app allowed me to view what
Ian was doing inside the penthouse – in real time. So far, I
knew he was alone and he was on his way out to the pool to
go for a swim, with a towel around his neck. Just as I pulled

into a parking spot near his building – I saw him on the screen of my phone as he dove into the pool. I had everything I needed already on my person; including a Philips screwdriver for the faceplates, so, I could remove them. I also had the trigger to detonate the C-4. I left the rental, and casually walked toward his building, because I knew there were several CCTV cameras in the area and the last thing, I wanted to do was draw unnecessary attention to myself. Ian's building had a doorman and the gentleman was preoccupied helping a resident into a waiting limo. I walked right past them and entered the building's lobby. I was wearing a light grey sweat coat under my leather jacket; I had the hood covering my head. Last thing I wanted was the building's security cameras to notice my face, so I intentionally kept my head down as I went over to the elevators. I pushed one of the buttons, going up. The elevator doors opened and I entered. I was relieved to see there wouldn't be anyone going up with me. I pressed the 33rd floor and waited for the elevator doors to close. On the way up, I figured I'd use the stairs when leaving – even though it would take longer.

When I reached the 33rd floor, the doors opened and I left the elevator, headed for Mr. Verlices' apartment. I had already made a key, so I wasted no time entering his apartment. The first thing I heard was music coming from the pool area. The tune was from The Allen Parsons Project – *Eye in the sky*. Apparently, he had the song playing on a loop, because I heard it repeat. I pulled a chair over to the door, so I could reach the smoke detector and pull it down. Next, I retrieved the receptacle faceplates, that I had installed. Finally, I went out *poolside*. Ian was rightfully startled when he saw me. "Who are you? And how did you get in here?"

"That really doesn't matter," I pulled open my leather coat, and moved my sweat coat aside, showing him, I was packing a 9mm Luger. "What the hell?" He was about to leave the pool, when I told him to stay put! I then went over to the radio and pulled the plug, killing the music. "What's this about?" Ian sounded quite nervous. "I'm here to ask you a couple of questions," I said, as I looked over at the PLEXIGLAS, and noticed the C-4 was still attached at the bottom of the glass. I was actually surprised he hadn't noticed it.

"Is this about money? You want money?"

"No. You worked for *Lane* and *Company* investments, *correct*?"

"Yes, *why*?"

"Do you have any idea how many people you hurt?"

"No."

"Do you care?"

"Are you with *Lane* and *Company*? Because we had a deal!"

"I'm not with Lane. What was the deal?"

"You know, that could get me killed if I tell you." I showed him the gun again. "Don't worry about *Lane* and *Company*. Right now, you should be worried about me."

"Okay, okay, I hear you. What do you want to know?"

"What did you do with the money?"

"I got to keep it, why?"

"Are you planning to return it?"

"Hell *no*," he said, unremorsefully. "It's my money now."

"Really, is that what you think? You mentioned you made a deal, with *who*?"

"The executives at *Lane* and *Company*. The company manages investments for global interests, including: Halliburton, Raytheon, Monsanto, Pfizer and Moderna. I was overseeing investments from the *big three*. Big tech, big finance and big media. I was working with so much money that I figured, I'd skim some off the top of each account. Nothing they couldn't afford. I mean they are *literally* worth billions of dollars."

"You skimmed *fifty* million dollars from one investor," I said, and thought of *Prometheus*.

"Look, I know. I got greedy. I wasn't in a right frame of mind. I began to think I was untouchable."

"What gave you that idea?"

"I had the goods on Lane and their many important global investors."

"How so?"

"You could say I had them over a barrel and they knew it. I was one of the very few insiders, who knew about the plan to connect the world to AI and I knew all the *dirty little secrets* that they didn't want known by the public."

"*What dirty little secrets*?"

"Well for instance, Lane gathers intelligence on their super wealthy investors, so they have something to use against them – in case any of them decide to go elsewhere and have another investment company manage their funds."

"That's a little *extreme*, not to mention probably *illegal*. What's their reason for doing that?"

"Well because Lane is actually bribing many of their global investors – threatening them that if they don't accept higher fees and play by their rules, they'll inform the media about their involvement with the five eyes –"

I interrupted him, "Are you referring to, *the* five eyes?"

"Yes, *the* five eyes, which it seems you're already aware of, are an intelligence alliance comprising of: Australia, Canada, New Zealand, the United Kingdom and the United States. They're working hand-in-hand with globalists who want to reduce the global population to a more sustainable number, because they're worried too many people will lead to global problems, including: *famine, disease and war.*"

"Reduce the population...*how*?"

"By any means necessary. With a manageable number of people, they could then use those individuals to *work* and *maintain* the artificial intelligence. I don't know if you've noticed, but artificial intelligence, also known as AI is growing considerably. For instance, now if you don't stop at a red light, you'll get a ticket in the mail, from a camera watching you, being manned with artificial intelligence. The plan is to attach *you* to your social credit score, which would increase your insurance rates for not stopping at the red light. Or let's say, you use your credit card to buy *beer* and *cigarettes* – both are terrible for your health! That information will soon wind up going to not only your doctor, but also the health insurance company you have. Eventually, cash will be obsolete, so you can be tracked and traced in real time. Everything is becoming automated and will eventually be consolidated into one ID, which you will be required to keep on you at all times. That's the coming *social credit score.*"

"Some of the things you mentioned I already know."

"Yes, but do you know the real names of the players behind the scene."

"No. Tell me some names."

"Honestly, I would if I could, but I took an oath. I swore on my life never to mention the *names* or dynasty families involved."

"That's too bad."

"Why? Are you gonna kill me?!"

"I haven't decided yet what I'm gonna do. However, before I got here that was my intention, because I've been contracted to end your life."

"I could give you ten million dollars, if you walk away now," he said.

"That's very tempting, but I think I'll pass. I have another idea."

"Anything!" Ian sounded anxious to find an equitable resolution.

"Return all the money to the investors – the ones who couldn't afford to lose their money."

"Are you crazy?!"

"Why is that crazy?"

"That would expose me, and I could go to prison! The press would be all over that. I made a promise to some very important people to disappear, and that's what I plan to do. It was all part of my agreement to keep my mouth shut, so the globalists can continue to do what they're doing, in hopes of reducing the population."

"So basically, you were paid off, with other people's money. Small time investors who couldn't afford to lose a dime, while the big three as you put it, continue to live lavish lifestyles. And you think that's fair?"

"I didn't say it was fair, but I also stole from wealthy investors. I didn't discriminate!" I heard him say. I then removed the trigger from my inside coat pocket and detonate the C-4. The blast caused the water to swoosh around and I noticed Ian saw the spidering effect on the pool glass. He attempted to leave the pool and I warned him to stay put. "I wouldn't move around in the water and cause waves. It won't take much to break the rest of that *plexiglass*." He immediately stopped moving. "You are messing with the wrong person!" he yelled! I looked directly into his eyes and said, "No. I gave you an opportunity to redeem yourself and you chose to continue to be a filthy thief. No one likes a thief. In fact, thieves don't like thieves, I find that ironic. Anyway, keep your eyes closed and don't look down." I then raised the 9mm and shot out the rest of the weakened glass. The breach caused a massive amount of water to gush over the side of the building. I watched as Mr. Verlice desperately tried to grab something, only to be forced over the side of the building with the rest of the water. I heard him scream as he fell to his death. "Easy come, easy go." I quickly got the last poolside receptacle, with the spy-cam embedded in it. I then left the apartment, and headed down the stairs.

TWENTY-SEVEN

Dante was able to get me thermite, from someone he knew, whom he called *Horus* – named after the mythological Egyptian god of war. Apparently, Horus worked for one of America's military defense contractors. Dante was of the opinion that thermite was used in the 9/11 job, to bring down the twin towers in New York City – to usher in the Patriot Act, as an excuse to take away US citizens' constitutional rights. I tend to agree with him, after doing my own research on the matter. That's why I decided to use thermite for my next job, because it burns extremely *hot*! I was inside the vault, testing a small amount of thermite on a sample of half-inch steel, when I heard the doorbell ring. I would have answered it, but it really wasn't a good time. The doorbell continued to ring three more times. I decided to go over to the vault's video panel, to see who was outside? The screen was approximately the size of an average iPad. I touched the viewer and moved the cursor to view outside. I saw Mr. Li Wong standing at the door. I pressed speak and said, "Hi Li! How are you?"

"Here to walk for dog!" he claimed, reminding me I had asked if he would walk Dakota, and keep an eye on her, until this job was complete. "I'm sorry Li, I completely forgot! Let me buzz you in." I buzzed him into my apartment and watched as he entered, closing the door behind him. I left the vault and met with him out in the living room. Dakota was already there, wagging her tail, hoping one of us would pat her.

"Where are you off to today?" I asked.

"Think might take her to *wiggly field*," he replied. "After come over to rest, in my home." Wiggly field was a dog park and a great place to take a pet. "Nice! I'm sure she'll like that." Last time he watched her, I offered to pay him. He refused to take any money, so this time I'm not taking *no* for an answer. "I know I offered to pay you before and you declined. I'm gonna give you something for your time."

"No, Mr. Sebastien! It's well."

"You mean fine?"

"Yes! Find."

"No, fine! Anyway, I'm gonna give you a hundred dollars."

"Oh no! Much too much!"

"Actually, with inflation it really isn't." I reached into my back pocket, grabbed my wallet and took out a one-hundred-dollar bill. I handed him the new hundred-dollar bill. He reluctantly accepted the money and I thanked him for his time. "Mr. Sebastien, mind if you answer a question?"

"I think you mean; do I mind if you ask me a question?"

"Yes, sorry. You believe *higher power* exist?"

"I don't understand your question?"

He took a moment to gather his thoughts, trying to

remember the English meaning to the word he wants to use. "Me worry about you. Me worry where you go from here when you die. You live *dangerous!*"

"I appreciate your concern. I think what you're trying to say is do I believe in *God*?"

"Yes! You knew me following Christians?"

"Yes, I know, you're a Christian. If I recall correctly, that was why you left China, because you wanted to be allowed to practice your faith?"

"*Yes*! You told me never if you are or not. You following *Christians*?" Li asked me.

"I *believe*, I just don't *practice*."

"Faith with no work is *dead*. Jesus gave up much to be with *us*."

"Yes, I know. He died for the sins of the world."

"Yesss! You following Him?" I gave Li a lot of credit, because he was quite persistent. I began to realize that was due to his faith. Something I couldn't say I had. Not with what I did for a living. "Li, I'm gonna be totally honest with you...*okay*?"

"Okay."

"I can't say I have faith like you. All I can say is, I hate the *evil* I see in the world and I do what I do, to make a difference. I don't know if that makes me a bad person or not, but at least I don't claim to be someone I'm not."

"I think reason for us being here is to make choice," says Li. "You have choice to follow *God or not*."

"I understand that."

"*No* there's more! Remember, Adam and Eve? From Bible."

"Yeah, *Genesis*."

"Exactly! Devil tempt Eve...speak her she can be liken a god. Due to Adam and Eve tempting every generation is cursed. I'm saying, 'cuz of that act it 'petuates continuous. Example will be, me or you be tempted every day. Something might make me anger, cause me to say or do something wrong. That is the tempt Satan did to Eve. He opened her eyes. We knew no sin, before him. Now say, you find wallet on ground. Lots of money inside! You take money but don't return wallet...that's stolen! Or man cheats on wife, by lust for her, that's example of that 'petuates of sin...the sin Satan brought on all of us, due to Adam and Eve's eyes being open. Understand, you Mr. Sebastien?"

"Yeah, I think I do. You're saying in life we're tempted every day by millions of things we do, whether it's telling a lie to a co-worker or cheating on your taxes, it's all temptations, bringing us *metaphorically* back to the Garden of Edan, where Satan tempted Adam and Eve. Only it's not them; it's us being tempted. I'll go a step further; Adam was a man who was responsible for bringing sin into this world, and Jesus had to become a man to correct Adam's mistake. Christ knew no sin, because He never allowed Himself to fall into the Devil's *schemes of temptation*."

"Yessss! *You do see*!" Li said, sounding excited!

"I do. I've read the book of Enoch and the Bible. On my research I came across something very interesting – *the attachment principle*. It's a principle where God created us to want to love Him. If you decide not to love Him, because you have freewill, you will ultimately find something else to love. For instance, a lot of guys love their cars. A lot of people worship money. I know a few people who love their job, more than they love their own family. When you love something, you put it first in your life – you care for it out of love. That's ultimately what God wants from us. The Bible calls it worship; when in all actuality it's simply putting God first in your life."

"Understand, I see," Li said, smiling. It was as if I had given him much to ponder over. "I told you I *believe*; I just don't *practice it*, by going to *church*."

"May me pray for *you*, Mr. Sebastien?"

"If you want."

"Mr. Sebastien me pray for your *protection*."

"I could definitely use that. Thank you."

TWENTY-EIGHT

My research on Sylvia Wixx had uncovered more disturbing behavior, concerning her involvement in the Church of Satan. Her Facebook page showed her cutting a male doll with a long butcher knife. The caption claimed: **THIS IS HOW YOU SACRIFICE A LITTLE CHILD!** I immediately remembered reading her file, and how her son Lucus was brutally murdered. She claimed she would be going to a cosplay event today; being held at Oz Park, along N. Burling Street. The event was open to only those who practice *witchery*, between the hours of 9 a.m. to 5 p.m. She stressed, *if you are not dressed for the event, you will not be allowed to attend.* I've heard of Oz Park, but I had never been there, so I did a quick search on the internet. I jotted down the address, logged off my fake account and left the library. It took me about thirty minutes to get to Oz. When I got there, I found a place to park, and that's when I saw handmade signs, directing cosplay attendees to where the event was being held. I followed the signs and I was led to a large open field; where the grass looked like it had recently been cut. I found a park bench and sat. I watched about three dozen witches prance around in costume. Luckily for me, I brought a small pair of binoculars. I removed the binoculars from my inside pocket, and scanned the group on the field, hoping to locate Sylvia. I had a mental image of what she looked like, so it shouldn't have been too difficult to determine if she was still here or not. It took a few minutes for me to find her – or at least I thought that was her. It was difficult to be sure, from where I'm sitting. I realized I couldn't just go over there, because I wasn't dressed for the event. I decided to go over anyway; just to ask what's going on? Maybe it would offer me an opportunity to meet Sylvia? I left the bench and walked toward the witches. As I got closer, I heard their chants to demons and even Lucifer himself, calling him the bearer of *light* and the bringer of *wisdom*. I found it rather odd, knowing what the Bible states about the devil. He's a *liar, thief* and *murderer*, who deceived Adam & Eve, claiming they could be as gods. The book of Enoch mentioned Lucifer was jealous of Almighty God and was cast down from heaven to earth, as a streak of lightening! While on earth he tempted Eve, in hopes of getting her and Adam to give up their God given *rights and dominion* over the earth. Even unto this day, Satan blinds and deceives mankind in hopes of remaining here on earth. He even accuses humans of allowing him dominion over God's creation by claiming we're *complicit*. Apparently, he's not alone, because he directs the actions of the fallen ones; also known as the *watchers*, to assist him in deceiving mankind into believing in many ancient gods. I was thinking all this, when one of the women noticed me and stopped what she was doing and said, "This is a cosplay event!"

"What's that?"

"It's a costume event," said one of the witches. This attracted Sylvia's attention and she left the group and came over to me. "This is a witch event. Are you a witch?"

"No. Just curious."

"Curious about the event, or curious about becoming a witch?"

"Does becoming a witch come with benefits?" I said, getting her to laugh.

"Well yeah, you get to practice *witchcraft*."

"My mother warned me about women like you," I said, teasing her.

"Oh yeah, did she tell you how *bad I can be*?"

"No, but I think I have a pretty good idea though."

"You can't join us, but would you like to hang around and meet with me *afterwards*? Maybe we can go out for a *drink*?" she said, sounding as if she was physically attracted to me. I played along, because I didn't want to discourage her, and lose any chance of getting her alone.

"I'd like that. However, I don't drink alcohol."

"We can go for coffee or tea...on *me*." She smiled, teasing me with the sexual innuendo, "I mean in a *cup*!"

"Of course. You see that park bench over there?" I pointed to the bench I had just been sitting, at a few minutes ago. "I'll be waiting for you over there."

"Okay." She returned to her witchery activities and I returned to where I was sitting on the bench. While looking out at the witches on the field, I felt my phone vibrate, then it rang. I wasn't expecting a call, but I answered it anyway, rather than allowing it go to voicemail. "Hello!"

"Sebastien," I heard a familiar female voice say. It took just a moment to recognize that the caller was none other than Olivia. "What's going on?" I asked. She replied, "I think I should be asking you that? While I was away, I couldn't stop thinking about what you said."

"And what's that?"

"When I was at the airport, on my way to *Odesa*...you mentioned you wanted to talk to me about something, but you didn't want me to miss my flight."

"I remember."

"So, what was so important?"

"Well for starters, I found out you lied to me. You told me you had a daughter that was raped and murdered by Miguel; that was a lie." I was half-expecting her to say something in her defense, but she remained silent. I continued, "One of my sources told me that you're actually working for the Russian mob, both you and your father. You wanted to use me to intimidate the Aguilera's, because your boss Mogilevich has been stepping on their toes; so-to-speak."

"Listen to me you little shit! I don't care what you know? But now that you do know the truth, I'm not gonna play games with you anymore. Truth is, there was never a file on

Miguel, I made it all up – the phony file and everything! You find him and kill him, or I'll make your life living hell, starting with your friend *Jimmie*. While you've been doing research on *me*, I've been doing the same on *you*. I know exactly where your friend lives, and his life-threatening illness."

"You bother him and you'll be sorry."

"Maybe I won't bother *him*. Maybe I'll visit with *your daughter*."

"Listen to me! I don't care that you're a cop! You mess around with my daughter and no one and I mean no one, will be able to stop me when I come looking for you, not even the *Russian mob*."

"You have twenty-four hours to get me Miguel's head. If I don't hear from you, I'll have you arrested on suspicion of being involved with the murder of Ian Verlice. Remember *him*? He fell to his death from his rooftop building, after his pool exploded. There's an open investigation concerning his death, because traces of C-4 were used to blow out the pool's glass wall. I have a sneaking suspicion you were involved and I'm pretty sure I can get a warrant to search your place. I might even be able to plant some evidence, which would lead to your arrest. After your arrest, I'd have a perfect opportunity to go after your daughter, and give her over to *Mikhail*. He'd probably take her out of this country and bring her to Ukraine, and you'd never see her again. Choice is yours."

"Listen to me! I need at least forty-eight hours. It takes time to do research and find him."

"Well then you better move fast, because I have to have it by tomorrow morning at noon. If I don't have his head, they'll take mine! And before that happens, I'll have you arrested and your daughter in transit, on her way to Ukraine. Do you understand?" I figured she was bluffing, due to fear! She could do a lot of damage to me in twenty-four hours; but I knew even she would need more time to do everything she was claiming. So, I played her game of chess; but with my chess pieces. "I do understand. So, I have twenty-four hours from *now*?" I said, with my mind racing!

"Exactly twenty-four hours; *not a minute more.*"

"Okay, I'll have your head."

"You mean, *Miguel's*?"

"Right," I said, letting her believe I was referring to him. She ended the call; leaving me with just a dial tone. I was on my way out onto the field to tell Sylvia something's come up, and we would have to make it another time; when I noticed her leave the group and she began walking toward me. As she got closer, she said, "You're an anxious little devil, aren't you?"

"Something's come up and we'll have to go out another time," I said.

"Oh, sorry to hear that! I was looking forward to spending the evening with you."

"Another time."

"Unfortunately, it won't be for a while! See, I'm leaving tomorrow for Europe. Going to London to visit with friends, and maybe do a little witchcraft there. You'd be surprised how many people in England practice!"

"Really? When will you return?"

"Not until the fall. I'm planning on spending the entire summer there," she replied. I decided to see her after all. "You know, since you'll be leaving tomorrow and I won't see you for a while, maybe we should go out this evening, after all," I said. I figured we could go out for drinks and I could convince her to go home with me. I also realized, Olivia hadn't given me sufficient time, and realistically, there was no way I would be able to research Miguel, find him and get his head for her. I figured while I finished this job, it would offer me time to think of what I was going to do with Olivia.

"Really? Are you sure?" she said, and smiled.

"Absolutely!"

"I'm all yours then."

"I've been thinking about what you said, concerning going out for drinks."

"Oh yeah, what are you thinking?"

"There's a great place I know, where you can have a few drinks and I can get a coffee."

"Sounds like you're trying to get me drunk," she smiled. "You're not thinking of taking advantage of me, are you? Not that I wouldn't let you."

"I just want you to enjoy yourself."

TWENTY-NINE

The Berkshire Room, was located on east Ohio Street and it was considered one of the best lounges in the city of Chicago. According to Rudy, it was a great place to meet with a friend, relax and have a cocktail. Sylvia and I were seated at the bar. She was having her second Manhattan, while I was nearly finished with my coffee. "Have you ever been to The Lodge Tavern, or Bar Allegro?" she asked me, while sipping her drink.

"No, never been to either."

"We should go, after here."

"It's getting late, I'd prefer if we have drinks at my place. That is if you're game?" I said, hoping she would get my drift that I wanted to wrap things up. Apparently; she was still sober, enough to recognize my intentions; or so she thought were my intentions. She smiled and said, "Let me use the ladies' room to freshen up. I'll be right back and we can go." I saw this as an opportunity to spike her drink. She left her place at the bar and walked off in the direction of the bathrooms. While she was gone, I quickly, yet inconspicuously removed a small tube of liquid from my coat pocket. I looked around the bar, to make sure no one is watching – I've been wondering *if* or *when* I'd be able to use this formula, as I opened the tube and poured its contents into her drinking glass. When she returned, she announced, "Are you ready?"

"Aren't you going to finish your drink?"

"I thought you wanted to leave."

"I do, but I'd hate to see you waste the drink. Besides, I have to pay the tab."

"Okay," she said. I called the bartender over to ask for the bill. While waiting for him to tally up the drinks, I watched her finish her cocktail. I smiled and said, "Was it good?"

"Oh yeah. You ever have a Manhattan?"

"No. I huh-I don't drink."

"Oh, that's right! Are you're in recovery?"

"No, I just don't like how it makes me feel. It dulls the senses."

"So, if we're headed back to your place to have drinks and you don't drink, does that mean you're going to have your way with me?"

"Something like that."

"*Something like that*," she repeated. "We'll see if you have the stamina to keep up with me. I can really be an animal," she smiled, with a devilish grin.

"We'll just have to find out, won't we?"

"Yes, we will, Mr. Sexy Pants."

I paid for her drinks and my coffee, before leaving a ten-dollar tip, for the bartender. Sylvia led the way, as we left the bar. "You're welcome to stay over if you like," I suggested, knowing she would be passing out in about five minutes. We made it to the rental; I opened the door for her and she got in. Just as I went around the vehicle to get in, I saw her slumped over in the seat. My initial thought was: *thank God*! We made it to the rental, without incident. Next, I made sure her airway was unobstructed, as I leaned her back in a comfortable position. I figured she was going to be out for a couple of hours. This would give me the opportunity to take her to the abandoned warehouse, over on Taylor Street, where I took *Murderous*. Since I had everything already set up there, I'll just had to tie her up and wait for her to wake. I drove carefully, being mindful of the speed limit and hopped I wouldn't be harassed by Olivia; after all I still had eighteen hours left. While driving, I had the radio on and I'm listening to one of my CDs from the band, Red Rider – the song was, *Lunatic Fringe*. I often listened to music when stressed; and this was the perfect song for how I was feeling right now. I was feeling tense about what Olivia said, concerning having me arrested, and with me out of the way; she planned on going after my daughter. When I finally reached the abandoned warehouse, I pulled the vehicle right up to the double doors, leaving the headlights on for visibility. I stepped out of the vehicle, so I could work the combination lock, that held the chain – securing the doors. I didn't use a lock and chain to keep people out – I did it, so I'd know if someone entered the warehouse, without me knowing. With the lock and chain off, I pulled open the doors, returned to the vehicle and drove it inside the warehouse. I momentarily kept the vehicle's headlights on, which allowed me some much-needed light, as I returned to the double doors to shut them. I had a portable generator in back of the rental. With enough electrical cord to reach the other end of the warehouse – where I had everything set up. I started the generator and attached the cord, pulling it along, allowing it to unwind. I then set up a spot light and returned to the rental, to turn the vehicle's lights off and get Sylvia from the passenger's seat. She was still out cold. I pulled her from the seat and carried her to where I had a chair at the other end of the building. When we get to the chair, I carefully set her down and tied her hands behind her – using a double fisherman's knot. I then retrieved the container of thermite from the rental and pour a line around her, completely encircling her. I could have waited another hour or so, to let her wake on her own; but I decided to quicken the process, with an antidote or countermeasure. The only way to give the corrective, was by syringe. I grabbed the needle and injected her right shoulder, pushing the liquid into her body. It took only a few minutes for her to begin to regain consciousness.

"Hello!" I said, seeing her wake. She looked confused, especially when she realized her hands were tied behind her back. "What's going on?"

"You took a little nap," I said, and I looked at my watch. "It's almost midnight."

"Why are my hands tied? And where the hell am I?" she began to frantically struggle to free her hands.

"Good luck with that! I realize this is all confusing for you, but you're here for a reason."

"Why?"

"I want you to tell me the truth about something. If you're honest, I'll give you the opportunity to free yourself and you can take off. However, if you lie to me, I'll kill you right away. Deal?"

"No."

"Well, you actually don't have a choice. You either tell me the truth and you get to walk outta here, or you lie and you die."

"Okay! What do you want to know?"

"I want to know about your son, *Lucus*. You killed him, didn't you?" I said, watching her body language and seeing her hesitate for a minute.

"Are you a cop?!"

"No."

"Well, who are you?"

"That's irrelevant."

"No, I'd like to know!"

"I'm a professional killer. I was hired to kill you."

"Are you going to kill me?!"

"No, if you recall I gave you an opportunity to tell me the truth."

"So, I tell you the truth and you'll really let me go?"

"I'll give you the opportunity to be free."

"What does that mean?"

"Look, do you want to get outta here or not?"

"Okay! *Yes*, I killed my son! It was a ritual killing. He was my first born – actually my only child. The church I belong to convinced me to sacrifice him, because he was my first. I was offered *wisdom* and *wealth* for doing it."

"How did that turn out for you?"

"I'm still waiting...it's a process of *trust*."

"You put your trust in the Church of Satan and allowed them to convince you to murder your boy; that's not only disgraceful – it's disgusting and shameful!"

"I told you the truth, now untie me!"

"I never said I was going to untie you. I said I would give you the opportunity to be free."

"You bastard! You lied to me! Untie me now!"

"Or what?"

"You either untie me now, or I'm going to put a curse on you!"

"Really?"

"Yes! I promise it will be a terrible curse, one you'll regret having done this to me."

"Now, you have me concerned," I said, with a little sarcasm. "I know there is power in curses, but you have to believe it will affect you, and I don't. So, I have a better idea. Why don't you call on Satan to untie you? If he's willing to make you rich and powerful, I'm sure he can easily untie you. What do say? You need a minute to call him?"

"That's a mockery! You asshole!"

"Why? He won't do it? And you know it, because you've been duped and you don't mean shit to him. He got what he wanted and you got nothing. Well, at least you will get to see him soon."

"I didn't say he couldn't untie me. I said it was mockery to ask him to do such a thing. It's beneath him..."

"I'm sure. While we wait for him to decide what he's going to do with you, I'm going to give you some very important instructions, okay? You'll want to pay close attention! You see that stuff on the floor around you? That's called, thermite. If it ignites it can burn right through steel."

"Why would it *ignite*?"

"*Pay attention*! The reason I've poured it around you, is because when I leave, you'll have exactly ten minutes to free yourself, or have the devil untie you."

"What are you talking about?" she said, sounding panicked!

"I'm going to leave you with a timer attached to a detonation charge. If you fail to free yourself before the ten minutes is up, the detonation device will explode, igniting the jet fuel that I'll be pouring on you in a minute."

"What?!"

"Yeah. The combination of jet fuel and thermite, will ensure the authorities, will never be able to identify you; not even by your teeth! By the time the fire department responds, and gets the blazing fire out – there won't be anything left of you...just ashes."

"Now wait a minute! You said if I told you the truth you wouldn't kill me."

"I'm not going to kill you...the timer, with the explosive in it is going to kill you. I mean, you do have a chance to get out of here, if you can get your hands untied." I began pouring the jet fuel from a nearby container, into the circle surrounding her. I doused her with some and poured the rest a few feet away from her – where I planned to set up the mini cam. The camera would allow me to see her progress, after I left.

"You have any last wishes, before I take your photo and leave?"

"Go to hell!"

"I'm sure you'll be going there soon enough." I removed the burner phone I had purchased with cash from my inside pocket. I told her to look at me and smile. She just stuck her tongue out at me and I snapped the picture anyway. *When Rudy gets this phone, I'm going to include a note – telling him this was my last job. This work had gotten too personal for me. First with Renée getting stabbed three times, and now my daughter possibly being used as a pawn by Olivia; to pressure me to do her dirty work.* Which reminded me, I had less than twelve hours left. I quickly set up the mini-cam and adjusted it, so Sylvia would be able to see it, without being able to touch it with her feet. I set the timer for ten minutes, and looked over at her, "You better either begin praying or working to get loose." I put the timer down into the jet fuel and gathered my gear. I could hear her plead for her life, as she struggled to get free. I turned off the spot light and wound up the electrical cord quickly, tossing it into the back of the rental. I then turned off the generator, opened the warehouse doors and got inside the rental. I quickly looked at my watch to see the count down. She had exactly six minutes. I used my index finger to scroll along my phone, to view the app, which would allow me to see her in the chair. I tapped on the app, before starting the rental and driving out of the warehouse. She hadn't made any progress yet. I drove off and stopped down the road. Waiting to be sure the device would go off on time. She struggled right up to the last few seconds – that's when I saw a flash on my phone, and heard a loud explosion! The warehouse began to burn, and I drove away into the night.

THIRTY

While driving I decided to call Rudy, first to see how my daughter was doing, after which, I planned to tell him that the last job was finished and so was I. The phone rang four times, before he answered. "Hey buddy, how's it going?" I heard him say.

"Not bad. How's my daughter?"

"My wife and I took her back to your place."

"Why?!"

"She wanted to go. She said if we didn't take her, she'd leave and walk home."

"Dammit!"

"What's wrong?"

"Can you get back over there?"

"I could, but it's going to take me about a half-hour. Why?"

"Never mind, I gotta go! I'll talk to you later." I decided to call Mr. Li Wong, and see if he could go and watch my daughter, until I get there. I had Siri dial his number, and I wait for him to answer. The call immediately went to his voicemail, like he hadn't answered any of his phone messages.

I called again, only for it to go to voicemail again. "Hey Li! Can you call me when you get this?!" Just as I end the call, my phone rang. I looked down at the number and saw that it was Olivia. "What's going on?" I said, answering it.

"Do you have him yet?"

"I'm following him right now," I lied, just to appease her.

"Are you aware of the time?"

"Yes."

"I stopped by to visit with your friend Jimmie. You can say, to prove I'm not fooling around with you."

"You stopped by...what did you do?"

"Let's just say, I put him out of his *misery*."

"You did what?!"

"Yeah. He had no fight left in him, at all. That's not why I'm calling though. I'm calling to tell you I have what you want. I have your daughter. Think of it as insurance; to ensure I get what I want, which is Miguel's head."

"I'm not going to be able to work under these conditions. You do realize, how difficult it is to get close to Miguel? Not to mention trying to do it, stressed out!"

"I'm sure you'll figure it out. In the meantime, do you want to say hi to your daughter?"

"Yes."

Olivia put Amanda on the phone. "Daddy!" I heard my daughter cry! She sounded very upset. I tried to reassure; not to worry. "Hey sweetie, don't worry! I'm gonna get you, *I promise*!"

Olivia returned to the phone, "You get me Miguel's head *first*!"

"Where will you be when I have it?"

"Call me when you have it, and I'll let you know?"

"Olivia!"

"What?"

"I'll get your head; you just don't hurt my daughter. Is that clear?"

"You're running out of time." She hung up, without saying another word. I rushed over to see Jimmie! Olivia was right, she put him out of his misery. I hugged his life-less body, before lying it back down on the floor. I wasn't concerned about crime scene evidence, because I had a pair of latex gloves on. "Jimmie, I promise I will get her for doing this. I don't want to leave you like this, but I gotta go get my daughter, before Olivia hurts her...or worse! I'll be back, I promise."

I left Jimmie's apartment, and just as I was getting in the rental, my phone rang and I saw it was Mr. Li calling me back. "Li! Is everything alright?!"

"Mr. Sebastien..."

"Yeah, I'm right here!"

"I sorry."

"For what?!"

"Saw strange woman with daughter. I spoke with her, she shoot me."

"You've been shot!"

"It's okay. Only in shoulder. Strange woman shoot dog too!"

"Dakota was shot!"

"Sorry. Dakota not moving."

"Li! I'm on my way!" For some reason the combination of *stress* and *worry* had me remembering a melody I often play on my piano. It was *fearless motivation* by Walter Bergman. I had that melody racing through my mind, as I hurried home. When I got home, I was in such a rush that I almost forgot to put the vehicle in park. I ran up the walk, where I saw Li waiting for me. "Are you okay?" I asked him!

"I be ok. Go to dog. Dog try to save your daughter. Strange woman shoots it." He pointed to the lobby of my building, with a bloody hand. I rushed in and when I got to my apartment, I saw that the door was open. I assumed Li was so upset, that he forgot to close it. I felt my heart swell for the first time since I can remember, as I rushed inside. Both the living room and dining room lights were on, and there on the living room floor was Dakota. I rushed over to her, falling down near her side! "Dakota! Dakota!" I lifted her head and saw that was she still holding on; but not by much! I saw her head move closer, as she gave me one last lick goodbye, before her inner being left her body. I knew she was gone, because her head drooped into my arms. I hugged her and said, "You did good girl. I know you tried to save Amanda. You paid the ultimate price, and I'll never forget that...ever!" That swelling feeling inside me, grew warmer and spread throughout my body. *This is what love must feel like*. I began to remember her as a puppy, until I recalled memories of her as an adult. "Goodbye," I said, as I patted her head, in gentle strokes.

"I sorry Mr. Sebastien," I heard Li say behind me. I turned to see him standing at the doorway to the apartment.

"There's only one person who's going to be sorry for doing this." I laid Dakota's head down on the floor. "Li, can you watch her until I get back? She killed my dog!"

"Yes, Mr. Sebastien."

Before I could leave my apartment, I had to get a few weapons from the vault. I grabbed everything I thought I would need, and exited the vault. On my way outside to the rental, that feeling of love I felt earlier for Dakota, was quickly waning – I was beginning to feel another emotion – *one I'm very familiar with! One called revenge!* Even if I wanted to go after Miguel, there wasn't enough time left to do it. With that realization, I decided to call Olivia and tell her I'm ready to meet. I dialed her number and waited for her to answer. She finally answered, "Hello."

"It's me, Sebastien."

"I know. I saved your name and number on my phone. Since you're calling, I assume you have what I want?"

"I do. Where do you want to meet?" I asked.

She told me to meet her at *Promontory Point*. She would be waiting on the limestones with my daughter. "Can you be more specific?" I said, remembering the layout of the *Point*.

She replied, "Look for me down by the water." I told her I was on my way. I had been to Promontory Point several times; it was a nice place with a great view of the water. The Point closes at eleven p.m. – it was nearly 4:30 a.m. I found a place to park, and grabbed my gym bag from the back of the rental. The same gym bag that I used to keep my sparring gear inside. I figured by bringing the gym bag, I could fool her to believe I had Miguel's head inside. I decided instead of searching for Olivia, I'd call her to let her know I was there. I called and she answered, "Are you on your way?" she asked. She sounded terse, and a bit rude.

"No, I'm here. Where exactly are you?"

"I told you I'd be down by the water! That's where we are."

"Okay, I should be there in a few minutes."

When I finally reached the tip of Promontory Point, I saw the outline of two people standing on the limestones. One looked like an adult and the other a child. As I went closer, I saw that it was Olivia, and she had Amanda by the arm, with a gun pointed at my daughter's side. "Is that Miguel head in there?" she asked, looking at my gym bag.

"Yes."

"Throw it to me!"

"Let my daughter go first!"

"No! You think I was born yesterday. You give me what I want; then I'll hand over your daughter."

"How do I know when you get what you want, you won't just kill us both?"

"You don't! But if you don't give me what I want, I'll definitely kill you both; starting with this lovely girl here. You know, it's a shame..."

"What is?"

"You have a daughter and you ignore her. While someone like me, who wished she could have a family, couldn't."

"Why's that?"

"Let's just say, I was willing, but *infertile*. That's life for you, people who should feel blessed and thankful *aren't*, and those who would be thankful and feel blessed, never get the opportunity. Isn't that a hoot? I'm the youngest of three girls. Both of my sisters had children; all boys! Handsome too! You ever wished you had siblings, Sebastien?"

"It doesn't matter now, what I wanted then...the past is the past."

"True. So, you don't have any regrets?"

"I do."

"And what's that?"

"I regret ever meeting you."

"Ouch! I like that you're honest, even while facing danger!"

"Why do you say that?"

"Because you have no idea what I'm thinking right now! I could have had a terrible day and you go and say something to hurt my feelings; even though you know I'm holding a gun to your daughter and I have my finger on the trigger. I mean, accidents happen Sebastien, you of all people should now that."

"I do. I don't know how deep your involved with the Russians, but you don't need to do this."

"I don't? Mikhail expects me to deliver! I gave him my word, not only on my life, but my father's. Besides there's more to it than just Mikhail. He's just the tip of the *iceberg*."

"What is that supposed to mean?" Right after I asked her that question, I heard a man's voice say, "It means she's a *double agent*!" The man who said that, came out from the shadows and apparently Olivia was very familiar with him, because she immediately used my daughter as a shield, between herself and the stranger. "Aaron, you come any closer and I will kill her."

"Olivia, tell him who you're really working for," said Aaron.

"How did you know who I'm working for?" she said, to the man I only knew as Aaron.

"Your contact in Ukraine was working with us." He looked at me and said, "Olivia here… was supposed to be working for her people, the Israeli government. However, she decided to go *rogue* and supply information to the Russians."

"Are you talking about Mikhail Mogilevich?"

"No. He's just a front. She's really working for the KGB, right Olivia? You're working with the KGB!"

"So what? I needed the money and they made me an offer I couldn't refuse. Mogilevich was the one who introduced me to the KGB. He said it would open doors to much wealth and opportunities!"

"Did it?" I asked.

"Not really. I wound up becoming indebted to Mikhail."

"Olivia, put the gun down," Aaron ordered. "There's a sniper with his gun trained on you. It's over."

"What do you expect me to do? You expect me to hand over the girl and let you arrest me for *espionage*?"

"*Yes*. The Israeli and American governments want to know what information you sold to the Russians? We suspect it has to do with new weapon technology for Israel and the electrical grid for the Americans. Not to mention your involvement with the Chinese. If you cooperate and give us all the details, we might not be as harsh – then if you resist."

"I have a better plan. You call your sniper and tell him or her, that I'm walking out of here with the gym bag, and the girl, and no one is going to stop me!"

"Come on Olivia you're being totally unreasonable. How far do you think you can get?" Aaron said, sounding as if he was trying to hostage negotiate with her.

"How far? I don't know. All I know is taking her with me, will allow me to get away from you."

"I can't let you do that."

"How are you going to stop me?" I heard Olivia say and that's when I saw Aaron touch the top of his head. Seeing him do that, appeared out of place and I knew I was right, because the next thing I heard was the sound of a rifle firing from a distance. The bullet struck Olivia on the side of her head, and she suddenly fell onto the limestones. Amanda immediately rushed over to me and I embraced her. With my daughter now safe, Aaron came over and joined us. He was a handsome looking older man, clean cut, with no facial hair to mention. "I work for Mossad. We've been watching you, ever since you left the marines. You're very good at what you do. Very thorough."

"Thank you."

"If you ever need a job, don't hesitate to contact me." He handed me his business card, with his name and cell number on it, along with a design of Israel in the background.

"I appreciate the offer, but I think my days of doing any more of this is over. I have a daughter who needs to spend time with her father."

"I understand."

I looked over at Olivia lying on the rocks. "What's going to happen to her?"

"We're going to notify her father, and arrest him for espionage. He too was involved with selling secrets to the Russians, by being a willing participant. I'm certain the Americans will want to interrogate him – concerning the Chinese as well."

"I'm sure. Well, thank you," I said to him.

"For what?"

"For saving my daughter's life, *and mine.*"

"It's all part of the job," he said, rather modestly, before walking off. I turned to my daughter and said, "Did Olivia hurt you?"

"No. What's going on daddy? Why did she do this? Who was that man? Why did he kill her? How do you know her?" Amanda said, sounding quite shook up and rightfully so. I was sure she would have many more questions for me; but for now, I just wanted to get her home safely.

"It's a long story sweetheart. I really can't get into it right now. All I can say is – *it's over* and you're safe." It was at that point, I decided to call Rudy and let him know, I wouldn't be working with him anymore. I took my daughter by the hand, and we walked back in the direction of the SUV rental. I had my phone to my ear when Rudy answered. I told Amanda to keep walking ahead of me, while I took the call, because I didn't want her hearing my conversation. "Hey Sebastien! Did you find Amanda?"

"Yes," I said. I lowered my voice so Amanda wouldn't hear. I watched as she walked farther and farther ahead of me. Obviously, she saw the rental, because she was headed right toward it. As she got even further away, I began to feel more comfortable, and I said what I was thinking.

"How is *she*?" I heard Rudy ask.

"She's doing well. The reason I'm calling is to tell you I'm out. *I'm done.*"

"Hey! Don't say that. That's not the Sebastien I know. Olivia taking your daughter was just a bump in the road."

"Excuse me!" If I said I was surprised at Rudy's comment, it would be putting it mildly. I was actually shocked! "You know what I mean?" he said, attempting to reword his comment. "What I said, didn't come out right! What I meant to say was, you have your daughter back...by the way, what happened to Olivia?"

"She's dead. This can never happen again Rudy. Not only did Olivia take my daughter hostage, she also killed *Jimmie* and *Dakota*."

"*Oh geez*! I'm sorry to hear that."

"That's why I'm finished!"

"Tell you what?"

"What?"

"Take a small vacation, you need it. I'll let *P* know you need two weeks off," he said, sounding as if he were trying to appease me.

"You're not listening, *are you*? I'm done! I gotta go!"

"Wait! Sebastien all I'm asking is that you take a little time and think about it. Don't make decisions based on emotions. I know you're worried about Amanda; we can figure something out concerning her safety in the future. You gotta believe me when I say I'm sorry to hear about what happened to Jimmie and Dakota! Heck, I'll get you another dog if you want?!"

"Another dog! You make it sound like Dakota meant nothing to me. Goodbye Rudy."

"Wait a minute! Don't hang up," he said, but I end the call and turned my phone off. I didn't want to hear from anyone, not even Carolyn. I met Amanda at the rental, she was waiting for me near the front of the vehicle. I went over and hugged her, just as the sun was beginning to kiss the horizon.

TWO WEEKS LATER

THIRTY-ONE

There's plenty to do in Chicago, whether you're a parent or *single.* As a parent, I tried to be a little diplomatic with my daughter, because I wanted her to value the time we spent together. Amanda told her mother about everything that happened; including what Olivia did to Dakota. I wasn't sure how Carolyn would mentally process all that information, because I knew how she felt about our daughter. She was just as protective about Amanda, as I was. I was pleasantly surprised, when Amanda asked to stay with me for a few additional weeks – claiming I needed to make up for lost time. Carolyn agreed, which was surprising to say the least! Since Amanda was going to be around for a few more weeks, I figured we could take an architecture boat tour – there was no nicer way to get an idea of the city, than by boat. Next, she agreed to go with me to the Art Institute of Chicago – it was a gorgeous art museum, with famous works from Picasso, among other great painters. Surprisingly, she wanted to see a Cubs game at Wrigley Field – the coming Wednesday against the

288

Padres. Both of us agreed we'd like to see the Willis Tower Skydeck – for different reasons. She wanted to overcome her fear of heights, whereas I wanted to see the expression on her face, when she realized exactly how far up in the air we were. *It's going to be memorable*! Finally, I wanted us to go on a tour of Frank Lloyd Wright's, Robie House, and visit the American Writers Museum. She on the other hand, wanted to either spend the day at Maggie Daley Park, where she could do some incredible rock-climbing activities, or rent bikes and stroll the lakefront trail. The trail was an 18-mile paved path that was perfect for just taking in the incredible views of Lake Michigan. I told her, we actually had time to do all of it! She was excited to hear me say that and we left my apartment, intending to visit the Art Institute first, and then the Willis Tower Skydeck. While at the art museum, I got a call from Rudy. "Hey Sebastien, don't hang up!"

"Rudy, this is not a good time."

"Why? What's wrong?"

"I'm with Amanda at the Art Institute."

"Nice. Can we meet afterwards?"

"Why?"

"I have something to give you."

"Can't you send it by mail?"

"No. I'm sure there's laws against it!"

"What are you talking about?"

"Would you please just meet with me after the museum?"

"I plan on spending the whole day with my daughter."

"Where are you planning to go after the museum?" he asked and he was persistent.

"What is this, twenty questions?"

"No really?"

"I'm planning to take her to the Willis Tower, next. Why?"

"What are we talking about time wise? Maybe another hour or so?"

"Probably," I claimed, not really concerned about the time. "Again, *why*?"

"Great! I'll see you there."

"Rudy! Wait!" I said, hearing him hang up. Amanda came over and said, "Who was that on the phone?"

"Rudy."

"What's he want?"

"He wants to meet us at the Willis Tower."

"Why? I thought you were finished working with him."

"Sweetie, I am. He said he wants to give me something – something he can't mail."

"I bet he just wants to try and convince you to work with him again."

"Well, I told him I'd meet him in about an hour."

"Good, 'cuz I'm ready to leave here."

"Sweetie this is art. You don't like art?"

"It's boring dad. I'd rather go see Willis Tower. Can we go now?"

"I suppose. I'll call Rudy when we get there and tell him I'll meet him outside, after..."

"Good, let's go!"

Willis Tower was more spectacular than either of us could have imagined! I was absolutely amazed at how the platform was constructed overlooking the city – allowing the brave to step out on to the glass ledge and look down at the city below. I stepped out onto the deck and asked Amanda to do the same. She was very nervous, and reluctant to even go near the edge of the retractable platform. "Sweetie, you have nothing to worry about. The platform isn't going to fall."

"I'm good here," she remained standing on the other side of the threshold.

"Hey, you're the one who wanted to overcome your fear of heights."

"I've changed my mind."

"Just step out with one foot."

"Nope."

I told her there was a boy looking at her from the other platform. He was standing out on it, and he didn't seem scared. My comment made her look and she saw him looking over at her. His stares boosted her confidence and she immediately stepped forward and said, "If I fall dad, I'm gonna tell mom it was all your fault!"

"I'm sure you would," I said, just as she stepped out and

walked to the center. She quickly looked down and said, "Oh my God! How high are we?"

"You don't want to know."

"Dad?"

"We're one thousand three hundred and fifty-three feet up."

"I really shouldn't have asked!" she said, sounding more nervous than ever.

"Sweetie, look at it this way...it's only one hundred and three floors."

"You're not helping!"

I smiled. After about two minutes, Amanda was ready to come inside. She stepped off of the platform and felt safe again. She turned to me and said, "Can we go for lunch? I'm getting hungry." I was surprised to hear her say that, knowing she lives on minimal fruits and vegetables. "You wanna get a pizza?" I asked, thinking of a great place near here!

"No. Something healthy that won't put on weight dad. Really, pizza!"

"What would you prefer, *salad*?"

"*Yeah*! Cesar, with no dressing."

"Sounds as appetizing as cut grass." I joined her inside, and we took one of the elevators down to the lobby. I was half expecting to see Rudy waiting in the lobby, to my surprise he wasn't there. I told Amanda to keep an eye out for him, as we exited the building to wait for him outside. "Dad! There's Rudy," I heard her say. I turned and see him walking toward us, holding in his arms a puppy. Not just any puppy, but a German Shepherd puppy. "See why I couldn't mail it!" he yelled over to us!

"Rudy!"

"Please don't say no!"

"No."

When he finally reached us, he put the puppy up near his face and said, "Hi Sebastien, my name is Dirk."

"*Dirk*? Dirk sounds like a porn star. Did you name him?"

"No. The woman who sold him to me named him *Dirk*. You're looking at two grand here."

I looked at the puppy. He was definitely adorable, but he didn't look like a *Dirk*. I could see by the size of his paws; he was going to be a large dog – a proper name for him would either be *Samson* or *Diesel*. Rudy asked me if I wanted to hold Dirk? I told him not particularly. "I know what you're trying to do Rudy…and the answer is still *no*."

"What am I trying to do, besides get this little guy a good home?"

"Probably comes with conditions dad!" I heard Amanda say.

"No. There's no conditions. He just needs a good home and since your father doesn't have a dog anymore, I figured the two would be a great match. Besides, if you don't take him, there's no refund – so I'll be out two thousand dollars."

"Let's say I agree to take him…I'm changing his name."

"To what?" Rudy asked.

"To Samson."

"Sammy?"

"No, Samson. You don't like that name?"

"It's your dog...you can name him *Ralph* if you want."
Rudy should have left by now, but he hadn't. Instead, he was
standing there looking at me holding the puppy. "Was there
something else?" I asked.

"There is. Can I have a word with you in private?" he said.

"Rudy."

"Please, it's very important."

"Okay." I told my daughter I'd be right back, and asked
her to hold Samson. I followed Rudy to the sidewalk, about
twenty feet from Amanda. He turned and hummed, "They
look adorable, don't they? I mean really, it's like a Kodak
moment. I should have brought my camera! That would also
make a great holiday or birthday photo."

"What's this about Rudy?"

"I admit Samson is a good name. Now that I'm looking
at him from a distance, I can see how you would think he
looks like a Samson. *Definitely*!"

"Rudy!"

"Okay, okay! You don't have to bite my head off. I have
an offer from Prometheus."

"Rudy, what did I tell you?"

"Look, he has this idea to start something called, *The
Lost Angel Files*. It involves missing and exploited children.
The idea is to find the children and bring the child traffickers

to justice. Prometheus is willing to pay for all expenses and bump your original fee by an additional ten thousand dollars, per file. That also would include all expenses, including hotel and airfare."

"Let's just say, I agree to think about doing it. How many files are we talking about?"

"As many as we can handle. It's completely up to you." He said and just stood there, looking at me. "Aren't you gonna ask?"

"Ask what?"

"Why he's asking for us to do this?"

"Why?"

"Well, I'm glad you asked! See, he's a mature man, don't ask me his age, because I don't know. All I know is he sounded mature, and yes, I got to speak with him over the phone on a secure line."

"Really? Lucky you."

"Anyway, his grand daughter was targeted for abduction; you could say she was an abductee."

"You saved me the trouble, you just did."

"Okay, I know you get grumpy when you're pressed for time. So, I'm going to get to the point."

"Finally!"

"His grand daughter was almost kidnapped. The couple that tried to nap her, knew Prometheus's son. Imagine that, a friend of the family doing that!"

"It happens more often than you think," I replied.

"Really?"

"Yeah. So, for him it's personal?"

"Yes. You game?" Rudy asked.

"Let me think about it."

"You do that. And while you're thinking, take a good look at Amanda. Imagine her missing and trafficked."

"I did, that's one of the reasons I left the business. Olivia threatened me that she was going to send Amanda off to Ukraine, and I'd never hear from her again."

"Well, think about the parents with missing kids. I'm sure you can sympathize with what they're going through. They could use someone with your specialty. Sebastien, you were born to help others."

"You mean, I was born to help you!"

"No...well, you and I have a symbiotic relationship..."

"How so?"

"I get the files and you complete them."

"We'll see, let me think about it."

"That's fair. Where are you two going now?"

"I'm taking her to lunch."

"Great! Where are *we* going?"

"I don't believe I invited you," I said, smiling. Rudy knew I was teasing him. He began to tell me all the great places he knew, where we could go for lunch. I reminded him we have a puppy with us. He replied, "That's not a problem. We can do take out!"

I just smiled, because I knew he meant well. "Dad, since we're doing take out, can we get Mc Donald's?" Amanda asked.

"No sweetie. Besides, what happened to wanting a Cesar salad?"

"They have salad at Mc Donald's."

"See what you started?" I chuckled, looking over at Rudy.

He just smiled and shrugged his shoulders

THE END